POWDER
MISSION

BY

HERBERT E. STOVER

CATAMOUNT
PRESS

an imprint of Sunbury Press, Inc.
Mechanicsburg, PA USA

CATAMOUNT
PRESS

an imprint of Sunbury Press, Inc.
Mechanicsburg, PA USA

For information about special discounts for bulk purchases, please contact Sunbury Press Orders Dept. at (855) 338-8359 or orders@sunburypress.com.

To request one of our authors for speaking engagements or book signings, please contact Sunbury Press Publicity Dept. at publicity@sunburypress.com.

FIRST CATAMOUNT PRESS EDITION: February 2023

Set in Adobe Garamond | Interior design by Crystal Devine | Cover by Lawrence Knorr | Edited by Jennifer Cappello.

Publisher's Cataloging-in-Publication Data
Names: Stovert, Herbert E., author.
Title: Powder mission / Herbert E. Stover.
Description: First trade paperback edition. | Mechanicsburg, PA : Catamount Press, 2023.
Summary: During the American Revolution, a critical shipment of gold from New Orleans is stolen. Martin Joe Richtier, the personal envoy of General Anthony Wayne, knows that he alone must bear the responsibility for its recovery.
Identifiers: ISBN : 979-8-88819-045-6 (softcover) | ISBN : 979-8-88819-046-3 (ePub).
Subjects: FICTION | Historical / Colonial America & Revolution | FICTION / Small Town & Rural.

Product of the United States of America
0 1 1 2 3 5 8 13 21 34 55

Continue the Enlightenment!

To
LESLIE

Also by
HERBERT E. STOVER

Song of the Susquehanna

Men in Buckskin

Copperhead Moon

By Night the Strangers

The Eagle and the Wind

PROLOGUE

ONE COULD be certain of just one thing about Anthony Wayne, commander of Pennsylvania's eight regiments in those perilous days of our Revolution, namely, that in battle, he would attack. Outside of this, the man was unpredictable, even to those of us who had been his neighbors and knew him well.

For the past five minutes, he had paced back and forth across the room while he delivered his tirade. Now he stopped and glanced sharply at the young lieutenant who stood at the door, then back to me.

"So, Martin Jon Richtier, I have reviewed your case, and your application for reenlistment at your former rank of ensign is refused. Your recent conduct bars you in spite of your record in the field and His Excellency's new medal, the Purple Heart, to which you are entitled because of your recent wound. I will not run the risk of other brawls and of having my officers disfigured with knives."

The rasping voice stopped but, from the eyes as hard and cold as the bayonet this general favored, it was plain he had not finished.

"Carmichal said you were not a gentleman and so would not duel with you. Then you thrashed him and nicked his ears with your knife. Richtier, you are no more of a gentleman than I am—we're soldiers and, before that, farmers. Your enlistment ran out while you were recovering from your wound but as soon as you returned to camp, trouble came. If it were not for your present civilian status I'd have you in the guardhouse and then up before a military court." Again the general looked sharply at the lieutenant who seemed to be getting some satisfaction from the fury vented on me.

"That will be all, Lieutenant Calvert. You may tell Colonel Lovett I'll see him in a half hour."

As Wayne turned to walk back to the table, which served as a desk, I managed a baleful look at the young officer who had raised his arm in salute. He did not finish the gesture but stammered a "Yes, sir" to the general's back and almost slammed the door as he hurried out.

"What did you do to the lieutenant, Martin?"

Wayne had seated himself, and it was my turn to be embarrassed and uneasy as I looked into the steady gray eyes.

"Nothing, sir. I just looked at him. Calvert's a close friend of Carmichal."

"Exactly," Wayne snapped. "That was why he was here—to know you were reprimanded and refused reenlistment. You've made me a deal of trouble. Captain Carmichal did not enjoy his thrashing or the injury to his ears. He has friends like General Gates, like Lovett and Leith. If you were in the army now, even I could not help you." He leaned back in his chair and studied the ceiling of this farmhouse kitchen for a long moment before he began talking again.

"God knows I need my officers and could have used you. You know that Howe's landed at the head of the Chesapeake, that the country is howling for us to defend Philadelphia at any cost. We have moved down from New York to the lower Delaware. For once, we could almost match Howe in numbers but most of our people are militia who will run; perhaps as you and I would if we found ourselves outgunned and outmatched. There will be battles, but I believe His Excellency is concerned to keep his army from destruction rather than to save a city. Martin, the great present need is powder. Little gristmills all over make it, but too slowly. Fort Pitt sends an urgent request for some of the precious stuff but there's none to spare and, mark you, if we lose this present campaign, our armies might well retreat to the Forks of the Ohio. His Excellency knows that country and has fought over it. Indians menace there today. Detroit frowns from the lakes and Tories gnaw from within. Young Clark wants to carry the war to the British in the Illinois country. All the danger out there could be averted with enough powder on hand to charge the frontiersmen's rifles."

Picking up a quill, he examined it carefully before tossing it into a box.

"'Tis said that down in New Orleans where the Spanish keep a sketchy peace with England, the arsenals bulge with powder. More, there is a strange rumor that our French friends in that city have gold for us. Lafayette hinted about it to His Excellency. God, Martin, how much we could accomplish with either of those things or both. With good powder in their flasks, militia would stand and fight. Knox's guns could thunder at the redcoats. With gold, we could buy the fruit of victory without spending blood for it. We could pay our soldiers; we could show farmers and suppliers that the new nation is sound and to be trusted. We could buy life for the cause."

Suddenly, he slapped the table with the flat of his hand.

"Martin, I have talked too long. Get you out to Fort Pitt and look about. Our old neighbor, Leonidas Breon, is now an innkeeper out there and will get any word you have through to me. But do not let boredom get you into knife fights. Your blade has made enough trouble. A doctor at Pitt is said to be a kingpin among the Tories. His agents may be here in Philadelphia County. Then there is always that man Gibson with his bluster. Go out there until this Carmichal business cools down. Behave as though I were a young man out there; act as I would act."

He rose as I snapped my hand up in salute.

"Yes, sir," I said, "I'll be going and hope I shall be smart enough to do as the general says."

He came around and placed his hands on my shoulders.

"Come back to me, you rawboned, redheaded hellion; I'll be able to show you some rare fighting when the Fourth Pennsylvania has learned the bayonet."

He grinned and shook my shoulders.

"Someday, mayhap, I'll take that knife from your belt and make you carry a sword. Yes, I'll fashion a captain of you and, who knows, I may ruin a good farmer to make a gentleman out of you, though God knows what we want with more of them."

Then, with all formalities over, we were shaking hands and saying, as we had so often done:

"Goodbye, neighbor, until better weather."

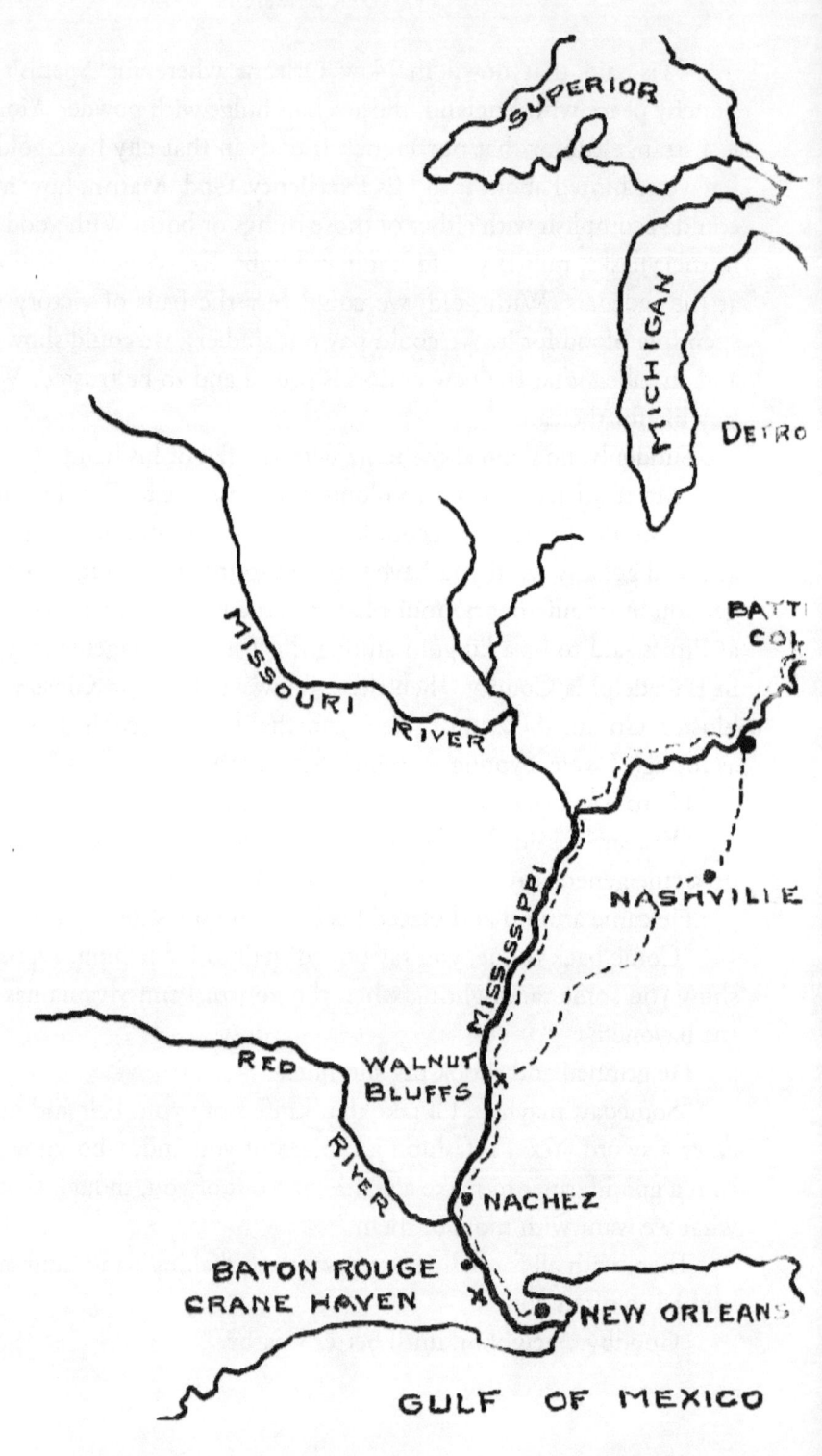

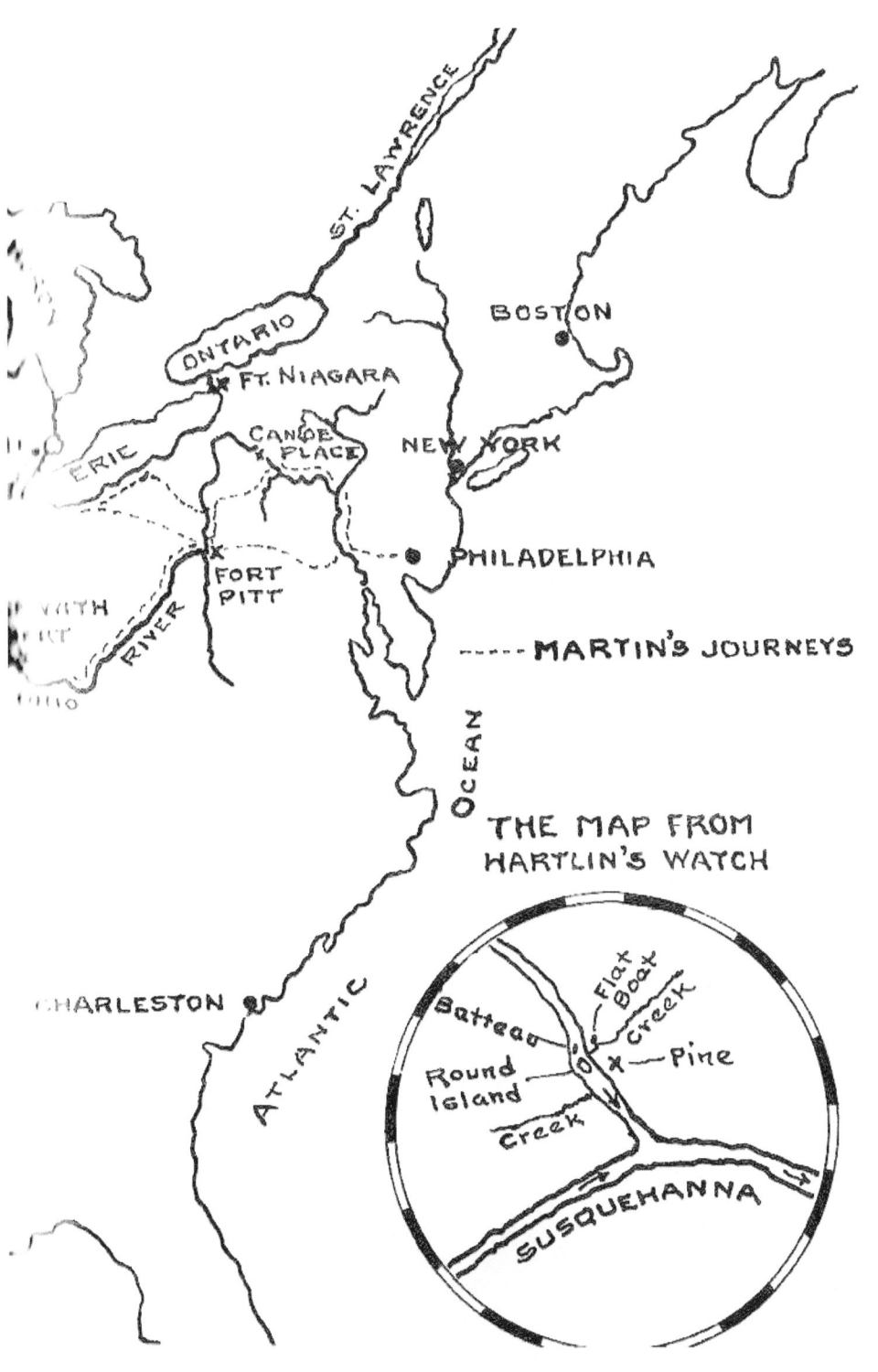

ST. LAWRENCE

BOSTON

ONTARIO

Ft. NIAGARA

ERIE

CANOE PLACE

NEW YORK

WITH ITT

FORT PITT

OHIO

RIVER

PHILADELPHIA

------ MARTIN'S JOURNEYS

OCEAN

THE MAP FROM
HARTLIN'S WATCH

CHARLESTON

ATLANTIC

Batteau

Flat Boat

Creek

Round Island

Pine

Creek

SUSQUEHANNA

CHAPTER ONE

LADY LUCK had been with me so often in the dangers of this war that perhaps I had begun to rely on her as a friend and ally, forgetting she is blind. This morning on the hillside a little north and east of Fort Pitt, she had seemed to smile, and then she turned her face from me suddenly. But, I knew it was my own carelessness, together with the excitement of the kill, that had brought things to this pass. The bear and I had blundered on each other at the side of a small natural clearing. She had tried to frighten me by going up on her hind feet; too close for a shot, I had snatched out the long knife that bewhiskered Tom Gisack had taught me a long time ago how to throw. Holding the weapon by the blade tip and giving it a spinning toss, I had sent it straight to its mark.

Now, kneeling there in the sunlight, it seemed for a moment that this Martin Jon Richtier, with his big bony hands spread out on the fresh bear hide, was not I but some careless person whom I should have warned to be cautious in these Indian-dense parts.

The two Indians had come up so silently that I had not seen them until they were too close for me to do anything but make a last desperate plunge that might take one of them with me before a bright hatchet went home through my thatch of hair. Dying with an enemy, however, is small satisfaction. My short heavy-barreled rifle lay fully cocked a bit to my right, and the heavy knife with which I had dispatched the angry bear was somewhere between my knees and the rolled-up skin. My slightest movement would be a signal for these men to act; I dared not risk fumbling for the keen heavy blade.

General Wayne had warned me that boredom usually brought me trouble. He had repeated the caution just before I left him near Philadelphia and came across the mountains to this outpost fort. But three days after I came to Fort Pitt, I had so wearied of the tedium of garrison life that I had to go hunting in spite of local warning about danger to solitary hunters in these hills where an Indian found a scalp easier to take than a beaver skin. It was only the second bear I had killed with a knife, and my excited triumph had made me reckless. So here in this tiny clearing within cannon-shot sound of the fort, it looked as though I, like the bear, had come to the end of the road. It was not fear that troubled me so much as the bitterness I felt about my own carelessness.

Cautiously, I set the toe of my right moccasin against a stone for purchase and felt the tingling run of tensed muscles along calves and thighs as I prepared to spring; then my eyes lifted slowly, noting everything, from the bright blood of the bear on the sassafras leaves to the two Indians. The one to my right was closer than the other.

This man was a big fellow with broken and muddy moccasins above which he wore long leggings and a red breech-clout. His tow cloth hunting shirt looked respectable enough and was only moderately dirty for a woodsman's. But the odd thing about his dress was a small round skin cap of some kind of brown fur in which was fastened with a piece of white twine a single bedraggled owl's feather. The second Indian was little more than a tall boy, naked but for breech-clout and moccasins. Like the first, he carried a cocked musket loose in his right hand, and his narrow thong belt carried both war ax and knife.

Neither Indian could have repaired his toilet for some time. What paint showed had run into dirty smudges on their faces. Then, as I stared, to my tremendous relief, I saw the big man was smiling. He had broken front teeth and his nose was twisted a bit to one side, but there was no mistaking the smile. He pointed with his free hand to the pile of bear meat.

"Good, much good," he grunted. "Buy."

The second Indian had not moved; his beady eyes searched the clearing, then came back to my face. The hand holding the musket came up a little, then the older man scowled at him ferociously and the gun went down. No doubt the young man could see little reason for palaver since it would be easy to take both the meat and a scalp. I had a moment's chance to find the knife. Scowling, I pointed to the muskets. Both Indians promptly laid them down, and I slid my big blade into its sheath and answered the two men as they raised their hands in the peace signal.

Carefully repressing any signs of the relief that flooded through me, I stood up on legs that felt a little wooden and watched the big fellow nod his satisfaction. He was pointing again to the bloody meat.

"Buy—you sell?" he asked.

The boy was watching closely and seemed impatient with his companion, for he took two pennies from his pouch, gestured toward the meat, and held out the money.

"Buy," he grunted, then he, too, smiled.

The older Indian pointed, then led the way to the edge of the clearing where one could look down the slope. I knew that one of the great trails toward the lake ran down there, and now I could see that some sort of company was approaching along it. The Indian took from his pouch a single mauled red squirrel and shrugged his shoulders. The matter was plain; these men hunted for that company down there, they had had poor success, and wished to buy my bear. I led them back to the meat, knelt, and gravely laid the pieces apart so they could inspect it.

"I will sell," I announced with some finality.

At once, the older man began to pick up the meat and pile it like firewood on the arms and shoulders of his young companion. It was a small bear, and in the end, the boy carried all of it, the bigger man making the concession of carrying the two muskets as we started down the hill. Suddenly he stopped and gestured toward the hide. It was a summer one with slipped hair and so was of little value. I motioned for him to take it.

"I have no use for it, my friend. Take it."

His smile was broad enough to show that only his front teeth were broken. He snatched up the bloody skin and draped it over his shoulder like a blanket, after which he strutted forward, leading the way down over the hill toward the trail.

The company that came up a few minutes after we arrived and after the young Indian had been permitted to pile his burden on some leaves, was a motley one of white men and women, and Indians. There was probably a score of people, six of them being Indians and three or four women. The leader, who stopped before us, was a tall man who carried nothing but a green ash cane. He was a bit stooped and was dressed more for the streets of a town than for forest traveling, and he looked like some kind of a professional man, either a lawyer or a doctor. The big Indian jabbered something to him and he seemed to understand, for he nodded his head.

"The boys say you'll sell this meat?" he asked, and I nodded, then started to explain but he cut me short with a snapped question.

"Who are you?"

I did not like the sharpness of either his eyes or his voice and I felt my temper rising. Then I remembered that this man was a customer and I had no use for a pile of bear meat. So I answered civilly.

"Martin Jon Richtier, sir. Lately come to these parts trading. Who are you?"

It was my inquisitor's turn to show annoyance, and his eyebrows drew down. But he, too, thought better of it.

"Our company is from Fort Pitt bound north for the lakes. We do need your meat, but money is scarce with us."

Minutes before, I had seen what I wanted. It was impossible to buy powder at the fort; Wayne had indicated the shortage out here. Sometimes the military would issue small supplies of the precious stuff but only for military purposes. Now I saw that the powder horns of the armed members of this body hung heavy from their shoulders.

"I don't want money, but I'll trade the whole of the meat for two horns of good powder. The bear's young, sir, and in good condition."

The leader looked at me sharply, then he smiled at my eagerness but he did not bicker. At his gesture, one of the Indians went to a pack horse and took from under the tarpaulin two of the leather powder flasks usually issued to soldiers and brought them to me. It was good powder, that was plain when I cupped my finger and thumb about the nozzle of my horn and began pouring, watching the black glistening grains slide in and pile up. Occasionally I held up the horn so I could see how full it was becoming, and I had to tap it twice in order to empty the first flask into it.

"That's a nice horn," the leader commented, gesturing toward it with a long forefinger, and I nodded.

"Yes, sir, I did make it pretty fancy, what with the scraping and the pictures. It's a kind of record like the Indians keep."

The Indian had taken the second flask to hold for me while I emptied the first. At the leader's gesture, he returned it.

"Put that in your packet, Richtier. By the by, my name's Hartlin, Doctor Hartlin. What do you do at home—farm?"

His question pleased me.

"Yes, it's a small place but good land along the Schuylkill.

There's forty acres of it planted mostly with potatoes and wheat. I brought a pack load of our own flitch west to trade."

The doctor glanced at his company, already beginning to move on after the Indians had packed the meat onto one of the horses. He spoke again to me, and his voice was grave.

"That would be a good place to stay—on your farm. A fellow with a good Dutch name like yours has no business being away from home in these troubled times."

I half turned and now saw the girl almost at the end of the line. She was walking, leading a saddled horse, and she looked directly at me. It was her hair that caught my fancy because it was dark brown with a hint of red in it. Just now she wore it loose about her face and the mass of it seemed to be cut short at her shoulders. She looked so alive that there was nothing in common with these other people whose evident discouragement showed in their bowed shoulders and on their faces. The birch twig in her mouth gave her an air of nonchalance and her dress was that of a frontier boy—all soft buckskin with the shirt open at her throat where she wore a string of bright beads.

I stared too long. Hartlin spoke again and, thinking it had been to me, I replied, answering the comment I had heard.

"Yes, sir, I like the farm. I hope you like the bear meat; it's almost as good as pork if it's well-cooked."

He had not spoken to me but to someone else, and he moved on with the others. The Indians were hazing the pack horses impatiently.

Presently the girl passed me and I started to smile at her, but she looked through me at the hemlocks as though I were not there.

It was a direct snub and it was annoying, for I only meant to be friendly. She showed plainly, however, that she wanted nothing to do with a wandering hunter who sold meat. Then I brought my mind back to what happened. Selling that bear for powder was a good piece of business.

But I had not walked a half mile down the trail toward the fort when another thought struck me so hard that I stopped. Wayne had spoken of some doctor who was a Tory leader out here at Pitt. The man with whom I traded called himself Doctor Hartlin; in fact, he had emphasized the 'Doctor' part of his name. And he and his company were bound for the lakes where there could only be British and Indians. After a little I shrugged my shoulders; Doctor Hartlin and his Tories would be the business of the military authorities. Besides, my friend Leonidas Breon, with whom I stayed down at the Blue Heron, could tell me all I wanted to know.

I felt pretty good, excepting that the girl had flaunted me. The day was turning out well. True, I had been careless, and back there on the hill I had felt that I had come to the end of the road, but those Indians were disposed to trade. Civilized Natives; there was some chagrin in knowing that they had frightened me.

A mile farther on I found a small open glade where a spring broke out from under a mossy bank. There I built a small fire and cooked bacon and toasted a piece of cornbread. After all, bacon is better than bear meat, though I could eat the latter with a relish when hungry. The meal finished, I sat smoking and doing little else except listening to the tiny sounds in the woods about me.

The pipe finished, I leaned forward to tap out the ashes when I heard the sound of a horse coming fast. One surprise a day was enough so I examined the priming of my rifle, loosed the knife in its sheath, and stepped partly back of a tree. Then the horse appeared, and the rider was the girl who had been with Hartlin's company. She was a real horsewoman, for when her mount took fright at me and leaped out of its stride to come up on its haunches, she fought it down and rode past me, her face showing a mixture of anger and scorn.

"Lout," she snapped at me, then was gone before there was any chance for a reply.

There it was again; in little more than an hour this girl had twice managed to annoy me with her indifference, and there seemed no reason for it. The provoking part was that she interested me; she was so alive and different from her companions back on the trail. I wondered why she had been with them and now was returning to the fort. But there was no profit in speculation so I picked up my things and followed down the trail.

The Blue Heron is a huge log and clapboard place a half mile east of the fort on the old road. Both General Wayne and I knew Leonidas Breon well. In fact, he and I had been friends since boyhood, though Lon was a bit older than I and just a bit younger than Wayne. Our homes were a short distance from the Wayne estate. Lon had done well down home and even better out here in the five years he had operated the tavern, for he served good food and had a knack for getting on well with all and sundry. It was pretty natural that General Wayne, with his passion for keeping informed, should have contact with Breon. Certainly, the man had judgment far beyond his years.

Purposely I came in late for the supper served in the dining room. It may be that Wayne's refusal to reenlist me had made me bitter, but I did not care much for the people out here in this frontier post at the meeting of these big muddy rivers. Lon saw me come in and grinned.

"Late again, Martin. Well, I expected it and kept a bowl of boiled turnips and beef warm for you. You can eat in the common room."

He had turned away when he seemed to remember something and came back to me.

"Just watch your step a bit this evening, Martin. Remember what Wayne said about a man named Gibson."

He gave me no chance to tell what had happened during the day, so I went on into the big common room, placed my rifle and other gear in the corner, and sat down at one of the small tables that stood about the room. This was an inviting place when sunlight flooded it; this evening, with a small fire in the grate and candles burning in tin sconces around the walls, it was extremely pleasant. In a few minutes, one of the servants brought me a big blue bowl of boiled turnips, potatoes, and a knuckle of beef.

My first careless glance had told me the room was empty. Now I saw that two men sat in a far corner, heavy-shouldered men dressed in tow cloth hunting shirts, with their rifles and powder horns in the corner back of them, as were mine. The older man was bearded, and when he raised his mug to drink, I could see that one eyelid drooped, making him look as though sighting a rifle. The second man was much younger, smoothly shaven, and with the round type of body that suggests fat but is all muscle. The odd thing about the two, which held my glance for a moment, was that each wore in his cap a small tuft of what looked like sheep's wool.

Dismissing them from my thoughts, I fell to the food, losing my momentary annoyance at Lon in the excellence of this cooking. Presently I laid down the big spoon, took up the bone, and sliced some meat from it with my knife. I kept thinking of the girl back there on the trail and wondered what she was doing with Hartlin's company.

Through my preoccupation with these thoughts and the food, I heard the two men talking but paid no attention until suddenly a word or two cut through and I looked up.

"Likes his bones just like a feist dog," the younger man said in contemptuous tones he did not bother to lower, and the other man nodded his head soberly in agreement. The young fellow pointed.

"He's got a full powder horn just like any other damned thieving Tory. I wonder, John, where did he steal it?"

To be called a Tory was a great deal to take for a man who had marched north with Nagle's riflemen to Boston, who had fought with Wayne from Long Island to his present position on the Delaware, and who had been mustered out because of a wound. But here was trouble once more as it had been with Carmichal who had his ears notched for his pains. Disgust rose in me. I had been an officer; now I must face common rowdy trouble in a barroom. But even Wayne, with all his warnings about using my knife, would not have put up with this.

I balanced a sliver of meat on the point of my knife and tried to put all the insult I could compass into my tones.

"Down our way," I drawled, "we have an apple we call sheep's nose. It really doesn't amount to a damn, but it makes me think of the other end of a sheep when I see people wearing wool on their caps. Looks like a rabbit's tail; maybe they're afraid to tackle a wild bunny."

There was no doubt that the slurs had gone home; the young man was on his feet yelling.

"John!" he cried. "He's insulted the Lambs. Wait till I trim his feathers."

"Wait, Eben Drough, wait." The bearded man's effort to restrain his companion was limited to that, and he had scarcely finished when I threw the round beef bone at the charging man. I had killed too many water snakes with stones to miss, but the missile caught this Eben Drough high up on the head and, while it did not stun him, it did bring him to his knees. Shaking his head, he rose just as Breon ran into the room. The older man stopped him.

"Keep back, landlord. It's still man to man."

"You dirty scut," Drough was bellowing. He had his knife out now and was brandishing it wildly while he came forward, weaving in and out among the tables. Yet I noticed he did not come too fast.

It was a matter of timing. With one movement, I rose and snatched up my stool. Then one step forward and I caught the point of the flourished knife on the seat of the stool and wrenched the weapon clear of the man's grasp. As he jerked back, my toe caught him behind the knee and he sprawled for the second time on the floor. I looked down at him a moment, then jerked out the knife and threw it overhand at the logs across the room where the blade stuck and quivered.

If Drough was surprised at what I had done, it was now my turn, for the young fellow was sitting on the floor, looking from the knife to the bearded man. They were both smiling!

"John Mcfail," he said, "the man will do. Did you see how he handled that knife?"

The man addressed as Mcfail was coming forward, holding out his hand.

"Your hand, friend. Here's a Dutchman handling a stool like it was a Scotch target. Shake hands, you red-haired hellion."

Both big men, we looked into each other's eyes a moment and there was something infectious in that grin of his. I grasped the proffered hand, and presently Drough was up and shaking hands as well.

"Richtier, I was trying to bait you; I hope you'll not hold it against me."

Breon stepped up.

"Martin, these boys know your name. The oldster is Sergeant John Mcfail of the Lambs. The tubby fire-eater is Eben Drough. He's a corporal of the same company when George Gibson doesn't have him reduced to the ranks for fighting."

Of course I had heard of the Lambs and their fighting in Virginia, and their return to help guard this river country. Gibson—that was one of the men Wayne had mentioned. No doubt Breon used his name now to caution me. At Mcfail's invitation, we went to his table.

"I didn't mean to insult the Lambs," I explained. "But when you're mad, you say anything that comes to your tongue." Drough's answer was to reach round and clap me on the shoulder with a heavy hand. When the ale was served, I pointed to the powder horn that hung from my rifle.

"Maybe you men can help me. I traded a bear for that horn of powder and another flask just this morning. I thought powder was scarce out here."

Breon turned from walking toward the bar and came closer; Mcfail leaned forward, his voice soft when he spoke.

"And with what man did you trade, my friend?"

He remained silent while I told him of the bear, the two Indians, and the company bound north under the leadership of Doctor Hartlin. There seemed no reason to mention the girl in my story. Drough spat on the floor when I finished.

"That would be Doc Hartlin, hardest and slyest Tory in these parts. He'd have been hanged if the commandant had done his duty. He's the man that wants settlers out of this country so the Indians can trap more fur. I'll bet he's heading for Presque Isle or Detroit."

Mcfail nodded and spoke musingly.

"And if Doc is pulling out, it may mean trouble. It could be an attack on the fort's coming. George will have to know about this. Powder's too scarce to trade; wonder where the old devil got the stuff?"

The sergeant stood up abruptly; Drough waited a moment, then followed, after which they slung on their gear.

"Wait," I said, "that is if you don't mind shooting Tory powder."

Both men, a bit shamefacedly, allowed me to divide the second flask of powder with them while Breon stood looking on, a little grimly, I thought. Mcfail finally pushed the stopper into his horn and spoke for both of them.

"Richtier, Colonel Gibson wanted us to find out about you a little after you came to town. Tonight we were sort of testing you. George would like to see you if you'd come along."

The remark puzzled me a little, but then I thought Gibson might be wanting news from the east. At any rate, I had Wayne's word. This might be an opportunity to do something. Breon said nothing, but when both the riflemen turned their backs, he nodded to me.

Picking up my arms, I followed the two outside and along the rutted road to the fort.

No sentry stopped us at the gate, at which Mcfail swore softly, then commented, "Any gang of Senecas or Ottawas could pick up a mess of scalps around here most any night with a little hatchet work. Our commandant believes in being accommodating and leaves the gates open so our Indian friends won't get splinters in their bellies when they climb the stockades."

Colonel George Gibson was alone in the big ground-floor room of his cabin when we three filed in. He had been writing and glanced up at us. The officer wore no insignia and was dressed, as were his men, in tow cloth and buckskin, but he did wear a white shirt open at the throat. His face was heavy, with drooping eyelids that made him look sleepy. There was a touch of gray at his temples, and he frowned at Mcfail, who was ahead.

"What's the trouble, Sergeant?"

The voice was deep, with a resonance about it that seemed to fill the room. Mcfail shook his head.

"No trouble; we just got acquainted with Martin Jon Richtier, but that's personal. Doctor Hartlin and his friends pulled foot this morning; Martin here traded with him for powder."

Gibson made no comment, and Mcfail nodded his head, then questioned, "You heard about it, George?"

"Yes," Gibson said, his voice sharper. "Heard it over at the barracks. Thirty of them walked out with nothing put in their way, taking with them what was left of the stock in the old Trent trading post. You boys get to your quarters; I'd like to talk with Richtier, now that he's here."

When the door had closed on the two men, Gibson rose and came round his table to shake hands. I marveled at the size of the man for he towered a head over my own six feet.

"We know each other's names," he said affably. "I'm from down east, too, where my wife operates our small gristmill. That's in Lancaster County."

He glanced back at the table.

"The boys said you were here a few days ago. I need a man of some education who can take a little danger with his work."

His big fingers snatched up a letter from his table and shook it open.

"Here's a letter from Wayne. He says you are twenty-eight years old, lots of fighting experience from Boston down to the Delaware. You were a scout, took a bad wound, and were discharged from the service to recuperate. Now you're eligible to reenlist at your former rank of ensign. The letter hints at a promotion."

He flung the letter down, motioned for me to take a chair, and resumed his own.

"That's official, one officer to another. On the hearsay line, I've heard of some trouble with another officer whom you thrashed and marked pretty badly. It's my notion that Wayne sent you out here until trouble blows over. Am I right?"

Temper boiled in me at his easy statement of almost exactly what had happened. Wayne had not told me he was writing to Gibson. I leaned forward.

"Did General Wayne tell you that last part?"

He looked straight at me.

"No," he answered without excitement and went on talking. "Fifteen of my best men are about to leave for New Orleans to bring back Spanish powder through British territory. They'll go down with a flatboat and a bateau, each loaded with whisky, corn, split pine shingles, and bear hams. The merchant, Oliver Pollock, is managing the powder deal, with Virginia paying the bill. The men who go risk their necks if the British get them, for they won't be uniformed. Lieutenant Linn is second in command, but I need a man to keep accounts, handle the money, and help a bit if the going gets bad. I want you, Ensign Richtier, if you'll go."

Temper was still high in me as I looked at the big man, but I was remembering my general. If he had written Gibson he must wish me to join the man's plans. The colonel smiled.

"You want to tell me to go to hell, Ensign, which I shall probably do someday, but now—I am going to New Orleans. Come with me."

He rose abruptly, slapped on the back of his big head a cap bearing a small tuft of wool, beckoned with a wave of his hand, and I followed him outside and to another cabin where a sentry watched before the closed door.

"It's all right," Gibson said to him after the man had presented his musket. We went inside.

There was no furniture in the candlelit room except four blanket-covered benches standing side by side. Taking a candle from its sconce, Gibson stepped to one bench and raised a corner of the blanket, holding his light so I could see. He repeated this with all four, then commented, his voice dry, "That's the Radel family. Seven Indians and a white man did it. Radel tried a week before to get some powder and couldn't. My boys got to the place while the cabin was still burning, but it was too late for the Radels.

"Powder," he growled, then gestured savagely with his broad hand. "They didn't butcher the little girl too much as you saw, but her folks are bad—under the blankets."

Shadows fell on the tall man's face, showing deep lines as though he had aged suddenly. One huge hand knotted into a fist.

"Richtier, I'll get powder to the folks around here so they can shoot back at the enemy when they come gobbling out of the brush in the mornings. I'll get powder here if it takes every Lamb from my flock, and you, too, Richtier."

I thought of the little girl lying there so still under the blankets and the horrors she must have experienced until a tomahawk brought a certain mercy to her.

"I'll go, Colonel Gibson."

He did not even nod as I walked out.

Breon was waiting for me and agreed that I probably had made the right decision.

"Never could figure George Gibson, but he's a fighter and men follow him. Wayne would want somebody along on the trip for there's a lot of money going and maybe George has to be watched when gold clinks."

Oddly that night, before I slept, I did not think of death, which had come so close in the morning, or of the Lambs or Gibson. No, I thought of a girl who rode a tall horse and who had been so disdainful.

CHAPTER TWO

GEORGE GIBSON certainly acted promptly, for by the time I came down for a late breakfast, the two riflemen, Mcfail and Drough, were waiting to explain the expedition and to instruct the new recruit. Neither mentioned whether Gibson had routed them out of bed early in the morning or late at night to give them their instructions concerning me.

"George is glad you're coming," Mcfail commented, "so he sent us early. Maybe he thought you'd change your mind."

Over bowls of Breon's excellent cornmeal mush and milk sweetened with maple sugar, Mcfail outlined the plan. Last night the thing had looked visionary; now, as the sergeant talked, I could see the importance of the expedition. A merchant named Oliver Pollock, who had influence with the Spanish, was already negotiating the sale of tons of the precious ammunition to the colonies. Our part was to take a flatboat loaded with produce down to New Orleans. The fifteen men chosen for river skill would be dressed as immigrants. We would take along a bateau and would represent that these immigrants would sell their produce in New Orleans and then use the bateau to take them to some place of settlement in Spanish territory. Actually, we would use this fast, easily handled craft to get the powder upriver to Fort Pitt.

The company was limited to fifteen men because a larger body might excite the suspicions of the Tory spies in Fort Pitt. Also there must be no inkling of money or valuables to be taken, for the spies of the river pirates were everywhere. So the least word might get us into trouble or lead to capture. If the British took us, there might be hangings since we were not in uniform; the river pirates would simply shoot us for our property.

The mention of Pollock added to my better impression of the venture to which we were committing ourselves. I had known him when I went to school in Philadelphia, and he had come at times to my farm to buy cured pork. A man of that caliber would not likely be involved in a wildcat scheme. Mcfail was leaning forward, tracing patterns on the table with his spoon.

"The British can claim we're passing through their territory anywhere along the rivers. Near New Orleans, they patrol with whaleboats. It's getting through them that will make the trouble; the pirates just mean plain fighting."

It was Drough's turn to cut into the conversation.

"They'll even have a couple of women on the flat to make us look like real movers."

I looked at him in surprise. When I asked my question, I did not anticipate the real information I would get.

"How on earth will women get back? They'll be dead weight when the boat goes upstream."

Drough shrugged his heavy shoulders.

"Likely George found somebody who wanted to go to Philadelphia on Pollock's ship, which takes more than half of the powder up there. Anyway, our concern is seeing to the fighting and getting that bateau back to Fort Pitt."

But I did feel a concern. This expedition, this powder deal, could make a tremendous difference to our cause. I knew too well the shortage of powder in Wayne's regiments, a shortage that turned our general's attention toward the bayonet. Also I remembered what Breon had told me of a Colonel Clark who had been shuttling back and forth from Virginia to Fort Pitt, trying to organize an expedition against the British forts in the Illinois country.

When our breakfast was finished, Mcfail summoned the landlord by slapping on our table with his broad palm.

"Breon," he said grandly, "bring in the damage for the three of us, and while you're figuring, remember this is the best mush I've eaten anywhere west of the mountains."

I protested when the sergeant paid not only for the breakfasts but for my own last two days' reckoning.

"You're one of us now, Martin. George would be put out if I didn't pay your bills."

Grinning, Drough took from his pouch one of the small tufts of wool and fastened it to my hat band. Last night we had fought about this emblem; today I felt pride in being allowed to wear the insignia of this devil-may-care company. Breon saw the action; presently he shook his head deprecatingly, and the peppery Drough bridled at once.

"Martin's one of us now, landlord. What's wrong with that?"

Breon arched his eyebrows and spread his hands.

"Nothing, nothing in the world, my well-fed friend. Only being a Lamb is such a poor way of growing old. They tell me that there's less than forty of George Gibson's first hundred that are still hale and hearty."

Drough smiled.

"Well, me and John are still up and about and able to drink your ale."

Breon's eyes twinkled.

"Yes, some men are born not to die in battle, so the old saying goes."

If Drough understood Breon's reference he chose to ignore it, and shortly after, he and the sergeant left. There were many things left for these two non-commissioned officers to do since the boats would leave the following morning, the weather being right.

Alone again, Breon and I sat opposite each other at one of his small tables.

"Lon," I said, "the thing is big. Pollock's in it, powder will get through to His Excellency, and God knows how much he needs it."

Breon nodded.

"Yes, a lot will depend on the few of you. Clark was here a week ago with his plans for the west. If you bring powder, he will take his chance at capturing the British posts in the Illinois country. If Pollock gets his shipment through, it might change the course of the whole war. Martin, did Gibson mention gold?"

I shook my head slowly. Breon drummed on the table.

"I've a notion that Wayne knew a lot about this expedition. Perhaps he wanted you to watch Gibson. The man's brave to foolhardiness, but he's known to be a bit tricky about money . . ."

He did not finish, but a little later I went down to Gibson's quarters where I met Lieutenant Linn, a man I liked at first sight. Perhaps a few years older than I was, he was a quiet man who looked you directly in the eyes. Dressed in a good blue coat and a cocked hat, he did not look like a man to undertake a dangerous mission until you looked back again into those direct blue eyes There was never any fear in them, only confidence. Gibson explained my duties.

"Your job is to take charge of the money, to make an inventory of what is on both boats. Start on the bateau then get over to the flat where your quarters will be."

He glanced at the quiet Linn then continued.

"Lieutenant Linn and I will go to Wheeling on horseback. We can't have Tory spies see us start with you. The river pirates must not know we carry money; outside of Mcfail and Drough, none of our own men know we do. A pirate like Colbert would get a full tribe of Indians together to rob us if he picked up the least word."

Crossing the room to a chest of drawers, he took out a buckskin bag sealed with wax.

"Here's the money, Martin, and your charge. There's eighteen hundred pieces of eight, or dollars as we like to call them, in that bag. There are British sovereigns, French louis d'or, and Spanish coins to make up the amount. The Dons want hard money."

He thumped the bag on the table until the coins jingled.

"Men, there's powder for Clark, powder for Washington, powder for our own farmers to blast back at those scalp hunters. Gentlemen, the Lambs are playing for big stakes; fifteen men are going to come close to winning a war."

Somehow the man did not sound boastful to me, and I took charge of the bag with a feeling of humbleness. To me, it seemed to weigh more than heavy gold for I could see the tattered regiments with whom I had marched, the tense officers, and the long lines of red-clad, splendidly equipped soldiers they must meet and defeat.

The morning of our start was what we wanted, with a misty rain discouraging anyone from being on the wharf who did not have business there. Drough met me and we went on board the bateau. It was a good double-ended boat with a narrow cabin amidships; narrow to allow for the men who would pole it upriver. The flatboat was tied up close by, looking exactly like a big box with another upset upon it, leaving only about six feet of free deck fore and aft. The name "Laura" was crudely lettered on her square bow.

"She's sure homely," the rifleman commented as we looked at her. "But she's double-planked with oak that makes her a sort of floating fort. They say she's as hard to handle as a mule that smells grain."

Sergeant Mcfail was to have charge of the expedition until we picked up Gibson and Linn below Wheeling. On board the bateau with me, besides Drough, were Orton Weigh, young Hoadley, who did not seem much out of his teens, and six other seasoned Lambs. Mcfail, Selin and Benjamin Frye, with Thomas Burnett, were on the flatboat where I saw also a black woman and, a few minutes later, a second woman who wore a huge sunbonnet that completely hid her face from my view.

Ahead lay two thousand miles of river travel that would take months. I thought hard about it and what we would accomplish if we won through. When I thought of those men I had left in the east it did not seem that we would be in time to help them. Yet I had the feeling that Wayne had a deep interest in this matter. Pollock was in it; Gibson seemed committed to the job. I did not like the man, but I remembered his earnestness back there in that room where the four blanket-shrouded shapes lay.

"If it takes the last Lamb from my flock," he had said, and: "there's powder for Clark, for Washington, and for our own farmers . . ." The man was surely committed to this enterprise.

It did not take me long to check the light inventory of everything on the bateau, but we had pushed off before I finished and went outside. The river was broad and roily, very different from our own eastern streams. Other boats were in sight, and the flatboat wallowed behind us. We were rapidly drawing away from her. A big, bearded man stood close to me as I looked. He spat into the water and spoke to me.

"It's slow stuff," he commented. "A feller just sits and grows his hair long going down, then works it off coming back up the current."

He spat again, a thin brown arc, and looked at me sharply.

"River boatin' is a job for men with strong backs and weak heads, none else. Should think you wouldn't care for it."

It was pretty hard to tell whether he was complimenting or deriding me.

On the second night, Mcfail directed me to come on board the flatboat where there was a tiny room for me in the aft portion of the boat back of the women's quarters and the cargo space.

"It's on account of that money," he explained. "The men might see you with it and talk, and that means danger from the British or pirates."

Just about noon of my first day on the flat, there was a light tapping at my door, and the black woman I had seen was there, carrying a tray.

"I'm Elsie," she explained. "Brought these fixins for your dinner. Coffee will come when I gets the hang of that there little brick fireplace we has. Land sakes, it's no bigger than a good-sized bucket."

She had brought me cold meat and excellent cornbread, which I ate with appetite.

Later, in the afternoon, I went up on the roof of the big cabin and sprawled there, watching the clouds, thinking of my farm home, of Wayne, of Carmichal; not much of each, but just allowing the thoughts to drift through my mind like the clouds above. Someday I'd get clear of this war business and could follow a team of horses while the plowshare turned over the rich brown loam.

From my position, I could just see the top of the hat of the man who sat up in the bow armed with a pike pole and watching for 'sleepers,' the half-submerged floating trees that are such a danger to river travel. Certainly, it was a drowsy afternoon and this a drowsy scene.

Half asleep, I saw her come up the ladder, and I raised myself on one elbow when I saw she was coming toward me. The sunbonnet had given place to a chip hat that rested lightly on her bright hair, and she was dressed in some sort of flowered gown. She was smiling.

I knew her at once, to my profound and shocked surprise; this was the girl who had been with Hartlin and his people, she who had treated me with so much scorn.

"You," I stammered, jumping to my feet. "What are you doing here?"

She laughed. Perhaps I did look funny, gaping at her and speaking in a voice half choked with surprise and anger. With a smooth movement that showed her rounded arm bare to the elbow, she swept off the chip hat, shook her hair free, then made me a low, mocking bow.

"I'm part of the domestic touch that Colonel Gibson thinks necessary," she explained.

"But," I spluttered, angry because I could not express myself clearly. "But you're a Tory; you were with Hartlin—"

Her steady gaze stopped me, and the smile had gone. Her eyes seemed wider and her voice was cold.

"Yes, I was with those people and I am whatever I am, which does not seem to be your business. Your name, Mcfail tells me, is Richtier. It may be you can speak more clearly in Dutch."

She turned her back, and I stared at her slim shoulders as she walked back to her end of the boat and down the ladder.

They had emphasized to me so often how secret and dangerous this powder enterprise was. Now we had on board with us a girl who foregathered with Tories. In days we would be running through British territory where a word or two from her would bring us into the shadow of a military gallows. This scornful girl could end our hopes for getting precious powder back home.

My first thought was to speak to Mcfail since our officers would not be with us for some time. But I dismissed that finally. The big sergeant did not seem quite the sort of person to understand, and I remembered that I had not spoken to him of the girl when I told of meeting Hartlin and trading with him for powder.

At our evening tie-up, one of the men was fortunate in killing a small deer and there was feasting that night with meat broiling on the coals. The girl ate with us and the men toasted her, using their horn cups and a small measure of whisky, which was a part of their rations. Later, at their urging, she sang for them, and her voice was sure and sweet.

Hours later, when all of us should have been asleep, I flung off my blanket and climbed to the roof. The campfires on the shore had burned down to small heaps of red embers and a light breeze was driving the insects away. With starshine on the water, it was very pleasant up here. A full quarter of an hour had slipped by before I realized that I was not alone. The girl was up toward the bow, apparently looking out over the river.

"So," she said when I approached her, "our farmer does not sleep well."

Her voice had the light mockery that irritated me, and I had learned how well she could carry off a scene.

"Who are you and what are you doing on this boat?" I demanded roughly.

"That is a fair question," she answered promptly, "especially when the man who keeps accounts for the colonel and who holds the money bag asks."

I could only stare at the white outline of her face. So she knew even that, our most guarded secret. When I said nothing, she continued.

"My name is Hester Jordan, and I am a young lady bound for New Orleans. I am well known to your colonel and Lieutenant Linn. Also, I have paid my passage; you, of course, are working your way like an honest patriot."

There was some venom in her words and I stepped closer.

"But," I blurted, "you are with Tories one day, with us on another. I'll have to do my duty and tell Gibson when he comes aboard."

"Dear, dear," the concern in her voice mocked me. "George will be so excited."

She swung half about so that she looked toward the bow of the boat and continued in the same light vein.

"It would seem that a young man who kills bears with his knife could manage to watch one woman spy and keep her from doing damage, especially when she's on a small boat. But perhaps she might whisper to birds about these boats. If you're uneasy, by all means, get help."

She had so thoroughly angered me by now that I stepped toward her, not knowing exactly what I would do. However, to my chagrin, I had not watched my footing. The cabin wall was flush with the side of the boat and I stepped off, dropping into a good four feet of lukewarm river water.

So I was denied even the dignity of swimming to save myself and had to wade back the length of the cabin and then swing over the bulwarks, being thankful that the men were sleeping ashore and there would be no witnesses to my fiasco. However, as I flung one dripping leg over the side, I was sure I heard a light ruffle of mocking laughter but, of course, I could not see her; the whole flatboat cabin bulked between us.

For three more days of monotonous travel I saw little of my fellow passenger, and when our paths did cross, we tried not to notice each other. But I was thinking hard. This Hester did not seem concerned about being reported to Colonel Gibson, and my mind went back to Breon's scarcely concealed doubts concerning the commander of the Lambs. My own doubts about the man would have been sharper had it not been for that evening when we looked at the bodies of the dead Radel family. Surely he was sincere about getting powder. Whatever else was in the wind would probably come to light in time. My business was to watch. Then, four miles below the tiny, stockaded port of Wheeling, we picked up our officers.

Gibson was effusive when he met the girl, calling her by her given name, and when I saw this meeting, it seemed wise to hold my peace, especially when I saw Lieutenant Linn's careful courtesy to our fellow traveler. So long as we rode this great river there could be no possibility of communication with Tories. The only fear was that word had been sent in advance of us, which would mean a fiasco to the expedition and possibly hanging for us.

The colonel presently had us all too busy for idle speculation, trying to make up in efficiency what we lacked in numbers. Breon's statement that the colonel was a fighting man was quickly proven as his plans went into execution. The more experienced rivermen grumbled at the work, but I was glad to learn more about handling these unwieldy crafts in defense.

The flatboat was to become our fort. Somewhere between fifty and sixty feet in length, its beam was a little over half of that, and the deck-cabin sides lifted directly above those of the boat part itself. Different from the average craft of its character, the cabin, which lifted a good seven feet from the bottom of the boat, stretched within six or seven feet of either end of the *Laura*. She was surely a homely thing but there was a lot of room inside her. While the planking was mostly green oak, Gibson reinforced the sides with bags of sand at places where riflemen would look out of small ports. Drawing little water, the flat could be edged in close to shore when we tied up for the night.

The bateau was simply a huge rowboat with both ends sharp. There was a cabin on this, but it was much smaller. This boat was built almost entirely of light lumber, pine and poplar. Therefore, the bateau would tie fast to the flat on the riverside at night; we did not plan to light from her.

Signals would come to us from the whistles carried by Gibson, Linn, and Mcfail. Extra rifles were placed close to the ports, and sharp axes were laid by in case we were boarded or if we wished to cut loose in a hurry. Gibson announced that we would not touch at any other ports going down, and the men did not like that.

"Men," Gibson explained, "lots of people depend on us to get through and back, as you ought to know by now. If we touch anywhere, somebody'll talk. And even if there're no Tories about, there are likely to be spotters for these river pirates like Colbert. They'd be glad to take two boats like ours and slit our throats to be rid of us. Colbert'd even turn the Red Sticks loose at us. We'll just keep moving and be safer."

Four nights after he gave that talk, we tied up where a small creek entered the river on the north side and found another party of a man and two women already encamped there. Their battered boat was festooned with nondescript farming gear, and the man was small, with shifty eyes and skin yellow from the effect of fever. His wife looked even worse. The second woman was younger, with a sullen face and straggly hair. The man said his name was Yates and that the woman, Bella, was his wife's sister.

Gibson was kind to these people in an open-handed way, giving them some of our provisions. I saw him stick a new ax in the man's chopping block. Once, during the evening, I saw Hester give the woman, Bella, something that looked like an article of clothing, and there was an odd look on Bella's face. I thought she protested against taking the gift. I walked down to one of the fires about which were four of our men, including Drough. Benjamin Frye was talking.

"Somewheres I've seen that woman—the young one."

Drough looked at the man for a moment, then snorted.

"That's it, Ben, you're always thinking of women so you think you know every one you see. Wait till we get to New Orleans; they say them Spanish women—"

He shrugged his big round shoulders, interrupting himself in whatever he claimed to know about Spanish women, but Frye frowned and spat into the fire.

When Yates and his wife saw us off in the morning, he explained elaborately that Bella had gone up the little creek to hunt for calamus root.

"Roasted, that's good for the stomach," he explained a little too elaborately, I thought, though I had little reason, beyond Frye's careless remark, to be suspicious.

Gibson looked thoughtful, his eyes seeming to retreat into the caverns below his jutting brows, but he said nothing for a number of hours; then I heard him speak to Mcfail.

"John, did you ever see Hen Colbert's wife?"

The sergeant shook his head and spat over the side of the boat.

"No, but she was a sporting woman back about Pitt. Say, did that Yates ever say just where he was bound?"

Gibson shook his head. Some suspicion must have been in his mind for we were given extra drill, and I think he went over every item of our equipment, cursing one of the men soundly for having a bad flint in place. To me, the bedraggled family might or might not be suspicious, but I felt better at seeing Gibson's precautions. So much depended on our success.

Again, the next night, there was another creek on the north side. From the middle of the river, there seemed to be a small meadow there that made the place seem a natural camping ground. As we moved in, we could see that this creek was wide and deep, running back through a tunnel of overarching trees. Back of the meadow was the usual tangled forest and the interlaced vines that make travel through it so difficult.

Two men worked the steering oars on the flatboat. Coming in closer, we could see the ashes of old fires. According to the drill, the flat would lie in close to the bank, the bateau on the riverside. The water shoaled; we were getting well in and there was no sign of life. Most of the men lolled about the decks, watching the bank or the steersmen. Twenty yards from the shore, the forward pilot snatched out his pistol and fired. He was answered by a fusillade of shots.

It had been a close call; a horde of Indians with some white men among them were hiding in the long grass as we warped in. Now they were on their feet, howling and firing. I saw the pilot, who had warned us, sag down, hands still clinging to the steering oar. Then Gibson's whistle shrilled and men leaped from the bateau to the flatboat. In a minute, all of us were under cover and I was at a forward firing post. From the corner of my eye, I saw Hester emerge from her quarters, carrying a rifle.

Elsie, the servant, followed her employer, laden with powder horn and huge shot bag. Gibson spoke to the girl and not too gently.

"Keep back and down, Hester. We can't look out for you, and don't use that gun unless they board us."

The riverbank was abloom with powder smoke and we, our ears deadened by the sound of our own pieces, felt rather than heard the blows of bullets on our stout planking. Then, from the cover of the smoke, they rushed us, scores of Indians and at least three white men, judging by their clothing.

In cases like this, orders were to throw two buckshots into our rifles on top of the regular charges, and when the attackers were splashing through the water toward us, Gibson's whistle called for a volley. Men went down in the water; there was a shrill screaming from the wounded, but, over all of it, a man's voice was yelling, urging the Indians forward.

Our men were firing at will and calmly calling their shots: "Third from left—center Injun with blue feathers."

The attackers broke, reeled up the bank, and disappeared in the dense cover. Close to a dozen of them were down in the water.

"That was Colbert," Gibson said to Linn. "Them Indians wouldn't rush like that without white leadership, and Colbert stands in with the Indians in these parts."

Linn looked sharply at his commander.

"Do you suppose, George, they know we carry money?" Gibson frowned, then he saw that probably I was the only one to hear Linn's question.

"Maybe," he said. "Maybe." He crossed over to me.

"If they take us, Martin, throw that bag overboard. That's an order."

Seemingly as an afterthought, he slipped one of his two pistols from his belt and tendered the heavy weapon to me.

"That gives you another shot. Try for the belly; pistols don't throw too well."

The second rush came right at dusk. This time, their men were well-spaced and the firing made long yellow stabs into the dimness of light. We loaded, fired, reloaded, and fired again as methodically as men work at machines. But it was hard to hold on those leaping, twisting shapes in the gathering gloom. Nevertheless, the attack was breaking when Gibson stood up from where he crouched at a port and yelled, "Drough, Beal, go topside! They're up there!"

I had no way of judging how Gibson knew we were boarded, but the two men, carrying axes, were leaping up the ladder. My glance back outside showed me dark forms going up the bank and merging with the shadows of the woods. Then there was the sound of a scuffle above us and a long scream.

Hester was standing under the shaded lanthorn, which had given us light to load and fire. I could see her face was pale and that her eyes were turned toward that ladder and the open trapdoor through which our men had disappeared. In a matter of minutes, they came down.

"All clear," Beal reported. He looked grim and wiped the blade of his ax on some sacking.

"There was two of them, a white and an Indian. The white man yelled when Eben went after him with the ax. The Indian made a fight of it. He took Eben's ax with him over the side—fast in his head."

Cold food and whisky went the rounds in the powder-filled confines of the boat. The shore was quiet, though we knew we were watched from the grass and bushes. Beal, making a second trip above, reported that he thought he had seen the glow of a campfire up the creek, then Gibson ascended the ladder. Returning, he called to us.

"Linn, Martin, Eben, and Selin Frye, get over to the bateau and wait for me. Careful; don't be seen from the shore."

In a quarter of an hour or so, he joined us. There was starshine but no moon, and after lying here this long, we could see pretty well. The line of shore was pitchy-dark from the trees back of the little meadow. We could see nothing there but knew they were moving, taking away their dead and wounded. Gibson drew in a long breath and then expelled it.

"Use the canoe we have as a tender, get up past the mouth of that creek, land, and come at those fellows from above. I think Beal did see a fire. Maybe they're ready to come down in the morning by water. Hit them before daybreak, when you've enough light."

Linn held us on the bateau for another hour, then tapped us on the shoulders and we went overboard into the big canoe that always trailed back of us on a line. We poled upstream, careful of lifting our poles because of noise. Past the creek mouth, we beached our craft and took to the woods.

We made a wide detour to the north and then came to the stream pretty far back from the river itself. There, fighting insects and listening, we lay for another hour. Frye insisted that he saw a glow of fire downstream from us and finally we stood up, our clothing soaked from the damp ground, and followed the creek riverward, using all the caution we could summon.

Frye was right; it was a tiny fire shielded by an upturned canoe, and a score or so of Indians and two white men were about it. From the faint glow, we were able to see that a number of canoes were tied up at the creek edge. A white man, standing close to the fire, was giving instructions. As the flames winked up, we could see he was tall and thin, with a hawklike face. Dressed in a dark coat, with a broad hat pulled low on his forehead and a sash thrust full of weapons, he looked what he probably was: a pirate.

"Colbert," Linn said after he had nudged me with his shoulder. "Try for him when we fire."

Once more, time dragged at our nerves. When he had finished talking, Colbert sat down before the fire and hugged his knees with his arms while he stared into the blaze. With his narrow face, he looked like some uncouth bird of prey. Most of the others sprawled about, sleeping.

Insects with stings like tiny drops of fire droned about us; the woods were full of light rustlings. As I moved my hand across my face to brush off insects, one of the men laid his hand on my knee. It was warm and perfectly steady. This sort of thing was an old story to a Lamb.

By common consent we came to our feet at the first daylight, our gunlocks clicking softly. No one in the camp moved. Colbert seemed to sleep. Then our rifles crashed out, tearing the morning quiet.

The surprise was complete enough, and we might have done real damage had we waited for more light. Perhaps too many of us tried for the man in the sash. I fired my pistol at him as he gained the brush. Two Indians lay dead by the fire, the rest had taken to the concealment of the close-growing timber.

Below us on the river, where our boats lay, there was a flurry of firing so we ran to the canoes and hastened down. But when we reached the small meadow, the attackers were vanishing again into cover. We had smashed the attack that was to have come from the creek as Gibson had guessed. Now they had had enough of it. The fight was over.

But Brady Scott had been killed. He had detected the first movement of the enemy as he piloted us in. Three others were wounded, none seriously, and Linn attended to these. We buried Scott in a deep grave. All of us stood by silent while Hester read from her small Bible.

Surely, I thought, as she read those old words, this woman cannot be a schemer. Once, her voice nearly broke as she read, but she put up her chin and continued as though she knew the words by heart.

We looked over our flatboat fort and found it little damaged but badly pitted by bullets. Gibson was now in no hurry. We remained at the place all that day.

"Just to show Colbert, if he's alive, that we licked him. It'll make river travel safer for the next flatboat."

Later, he talked to Linn close to where I was sitting, cleaning my weapons.

"I keep wondering why Colbert struck so hard. He might know about the money . . ."

When he did not finish, Linn spoke.

"Of course the Yates outfit warned Colbert. The younger woman did that. But how would Yates or the woman have known about the money?"

Gibson shook his heavy head and did not comment. Suddenly, an awful thought gripped me. I shook it off as one will the clutch of a hand. It could not be that she would do such a thing.

CHAPTER THREE

OUR VICTORY over Colbert and his gang of Indians and outlaws left us all with a cocky spirit, but there was nothing reckless about these Lambs or their colonel when it came to facing the possible dangers of our travel. As we would pull in toward the low, wooded shore that stretched on in infinite monotony, men with ready rifles searched the woods cover and the long grass. When the boats stopped, men with buckshot-charged pieces waded ashore while riflemen from the top of the flatboat covered them in case of ambush. While I had seen much of the woods and much of the fighting in the woods of New England, I was sure these men were the best I had yet encountered. They seemed to miss nothing: a dead weed in the grass, deformed trees, a trace of mud left by a turtle; they read the prospect before us as one does a book.

Uneasy as I was about this girl, Hester Jordan, who now spent a lot of time up on deck, talking with either Gibson or Linn, I felt better about Gibson. The man did not appeal to me personally, but he understood the business in which he was engaged, and the men trusted him. Something of the weight of my own personal responsibility lifted as I grew to respect his judgment. But I could close my eyes and see the long lines of ragged soldiers, the emaciated horses tugging at our few guns, the hungry men, the grim-faced officers of our eastern army. Somewhere about Philadelphia, they faced the enemy. By this time there must have been sharp engagements.

When I thought in this vein, impatience made me pace up and down in my narrow quarters. Our progress seemed so slow in view of the need.

The great Ohio River dwarfed our own Delaware and Susquehanna, but I had not suspected anything could be like the mighty Mississippi when at last we swung into it. It seemed not a river but a flowing sea on which our boats, big enough to contain all of us and our living, were lost on the great wild brown flood of water. Occasionally we sighted other craft, but for the main, ours was a great loneliness. The farther south we went, the more it seemed the banks of the river were lower than the water itself, for there were few bluffs. It was as though the stream flowed between two horizons when we were out in the middle of it.

Day after day dragged by, broken only by the limited amount of our duties. Noon cooking was done on a bed of sand laid on broad flat stones, which protected the planking from the fire. Before dusk of each evening, we would be running close to shore, hunting for a place to tie up. Travel at night, because of sandbars and floating snags, was impossible. Huge trees, half submerged, were the dread of all rivermen, for they could rip the bottoms out of the flimsy rivercraft. If the trees showed a bit, they were called sawyers; if they were all underwater, the name was sleeping sawyers or sleepers. In bends of the river, great masses of floating stuff had drifted in; sand had been washed on the debris until treacherous islands had been formed. Another danger was the presence of eddies that could whirl a boat about until the seams opened. Occasionally I would stand by the pilots and have them point out to me what they saw. Wide and deep though this river was, there were plenty of sandbars. Those under the surface could be detected by the way the water broke above them. One day, the pilot pointed excitedly.

"See that bar looking so smooth and slick? That's quicksand, brother. Step ashore on one of them smooth bars and you're a goner. Ain't even bird tracks on 'em. Wild things knows."

Gibson, Linn, Mcfail, and Hester occasionally played cards, but there were times when I saw she was reading a book. When we were close, we observed the ordinary civilities but, for the most part, she ignored me, though she was friendly to the other men. Often she would share the evening meal with the crews, and occasionally Elsie would cook something tasty to break the monotony of the regular food.

Sometimes at night I would lie in my narrow room and listen to the two women moving about, and to the murmur of their voices, though no intelligible sound came to me. Their quarters were up forward, then came the baggage compartment, then my small room. Here I kept the money bag, though I changed its location every few days. As a precaution, I had fastened it inside the sleeve of an old hunting shirt, and at any hour of the day or night, I was not too far from it.

Good weather was with us most of the way after the start. We had several rain squalls, and on another day a stiff wind threatened to drive us into one of the dangerous wood islands that lined a great bend of the river. I think Gibson would have welcomed some bad weather to keep the men busy, for they were surly at times about little things. Finally, he set a prize of a shilling day for the best rifle shooting. Targets were plentiful; bits of driftwood, rafts of wild ducks, and when close inshore, water snakes. Hoadley proved to be a remarkable shot, and the men finally ruled out Mcfail from competition because he won so many of the daily shillings.

Two long months of travel lay behind us when we had passed the mouth of the last great river that poured its flood into the Mississippi. So far, Gibson had paid little attention to me; in fact, he seemed to avoid me. Now, one evening, he came up to where I was sitting in the stern of the flatboat. I had been thinking how much easier it would have been to be back with my squad of the First Pennsylvania in Wayne's army. There, one had orders, direct and understandable. Here I was, thousands of miles from the struggle, uncertain of exactly what I should do but feeling that if this expedition were a success, it would mean far more than any other personal contribution I could make.

The night was not dark; I could see that Gibson was smiling by the flash of his teeth. He touched me on the shoulder with his big hand.

"I'd be wagering you're thinking of the army down east. Am I right, Martin?"

His guess was so good that I began to talk about things in the east, of our long marches and countermarches through lower New York, the Jerseys, and Pennsylvania.

"Howe had landed at the Chesapeake, Colonel. Most of our force was west of the Delaware and His Excellency was in a hurry. I feel he thought he could stop Howe."

Gibson tossed a chip into the water and sniffed.

"No, Washington will fight him, but he'll be careful of his losses. He knows that the city with its women, its liquor, and its society life will take Howe. No, Martin, His Excellency knows that his job is to keep his army intact. Someday, other generals will learn that towns mean little; an intact army much."

He was silent for a moment, then: "I have met the general. He does not like me. Nevertheless, I, George Gibson, who have seen some fighting, believe George Washington is a great commander."

This time he was quiet for so long that I asked a question.

"About the powder, sir, what—"

"Yes," he answered, interrupting me. "The powder will be there for us. Oliver Pollock has the young Spanish governor heavily in his debt for services to the city in famine time. The problem will be to avoid British interference. Half of what we get goes to Philadelphia on the merchant's ship. If the British have that place, it will be landed elsewhere. Mistress Jordan will sail on that boat."

I looked at him in surprise that would have been evident had it not been for the shadow. This had been hinted to me before, but now it was confirmed. So she was sailing to Philadelphia; I could not fathom this business and wanted to ask questions about Hester Jordan but held my peace.

"How long will it take us to get upriver with the powder, Colonel?"

He answered promptly, showing he had made the calculation before.

"You'll average ten miles a day, more down here, more above if you get help. Say, five to six months. We could do better with a pack train but there're Indians, land pirates, and the British. Besides, we may carry more than powder . . ."

He let the words trail away and did not finish. Soon he rose from his seat on the gunwale, walked up and down a moment, then returned to me and spoke earnestly.

"Martin, I've been watching you. Whatever happens, get that powder upriver. Even Linn doesn't know how big the job is. When you get upriver past the British posts, you'll have to get help or winter will hold you up. Martin, I've a feeling I won't be getting back with you. You and

Linn will have to do the thinking; Mcfail will take care of the fighting. Remember, from Natchez to Baton Rouge is patrolled British territory. If they get wind of what we're doing, they'll hunt us as they do foxes."

He departed abruptly with no word of good night, and he left me puzzled. Toward the last, he had seemed discouraged, but there had been the greatest stress in his charge to me. Next evening, after tie-up, he spoke soberly to the whole company.

"Remember, boys, you're farmer-immigrants downriver to sell your stuff and look about for land. If you can't find what you want, then you'll trade for a load of moist Creole sugar and maybe some Spanish wine. Keep clear of anything British; a slip of the tongue and some of us'll hang. Watch the liquor and the women."

He glanced at Hester and she half smiled as he finished.

"Women will try to pump you; keep clear of them."

We passed Natchez, a dim mass on the eastern shore, but below it, there were more boats on the river. Some of these hailed us and we passed back our answer.

"Out of Pitt with whisky, corn, shingles, and bear hams."

River trade, in spite of war, had never stopped, so our answer was a sensible one. We felt sure the British either at Natchez or Baton Rouge would not stop a trading boat; business was more important than war.

Several times during the last few weeks, I felt Hester Jordan looked at me as though she wished to tell me something, but I held to my stiff avoidance of her even though I could not shut her out of my mind, much to my chagrin. Certainly, I did not know what to do about her.

"One man to watch one woman."

That might be all right on the river, but New Orleans was different. Yet, Gibson and Linn seemed to trust her implicitly. After all, her errand to Hartlin and his party might have been to say an innocent farewell. Our last night on the river came below Baton Rouge, and I slept with my door closed against the mosquitoes.

There was no way of telling the time when I woke and lay quiet, sure there was someone else in the little room. My thought was for the buckskin sack hidden this night in the sleeve of a hunting shirt hanging to my back on the wall. Cautiously, I took out my pistol from under the blanket. Then I caught the vague fragrance I associated with Hester and I put the weapon down again on the blanket.

"Martin." The voice was little more than a whisper, and it was Hester's, making me angry that it should thrill me so. After a moment I answered, whispering, too, "Yes, what is it?"

She had come closer, for the perfume was more apparent and I could hear the rustle of her dress. It was dead of night; she had roused me from sleep but that fragrance made me think of sunny fields and daisies nodding in the breeze. Her fingertips brushed my arm and I was ashamed that this girl could stir me so much. But she was speaking again, her voice more tense.

"Martin, have you counted that money since we left?"

She surprised me so that I answered at once.

"No, the bag is sealed. I did not see the money at any time and did not count it."

She seemed to catch her breath before she spoke again.

"So," she said tensely. "You have not seen the money; no one has seen it."

Certainly, she seemed surprised that I had not examined what I carried. She touched me again.

"I wish we could examine the bag. There's no way of loosening the seal?"

"No," I answered coldly. "Nor would I meddle with it."

She stirred again and her dress rustled so that I knew she was moving away.

"I thought you would have seen what you carried, also that I could talk with you. There's something wrong, but you're Dutch and so stubborn and conceited. God knows what will happen, but the only way a man like you will ever learn is the hard one."

She was gone and I heard my door close softly. Certainly, I now had something more to worry about. If this girl were a British agent, she might well have an object in inspecting the money bag in my charge; if she were not, what could be her reason for trying to plant doubts in my mind? This money was vital. It would buy the powder, which would enable our people to strike back at the forces ringing about us from the seaboard to the back rivers. Uneasy, I reached back over my shoulder and thrust my fingers into the sleeve of the jacket to reassure myself that the buckskin bag with its precious contents was still there.

Sleep was out of the question, so I swung my long legs over the side of the cot and sat there in the darkness, thinking. Certainly, my own position was weak, and arrival at New Orleans would make it worse. I had seen Hester Jordan with Hartlin and his company, which surely was enough to make me suspicious of her loyalties. Now she was on this boat, and I had not reported my suspicions to my immediate commanding officer. If anything happened to our mission, much blame could rest on my shoulders. I filled my pipe and smoked it down to the heel, but it did not help my thinking; it only made me sleepy.

For our last few hours on the river, we moved through a throng of shipping of all descriptions, from canoes to tall ships. The current had become so light that it took all hands at the sweeps to bring our craft into the wharf. Here I saw a wondrous thing. The level of the river itself was a good six feet above the street below us along which rumbled two-wheeled carts drawn by oxen, mules, or small shaggy horses. Gibson, standing close to me, explained that most of the wharf was built on the great levee that holds back the river. Hundreds of ships, large and small, were anchored or tied up along this curving wharf, and as we came in, one looked north at the city itself. On either side of our anchorage, ship masts, stripped of sails, looked like an untidy forest of dead pines.

For a long, tedious time we had moved toward this place and had talked of it so much that my first glimpse of it was disappointing. Warehouses stood along the street below, some of them having overhead passageways to the wharf itself. The city sprawled, seemingly everywhere, with little regard for order, and the smells wrapped themselves about us: that of river mud, stale dead fish, and the mingled odors of many products like furs, sugar, whisky, and wine. Mcfail stood near me and sniffed the air as our flat bumped the wharf planking.

"Some smell," he grunted. "Just about every stink a fellow wants to forget."

Ropes made fast, our shaggy-looking crew stood on the planks, looking about. Young Benjamin Frye walked across to where he could look down at the street and came back almost immediately.

"Women," he said, disappointment in his voice. "Kind of a mixed lot. Gimme Louisville, where what's white's white and what's black's black."

But we were given little opportunity to look about; one of Oliver Pollock's agents, a tall, polite, light-skinned black man, came up and welcomed us. After two men were detailed as guards of the boats and cargoes, he took us to our quarters on the ground floor of a huge building sided with cedar shingles and standing just across the street from our section of the wharf. There were straw-filled bunks along the walls and a good fireplace at one end of the single big room where we could cook or sit in comfort if the evenings were chilly.

Sometime during the confusion that attended our docking and finding our quarters, Gibson and our women passengers disappeared, but the colonel came to us in the warehouse early that evening after which he made a careful inspection of both boats by lanthorn light. Back in our quarters, one of the men commented on the appearance of our leader, and Gibson held up his light, balancing himself back and forth on his heels and grinning. He now wore a fine blue coat with horn buttons, gray smallclothes, and bright buckles on varnished black shoes.

"The shepherd of a flock must be well dressed to see the governor, my Lambs."

He held up a huge forefinger like a parent admonishing children. "Mouths shut, boys; set a guard on our plunder until it's sold. There are those in this city that would steal your hair for the oil on it. You're farmers, small-time traders. Act dumb—"

He showed his fine teeth in a wide grin before he continued. "That shouldn't be hard for most of us. Some of you can talk a little Spanish, that's why you were picked. But don't use it except to listen with it."

His brows drew down until, in the poor light, one could scarcely see the deeply set eyes. He struck his thigh with his palm for emphasis.

"Keep clear of anything British. Remember, Baton Rouge is only about fifty miles above, and some of its garrison can be around here. By the way, I took Mistress Jordan to a hotel and I'll be staying downtown."

She was gone; I stood staring at Gibson, only half hearing what he said further. My foolishness in not denouncing her might be the ruin of our chances, and I could not understand my own reluctance to speak up. So much depended on this mission that I should have been ruthless; a few words from this scornful girl could wreck our venture. On the boat she could not have harmed us, but here even Gibson had warned of the presence of British soldiers and officers, to whom she could expose us.

The merchant, Oliver Pollock, visited us before noon of the following day. A small man, he was now becoming a bit thick about his middle, but he was dressed immaculately, as he always was, in a brown coat and breeches, with his shoe buckles polished until they gleamed. The man's eyes were sharp, if set a bit too close together, and he knew some of our company, notably the Fryes and Eben Drough. Sighting me, he cried out, "Martin, George said he'd brought you down. You surely get about, fighting in New England, then in the Jerseys, and now you're here; but, of course, not fighting."

He cackled at his correction, and some of the men, including Mcfail and Drough, eyed me askance when the merchant pumped my hand and patted me on the back.

"Saw your neighbor, Anthony Wayne, before I left. I was up at Waynesboro and saw your little farm on the visit. If you ever want to sell it, let me know."

It was my turn to smile.

"No, Mister Pollock, not before I sell my left arm. With the war over, I'll be back there raising potatoes, corn, and maybe wheat. Tell me, will we get our powder?"

Pollock glanced quickly to the door of our big room and frowned. "Careful, Martin. There can be no open speaking in this town where most walls have ears. There's some suspicion about your too-light cargo, even now, and they say you men don't look like farmer-immigrants. Likely, though, you'll get the powder."

He turned to the listening group.

"Try not to swagger; walk more like working people than forest hellcats. Humble pie is always safe, and the town's thronged with sailors who don't like rivermen too well. By the by, I'll advance you some money. One of my men will help sell the cargo you brought down."

Most of the men who were not on guard went over to the shops and taverns immediately after the merchant left us. This free money was hot in their pockets, though Linn gave them sharp orders before they left, finishing with: "Drink a little, but no women. They'd make you talk, and if we're taken on the way back, you'll hang for your loose tongues." I was busy with our inventory most of the afternoon and did not walk over into the city until early evening. Two blocks east of where we were moored was a huge open square lined with shops and houses. Here also were great willows and live oak trees. Everywhere there was a profusion of flowers. The wide promenade that stretched about the place was thronged with gaily dressed people. In front of some of the places were small tables where men and women sat drinking wine or coffee. As I moved on, I could see there was certainly a mixture of people; here were men dressed immaculately with high stocks about their necks, others wore homespun, and there was a sprinkling of men in buckskin. Strange foods were offered at booths. I saw something that looked like our sawyer worms found in rotten logs, only these were pink and the shopman said they were shrimps. I shook my head feeling that I would have to be hungrier to eat them with any relish.

When I had walked all around this promenade and was ready to return to the warehouse, I turned a corner and stopped full in my tracks for I saw Hester Jordan. She was dressed beautifully in a flowered gown and she walked with a man in the uniform of the British army, her small hand, partly covered with a mitt, tucked inside his arm. I turned, but I was sure she had seen and recognized me for she flung up her head a little, then spoke to her escort. Back of them, walking sedately, was the maid, Elsie.

Sheer anger made me stride toward them but, after I had collided with several people and had apologized in Spanish, I saw the futility of going to them. It seemed to me that I never did my thinking in time. Perhaps that was because for more than two years as a soldier I had taken orders. Responsibility for thinking rested with the officers. Even after I had been promoted to ensign, the lieutenants saw to it that I assumed little responsibility. So I had delayed, argued with myself, and now it was probably too late. I kept remembering how the girl's small hand had rested on the British officer's sleeve. But Gibson trusted her. Surely Hester Jordan picked strange company; first, Hartlin and his discouraged companions, then Gibson and the Lambs, now a British officer, resplendent in a red coat.

Fortunately, on returning to quarters, there was work to be done. Pollock's agent, Ferare, an exceedingly polite Spaniard, had come to help us dispose of the cargo.

"Also any land business," he said. "The men, I believe, wish to look at land."

Mcfail and four other Lambs went with me and the agent, who already had a buyer for our cargo. The unloading moved rapidly; huge black men, who were probably slaves, did the work. Finally, payment was made over a broad mahogany bar in the warehouse where our boxes, bales, and kegs had gone. Ferare handled the whole transaction; when the money was paid it was mostly in Spanish dollars. Gravely, Pollock's agent advised that the merchant would charge us two doubloons for handling the transaction, which had amounted, according to his calculation, to three hundred and twenty dollars. Mcfail glanced at me sharply then gravely took the cotton sack into which the money had been placed.

"And the flatboat?" he asked.

Ferare nodded.

"Mr. Pollock will buy the lumber in it at the usual rate, about forty more dollars."

We left the warehouse after effusive Spanish thanks and handshaking all around. When we emerged into the bright sunlight, Ferare looked at me with the suspicion of a smile on his tan face. When he spoke, it seemed to me it was too loudly.

"Now, your cargo was light. I fear there may not be enough money for land, but we will see."

Mcfail seemed about to say something; he looked annoyed, but I noticed a group of loafers on the others side of the narrow street and remembered Pollock's statement about the walls having ears. Perhaps our man Ferare knew what he was doing.

Now we saw another part of this city, shut off from the rest of it by a turn in the levee. Here were narrow streets with small houses leaning against each other. There were no sidewalks; one had to stay close to the buildings to avoid the mud and filth that lay in the cart tracks. And almost every building was some sort of public house, each crowded even at this time of day. Sailors were everywhere; we saw one flat on his back in the street mud breathing hoarsely in his drunken stupor.

A turn of the street and the houses were even smaller, but here were front doors like our Dutch ones, sawn across at the middle so the top could be opened and the bottom kept closed. Nearly all of these stood open, many with a single flowering potted plant set on a shelf fastened to the lower section of the door. Ferare pointed to one, grinned, and said dryly, "The lady of the house is busy."

Just inside others of these half portals sat women, scantily clad, who giggled at us as we walked past and beckoned with their eyes. Occasionally one of them would whisper loudly to a companion, "Kaintuck."

There was no keeping these young men of the Lambs from walking with a swagger. Considering the money that would shortly be distributed among them, I wondered how Linn and Mcfail could hold them in line.

Ferare found no land but returned us to our warehouse quarters taking other streets. There, after I had checked, each man received his share of the profits of the voyage; what was due to those who had shipped the goods was turned over to Linn, and he would give it to Gibson, who had made these arrangements himself. The Lambs took their money, eyes shining; it was not hard to guess that for the moment powder was not on their minds.

Nothing more happened in the remainder of the day and evening except that Linn kept us all busy transferring our meager belongings from the flatboat to the bateau. But the next morning, after he returned from a quick trip down into the city, he had startling news.

"The Spanish have arrested Colonel Gibson. British officers recognized him, said he was an enemy officer in disguise. To keep the peace they locked him up, but in the jailer's quarters."

We stood staring at the lieutenant. Now was the time for me to talk to Linn about Hester. She had worked fast, had trapped our leader. But Linn was in a peremptory humor.

"See that the bateau is in good shape. I want two men on guard— every hour. Better get some provisions in the craft; it could be that we'll have to leave here in a hurry. I'll try to see the colonel and get instructions."

Mcfail talked to me later, after Linn had gone.

"George Gibson's no fool, Martin. I think we'll get our powder, for I've heard Pollock has a ship all ready to sail for Philadelphia with half the black stuff the Spanish'll sell us. Washington could use it."

I nodded soberly, remembering the ammunition chests with Wayne's force. He waited a little before he continued.

"I've a kind of a hunch that our friend George Gibson don't go up-river with us. He's a show-off; he'd rather go to Philadelphia and let the dirty labor of getting the stuff upriver to Linn and us. These slick Spanish'll humor the British by pretending they'll get Gibson out of this city. And—he'll go on Pollock's ship."

I could not quite follow Mcfail's reasoning. He had both praised and cast suspicion on the Colonel of the Lambs. If Gibson didn't go upriver with us there would have to be a stronger reason for it. Certainly the Spanish could have slipped him upstream where he could have joined us on the boat, if they wished or if Gibson wanted it that way.

These Lambs were good men; I'd seen them fight and face danger casually, taking it in their stride as part of the day's work. Now they had jingling money in their pockets; they had been cooped up on the boats for a long time, and there was a thoroughly wicked city open to them. They proposed to enjoy it in their own way, and there was no holding them. Drough and Mcfail remained behind to watch our bateau after the others left in a body.

For myself, I took a long walk, this time getting well back into the city, marveling at the fine houses in spacious grounds with neighboring hovels set on pilings just outside these mansion fences. Poverty and wealth rubbed shoulders with each other. There were many pools of stagnant water covered with green scum, and thick snakes lay on limbs or slithered into the water as I passed. I did not like this New Orleans; it seemed old and suspicious. It stank of dead things, and I was anxious to get away from it and the smell of the slow-moving river that hemmed it in.

Our people were nasty and quarrelsome in the morning after their drinking, and it was hard to keep out of trouble with them. Benjamin Frye, with his talk of liquor and women, was the worst. Mcfail listened but spoke to me quietly so the others did not hear.

"They're like kettles with tight lids. Just let them blow off steam. If we have any row here, they'll land us in Gibson's jail."

Minutes later, Frye, crossing the room, stumbled over the sergeant's legs, staggered back, and roared at Mcfail.

"Get your damned Scotch bulk out of my way!" Then he spat at Mcfail's feet.

The sergeant came off his stool in one smooth movement, and the sound of his fist against Frye's jaw was like that of an ax blow. The younger man sagged; Mcfail grabbed his body and dragged it to the bunks. Turning to the others, he spoke quietly but wickedly:

"Two of them harbor police went by a minute ago. Any more yelling around here and I'll knock the hell out of him that bellers."

By afternoon, most of the men felt better and trooped over town again, leaving Mcfail, Drough, and me at the warehouse. Evening came with no word from our officers, and none of our crew returned for supper. But, just at the first onset of darkness, a nearly full-grown black boy dressed in ragged brown pants and a battered hat appeared.

"Got a letter for Mister Martin, or Mister Linn, effen Martin ain't here."

I took the folded piece of paper, sealed in three places. There was no name on it. Tossing the boy a small coin, I ripped open the missive while he scuttled through the door and disappeared. It was for me, all right.

> *Martin:*
>
> *They've taken the men for a party near Baton Rouge.*
>
> *It's to be tomorrow night in some tavern up there. Remember, that's British territory.*
>
> *—H.*

Mcfail whistled softly through his teeth after I passed the note to him and he had read it carefully.

"Have to get Linn," he declared. "This is his business now that George has himself in a comfortable jail. That British town's all of fifty miles from here. Just wonder when they started with the boys."

Either the sergeant was in luck or he knew more about the where-abouts of our officers than he told me, for he returned with Linn in less than an hour, and the lieutenant's face was grim when he had read the note.

"That caps it, and it's what we dreaded," he said. "When they get them boys on British territory, they're spies and face jail or a hangman. I told George it was too big a risk; the Lambs are regularly enlisted soldiers and should have worn them wool tufts anyway. Mcfail, you stay here and take care of things. Eben, you and Martin come with me."

The sergeant did not argue, in spite of his evident disappointment. Linn had a final word for him.

"If we don't get back in a couple of days, get word to Gibson. Better still, get some of Pollock's men to guard our stuff and try to see the colonel. The powder deal is about at a head."

He was busy strapping on his belt now and muttered half to himself.

"Twenty hours' start they'll have, and we'll have to find a boat. Let's wear all the military insignia we have so they can't call us spies, too."

In another hour, Mcfail found a boat for us, a small cutter manned by two men who regarded us furtively and did nothing about raising a small triangular sail until Linn gave them money. Mcfail had picked up a little more news in the short time he had been away from us.

"The boys was mostly drunk and went in a big bateau with a bunch of sailors. The only good word dropped was 'Crane Haven.' Mebbe that's where they took them, Lieutenant."

Linn nodded.

"I've heard of that place, Sergeant. It's only a few miles this side of Baton Rouge and a hangout for British soldiers. But I don't know more than that."

In our own north country, we could have found horses to do an er-rand like ours, and good men could even run that far. But here was a land of tangled forests, of marshes, of river bayous over which horses could not travel. The small sail of our cutter slapped against the mast, two smoky lanthorns hung at our prow, and the bilge water sloshing about our feet smelled foul and sour. Mosquitoes kept up an unceasing hum about our heads, and our boatmen were silent. It seemed that we were stationary on the oily-looking water over which our lanthorns flickered. I wished for one of those New England whaleboats with a good fisherman crew. Lieutenant Linn was sitting crouched forward a little, as though he could hurry our progress by straining his muscles.

CHAPTER FOUR

SOMEHOW, we wore out that night of tedium. I dozed at times, but do not believe Linn relaxed a moment. Whenever I would wake, he would be steering or speaking to one or the other of the boatmen. The unceasing slapping of the sail against the mast annoyed me at first, but by and by I was grateful for the rhythmic pattern of sound that made me drowsy.

The tardy morning found us close inshore, scarcely maintaining steerage way against the current; a light drizzle of rain had begun. Our two unhappy boatmen were huddled in their places, looking cold and disgruntled. Linn pointed to the single pair of oars.

"We've got to row to make time."

He took the first half hour of it, stroking the oars powerfully, but when he gestured to the taller of the men, who answered to the name of Charles, the fellow looked reluctant. Trying to keep up the pace Linn had set, he was limp and streaming with perspiration in fifteen minutes. So we three Lambs alternated at the oars, keeping the boat close inshore to take advantage of the backflow of the river, which was strongest here.

Judging by our occasional glimpses of the sun, it must have been about noon when Linn told the steersman to head into the mouth of a small creek. When he saw a dry bank, we landed, and Linn built a small fire about which we gathered gratefully. Linn divided with all of us the small store of dried meat and cornbread he had brought in a small bag.

"We'll rest a half hour," he said. "Charles, how far is it to Baton Rouge?"

The boatman shrugged his narrow shoulders. At this exasperating answer, I thought the lieutenant was going to do something violent, but finally, he grunted, stretched himself out on the ground, feet to the fire, and slept. Drough and I followed his example.

We had no way of telling how long we were asleep, but I am sure it was not more than a half hour when Drough, awake first, yelled. Our boat was standing out from the little creek into the edge of the river where the sail would catch the downstream breeze and where the current would add to its speed. Both of the boatmen had seemed too meek for such a performance, but evidently the pace Linn was setting had been too much for them, and they deserted at the earliest opportunity. They paid no attention to Linn's hail, except to huddle down more, so we could see only their heads and the upper parts of their shoulders.

Drough was profanely lamenting that he had not brought his rifle, but he drew his long-barreled pistol. Linn shook his head.

"Not that, Eben."

Drough grinned.

"I'll try for their mast; want to make them some trouble."

Resting the pistol barrel over a limb, his first shot threw up water at the prow of the boat; then he snatched out his second weapon, cradled it carefully in his big hands, and the three of us yelled in delight when the small mast buckled and the sail tumbled down on the deserters.

Drough whistled softly.

"Plain luck, that shot, but it'll give them boys something to think about going back."

None of us knew how far we had come, but from our map study on our way down and our glimpse of it through the mist, we knew Baton Rouge and this Crane Haven must be on the south side of the river, where we were. Granted that we had made reasonable time during the night, we should not be over a dozen miles from our destination.

There was nothing left to us but to walk, and we came out along the creek and started up the riverbank. The going was bad; mud, clutching brush, snakes, and potholes. After an hour of it, we turned back inland and found better traveling in the timber, but insects hummed about our heads in clouds, stinging our faces and necks, even getting up our nostrils until we seemed to breathe them. But finally, luck favored us a little, for at the end of the second hour we found a log canoe drawn up in a tiny creek, which we followed until we reached a crude cabin and found there, working on his skins, a black man who appeared to be a trapper. He did not know how far it was to Baton Rouge but was sure it was a good day's walk.

"You gotta keep back from the river and walk round the end of a big bayou is what'll take your time," he explained.

He had some fish in a live box and cooked them for us. There was plenty of cornbread, and the man seemed surprised when we paid him, so much so that he insisted on guiding us on our way for the first mile or so and then giving us directions as carefully as he could.

A day's journey, but we had to make it in less than half of that, so we set ourselves grimly to our task. Linn was silent most of the time; Drough was as voluble as he always was, talking of just anything that came to his mind. He puffed a great deal, sometimes looking distressed, but I noticed he was setting the pace. For myself, I wondered how this loss of the men, if we did lose them, would affect our venture; but I had the satisfaction that some of the powder was going through on Pollock's ship.

Darkness found us fighting our way through a tangle of trees and vines that finally ended when we came upon a road. Not a good one, it was still much better than anything we had found so far, and it seemed to be reaching in the direction we wanted to go.

Evidently, those who laid it out had in mind solid footing, and so the track wound out toward the river, then back inland. Seldom was it straight for more than fifty yards, but we followed it doggedly until suddenly Drough gripped my arm with his strong fingers.

"Music," he grunted. "Listen."

Both Linn and I could hear it, and in a few hundred yards more it was plain; the sound of violins with drums keeping time.

"That's our party," Drough said grimly. "Guess we're a little late." We started to run.

Crane Haven was a huge two-story log building standing in the center of a small meadow. The moon was out, shining on the dark roof of the house and the closely clipped lawn. To our right, the river showed

and there was a wharf where boats were moored. Close up, we could hear
the dancing, the whooping of men, and an occasional shriller shout from
women. Weary, briar-torn, we stood quiet for a little.

Crane Haven. There was something eerie about a place of pleasure
here in the forest where only the moonlight appeared kind. There were
only three of us—perhaps Linn was calculating how much we could do.
For myself, now that we were here, I was not at all sure of what we could
do, but Drough seemed to have no thought but of the excitement that
lay ahead. With his hand on my shoulder, we walked with Linn to one of
the windows glazed with some sort of oiled paper, which the lieutenant
slit carefully with the point of his knife so we could look into the room.

The place was lighted with a score or more of tin sconces bearing
small sheaves of candles. There was a wide floor and a long bar. Here
was a party with men standing along the wall or lolling against the bar,
watching the dancing. Our own men were on the floor, and the girls
with whom they danced ran all shades of hair and skin, from coal-black
to bright blonde, like the one who was clutched close in young Hoadley's arms. Over her nearly bare shoulder we could see the silly grin on
the boy's face. The women were alike in some things; they wore loose
wrappers cut extremely low, and they hung onto their partners. Ben Frye
passed so close to our window that we caught the reek of the perfume his
light-skinned partner wore. Two bartenders worked busily with bottles
and glasses.

We had not watched long before we heard another sound cutting
through that of the revelry, a rhythmic tramping that I understood at
once. A file of disciplined men was approaching. Linn whirled on us as
he heard it.

"We've got a full minute to get them out! Come on!"

The main door swung open at his push, letting the reek of rum,
perfume, and sweat strike us in the faces. Then we were inside—three
men. Linn whipped out his small whistle, and the blast of it cut through
the noise. Three sharp notes, the gathering signal of the Lambs. Another
moment and he repeated the signal.

I saw men on the dance floor hesitate, then let their arms drop from
the partners they had been clutching and pawing. They might be drunk,

but they were Lambs, and they had heard that call too often to ignore it. Their officers never used it unless the matter was urgent.

"Lambs!" Linn shouted. "Up and out of this; soldiers—"

There was no time for him to finish his warning; there were three outside doors to this big room, and each now framed red-coated British soldiers, their bayonets glittering in the candlelight. Through one door, a young officer pushed past the soldiers into the now quiet room. He raised his hand.

"I have orders to arrest eleven American spies, rebels against their lawful King and now out of uniform in His Majesty's dominion." Gibson had been right, and so had the others, in believing the British would treat us of the expedition as spies. Of us all, Linn was the only man who wore a uniform coat, though Drough and I flaunted the wool tuft of the Lambs in our caps. The officer, a young fellow, having delivered his dictum, glanced round with all the usual arrogance I had come to expect from such men. Someone by the wall moved.

"Keep your places," the officer snapped. "No one leaves."

The half-naked girls huddled together near one corner of the room, plainly frightened. Likely they had been hired with no word about the plan in which they fitted. The young officer looked them over and raised his nose a bit in the air.

"Get out, you."

Some of the riffraff slunk past the soldiers as the girls ran out, but nobody paid any attention to them. The soldiers in the doorway stepped into the room, and I counted a full score, which included a sergeant and the young subaltern.

In those days of the Boston siege, when I had seen so much tavern and barroom fighting, it had been noticeable that some little thing precipitates a fight. Men may be all ready, cocked, and primed mentally for the fray, but something must set them in motion. Now there was hardly any movement in this long, low room excepting that some of our men were carefully and slowly edging away from the file of soldiers. The red-coats were holding their formation. It was Drough who did it, and I am sure his quick mind told him we should act before our enemies were well set. Probably what he threw was a bullet from his pouch. He had tossed it with a quick movement, and it splintered the glass of some bottles that stood on the bar.

The British lieutenant leaped forward to seize Drough, his drawn sword lifted high, the other hand outthrust to grasp his quarry. Doubtless this young redcoat had been schooled to believe no one would ever strike a King's officer, but this was the stout rifleman's opportunity. Even so, he did not use his fist but the heel of his hand caught the officer full on the point of his chin with such lifting force that the man was hurled across the room into the arms of the soldiers. Then, as quickly as this had happened, two soldiers back of Drough whipped up their muskets and one drove his bayonet clear through the woodsman's neck. One of Drough's hands came up toward his mangled throat, the other groped for his pistol, and under the candlelight, I saw the look of utter incredulity on his round face as he sank to the floor.

I scarcely heard the beastlike roar from our men along the bar, for I had lived with this man at my feet, fought with him, laughed with him, trusted him, and he had been killed by a thrust from the back. As I bent to lift the dying man from the floor, my hand brushed my knife hilt, and I whipped out the heavy blade, the one I had used on the bear. I had time to remember, too, how Drough had approved of the way I threw his knife in the tavern back there at Fort Pitt.

Nothing in the British Manual of Arms had taught these soldiers how to fend off a thrown knife or to stop the rush of maddened men who were too close for the bayonet. I put every ounce of my muscle back of the throw I made, and the broad, keen blade went through the soldier's throat as his bayonet had done to my friend. The second of those two attacking soldiers went down a moment later, clipped by a hatchet.

The room was a hell of action, for some of the Lambs had knives and pistols. Others used stools; Linn used his short officer's hanger to parry the thrusts of the revived lieutenant's rapier. Stools flying, bottles smashing, bayonets jabbing; I would have thought no one could have come through this chaos unwounded, had there been time to think. A glancing blow from a musket butt dropped me to the floor, and I fell over Drough's body. There I snatched out one of his pistols and fired it at another soldier with a musket butt raised high to smash it down on

Linn's head. The second pistol flashed in the pan, but it did make a fine club when I was on my feet again.

The soldiers had bunched around their officer, who was grasping his arm where a slash from Linn's weapon had laid it open. They were trying to get through the door and I saw one Lamb, Selin Frye, I think it was, stand and snap an empty pistol at them three times, then he hurled the weapon and knocked a grenadier down.

The soldiers had had enough of it, and our men were wild with anger and the heat of battle. We had cleared the room, and the Lambs drove the soldiers across the clearing and back toward town until Linn's whistle shrilled the recall.

Drough was dead, his clothing soaked with blood and foul from our fighting above him. There were three dead soldiers, one with my knife in him. I looked down at him for a moment and did not retrieve the weapon.

"Keep that knife in your belt." Wayne had said that, but I was sure he would have approved this thrust.

At Linn's barked order, two men carried Drough's body out and down to the landing where a big bateau was tied up. There were no questions and little talking, but we put our dead into the boat, and Linn cut loose the mooring ropes with his sword.

Of the fourteen of us, one was dead and several were in pretty bad shape, but with Linn to steer, we swept the boat out into the current and then bent hard on the ash oars. It behooved us to get out of this place before a strongly manned British whaleboat came down upon us. With what we had done in Crane Haven, we would receive short shrift as prisoners.

Gray morning found us well downriver, almost to the city. We pulled in closer to shore, wrapped Drough's body in the best blanket we could find in the boat's locker, and fastened the anchor to the swathed form. Before we slid it into the water, Linn fumbled under the blanket a moment, and after Eben Drough had gone his way, the lieutenant gave to me the object he had taken.

"Here, Eben would want you to have his knife. Yours is gone."

I took the heavy weapon in its broad, soft leather sheath, which was stiffened with bone where the blade touched. I had caught this blade a long time ago with a stool in the Blue Heron. It felt good in my hand, this buckhorn haft.

After the burial, we pulled in much closer to the shore, which was here covered with dense brush. At Linn's orders, we climbed out and waded to shore; he remained in the bateau. When he had chopped a hole in the bottom, he leaped out, and with his shoulder pushed the sinking craft away. The eddy here had its way with the craft; before we were all through the fringing brush, the bateau had sunk. Our bedraggled crew moved off on the way to New Orleans.

Plodding along toward the city, wading in mud and avoiding snakes, I tried to think my way through this happening and bring some sense out of it. Undoubtedly the British were suspicious of us from the first; perhaps they knew our errand. Hester could have told them, but if she had, why had she warned about the Crane Haven business? Everything about the girl was a contradiction. One moment, she seemed clearly Tory, the next she was warning us. Also, I thought of her voice, reading from the Good Book back there after we had beaten off Colbert's savage attack. So much and so many depended on the success of our enterprise; so little could wreck it.

George Gibson lay in a comfortable jail. It was idle to speculate about what had brought him there. Eben Drough, with all his lightheartedness and courage, was dead. Back at Pitt, Landlord Breon had hinted: "Some do not die in battle." Yet Drough had died in a desperate struggle, with the Lambs outnumbered. I would remember his eagerness, how he had forced the march, and how his warm hand had rested on my shoulder as we looked in at that window of Crane Haven.

By late afternoon, and by devious ways, we were all back in the warehouse, a battered, ashamed, and despondent body of men. In their eagerness to spend the hard money paid to them, they had taken the arrest of our commander with little comment; they had left the success of the mission to their officers, as was characteristic of soldiers in all times. Now they realized what a price had been paid for their fling.

Linn did not upbraid them. Assisted by Mcfail, he moved about among them, dressing some bad cuts and many bruises. Both officers did their work efficiently with little regard for groans and wincing from pain.

It was simply a case of repairing a fighting arm. With the men patched up, there was a most careful inspection of all weapons. Knives and hatchets were honed and new flints put in pistol and rifle locks. These things done, Linn ordered the men to shave, bathe, and get their clothing in shape. Each man had to set the wool tuft in his hat or cap. All finished, Linn nodded to Mcfail.

For a full minute, the sergeant paced back and forth before the line of bandaged and worn-looking men; then his voice snapped.

"You're a hell of a trade for him dead back on the river. You've had your fling now with loose women and mixed liquor. From now on, you work. We'll get that powder and take it upriver if it drags the heart out of the last one of you that followed a British pimp upriver the other night. Now, get to your bunks, you, you—" Mcfail's voice failed from sheer rage, but the men leaped to obey and be free from that lashing tongue.

Coming out of a deep sleep-fog, for an instant I saw Drough's staring eyes, saw the bright glint of the bayonet protrude through his throat. My hand, fumbling for my knife, was suddenly caught in a strong grip. Linn was standing over me, shaking me awake.

"Get up, Martin. We must go to the governor's office."

He gave me time to wash sleep from my eyes, tidy my clothing a little, and to get the money bag from Mcfail, who had guarded it while we were upriver after the men.

"Pollock sent word the deal has gone through," Linn told me. We went in some style, riding in a carriage drawn by two horses not much larger than ponies but driven by a huge black man. Occasionally Linn would look at me. Once he grinned.

"We're soon out of this, Martin. I'll be glad to see the last of the city and be on the river again."

Abruptly I touched his arm.

"Linn," I said. "How about this—"

I stopped there, having meant to ask him about Hester Jordan, but I found I could not do it.

"Yes," he said when I did not finish. "What is it?"

"Nothing," I answered grumpily and shifted the weight of the buckskin bag. I thought he was smiling at me.

Our equipage drew up before a wide whitewashed building that seemed to be made out of some kind of mortar. There were big doors at which stood two sentries, and we stepped out, the lieutenant walking ahead, I following with the bag under my arm.

After we passed two more sentries, we stepped into a huge, ornate room with a wide table at one end about which were set some heavily gilded chairs. Back of it sat a handsome young man not much older than Linn. He was dressed simply in light brown clothes and wore a carefully adjusted stock that seemed to tilt his strong chin into the air. He wore his hair unpowdered, and there was a thin line of mustache across his lip. At his left, in a braided uniform, was a slightly older man, some sort of military officer, and on his right was Pollock who got up as we entered and came to escort us up to the table.

"Your Excellency," he said as we bowed to the young man back of the table, "I present Lieutenant Linn, whom you have seen before—"

Linn bowed, holding his hand over his heart.

"And Martin Jon Richtier, who keeps Colonel Gibson's accounts."

I tried to imitate Linn's bow as I had been schooled to do in Philadelphia when a boy, but I am Dutch, with a spine a little too stiff for formality. In doing my best at it, I nearly dropped the money bag. The man back of the table would be Ungaza, the Spanish governor, who was reputed to be no friend of the English. He smiled gravely, and the military officer gestured toward some chairs.

Pollock seated himself beside me, and I placed the leather bag on the table. In another minute or so I would be rid of my charge, and for an instant, I felt a thrill of pride in having a part in this enterprise. Washington's men along the Delaware, men on lonely frontier farms, they would fight the better because of what the contents of this bag would buy.

"Your Excellency," Pollock was saying, "we will now pay you for the goods you have so kindly spared from your ample stores. In this bag is the equivalent of eighteen hundred pieces of eight."

He smiled deprecatingly.

"Of course, it is not all Spanish money, but it amounts to the sum I have named, and it is in coins."

Suddenly, impatience tugged at me. These men were too leisurely, and I felt the British would be hunting us. I wanted to beat on that long table and tell them to hurry. Ungaza broke the tension when he leaned forward and spoke in his pleasant voice.

"It might be wise to get the matter over; open the bag."

With something of a flourish. Pollock opened the small sack of deer-skin and turned it upside down on the dark wood of the table. Out cascaded a pile of bright English pennies!

None of us moved; the military man's face turned black as a thun-dercloud; there was the hint of a smile about the governor's lips; Pollock's mouth was open; he was staring at me. Linn looked straight ahead.

Pollock made the first move, which was to gesture to one of the sen-tries at the door. The man came over and escorted me from the room, down the hallway, and out of earshot. There, he stood by me, his face expressionless. I could not help but see that the lock of his gun was rusty.

No one can ever guess how long those moments were as I waited. This seemed the end of the road more definitely than back there on the hillside when I knelt by the bearskin and expected the attack of the In-dians. Certainly, I could never live down a failure so costly to the Patriot cause. Finally, I was summoned back to the room but given no chair, and Pollock's voice was cold.

"Martin, I have just covered the loss with funds of my own."

He gestured with a pudgy hand, and I saw the pile of gold pieces before the governor, who also had the bag with the broken seals.

"You were given this bag in Fort Pitt by Colonel Gibson?" he ques-tioned, and I had to clear my throat before answering in the affirmative.

"Did you see the money at any time?"

I shook my head and Pollock snapped: "Answer me."

"No."

"Did anyone else handle this bag?"

I thought of Mcfail, who had guarded it while I was with Linn on the trip to Crane Haven. But I would have staked my life on the sergeant, so I lied.

"No."

Pollock half smiled, and I wondered how much this pudgy man in the brown clothes knew. He put his next question.

"Were you warned at any time that there might be something wrong with the bag of money?"

Standing there, facing the governor and the others, I could remember that hint of perfume, the soft, impatient voice in the darkness on the flatboat. I had trapped myself by not telling Gibson or Linn everything. She had suggested the possibility of something being wrong; she had told me I would learn the hard way. So—she knew about the money. Looking directly at Pollock, I lied again, and I wanted to take that soft throat in my hands and press it, for I felt he and the girl had something in common.

"No."

The officer apologized to the governor and walked to the window. Pollock took out a piece of paper and wrote rapidly with a quill the governor extended to him.

"Martin, I have here a bill of sale for your farm on the Schuylkill. It so happens that I had a customer for it before I left home. Since I have covered your loss with my money, you will transfer your place to me. Sign here, and the governor and Lieutenant Linn will be good enough to witness the transfer."

Fury was strong in me as I took the quill. Surely I had been cheated outlandishly and cozened by this girl and now Pollock. The merchant knew how much I loved my land, but he knew I realized the importance of the powder deal. I wanted to see Hester Jordan once more, to vent my anger on her. Pollock was waiting.

Rage must have run down into my fingers, for I mashed the quill. Linn took it gravely, put a point on it, and handed it back to me.

I signed.

At the door into which I had gone blindly, a hand was placed on my shoulder, and I turned to look directly into the eyes of the governor. We were about the same height, both strongly built, though his hands were smooth and soft.

"Martin," he said softly. "I believe you have been betrayed. There is no dishonesty in your eyes or on your face."

Both of those fine hands went up on my shoulders.

"I am not much older than you, my friend. Yet, I have learned that Fortune does not always frown."

Somehow, in that tangled city, I found the place where Hester Jordan was staying, and Elsie was at the door. One glance at my face and she cowered back so that I had only to push her aside and enter. Hester came out of an inner room, and once more her hair was loose about her face. The garment she wore clung close to her body.

"You," she said. "Why don't you get out of this city before—"

"Before your British friends hang me?" I finished. "How did you know about the money? Did your Tory friends get it?"

Her eyes were steady while I ran on, fury choking me occasionally.

"Drough is dead, he that loved your singing. They're after us like wolves. If a single grain of powder gets back to Pitt, it will be a miracle. Your work is well done."

Suddenly her eyes blazed, her lips curled.

"You poor fool," she said. "I tried to help you, tried to warn you, but there was no breaking through your stiff-necked Dutch stubbornness—"

I strode forward, and my big rough hands dropped on her slim shoulders and I shook her until her hair fell across her face.

"They hang spies," I gritted. "Your white neck should be fitted for a noose, but I should break it for the sake of the men who have already died and those who will—because of you."

Her eyes did not waver, and I was close enough to see there was no shame in them; only blazing defiance. Then, suddenly, my hands were weak; I was conscious of the fragrance of her, the disdain for me, and the courage. I recalled that she had held a rifle when Colbert attacked and that every Lamb would now be a British prisoner save for her warning note to me. Others trusted her . . . I dropped my hands, then raised one and brushed her shoulder lightly where I had gripped it. Then I turned and stumbled from the room. At the door stood the faithful Elsie, a musket in her hands. But I paid no attention to her weapon or her mumbled threats.

CHAPTER FIVE

NEITHER Oliver Pollock nor our colonel visited us again, and there was some hard talk about it among the men. But Gibson's presence with us might have entailed further notice. The British might then have insisted on the arrest of all of us, as they had first done with our leader. Mcfail was more or less outspoken for a man who usually kept his counsel about his officers. For myself, I kept thinking of that short talk with Gibson on the way down and how hopeless the man seemed to be. However, as friendly as Ungaza had proven, Gibson might have been spirited upriver to some place where he could rejoin the expedition if he had so chosen.

The competent Linn took entire charge, insisting that we prepare to leave on short notice. Oddly, so far, there had been no effort on the British part to locate or apprehend us. I did notice that the usual shore patrol of police had been taken over by fully armed soldiers and that they passed our quarters twice in the hour instead of once as the police used to do. Also, we all noted that our part of the levee was as deserted as though we had the plague.

At dusk of the day following the payment of the money, we pulled away from our wharf with Linn steering. Something over two hours later, and perhaps twelve miles above the city, we took on our cargo from a tall, dark ship that was moored in the shadows of the shore woodland. A plank runway was sent down to us from a port in her side and the kegs rolled down; one hundred fifty-six of them, each weighing fifty pounds. My job was to stand by and check the cargo as it came in. The interior of the bateau's cabin was pretty dark and my eyes seemed a bit blinded by the lanthorn. As the kegs were stacked, I had the impression that we already had some cargo before taking on the powder, but I was too busy to check. They were sending down the containers pretty fast, and our men were in a hurry for there was something eerie about the dark river and the shadowy bulk of the ship looming above us.

Linn had boarded the big craft as soon as we tied fast to her. When our tally was complete, he returned to the bateau, accompanied by a tall, taciturn man with whom he inspected our stowage, using the lanthorn with which I had worked. Satisfied, Linn directed that the precious rank of kegs be covered with sailcloth against the dampness of river travel. My ears are quick, and I noted that Linn and his companion talked in French instead of Spanish.

With the sound of the ship taking up her anchor, we set off upriver, half of us taking a turn at the oars, then, in a half hour, giving over to the rest. Probably every man of us was glad to get out of this city of intrigue, of snakes and swamps. We had the powder for which we had come, and no matter how great my own personal loss had been, I was relieved that whatever evil thing stirred in the city we had left, it had not stopped our venture. Pollock's ship would bear powder for Washington's empty caissons; we would take the stuff to Clark and the frontiersmen who held the west.

Linn and I had an occasional chance to talk a little, and I spoke of the seeming ease with which we had come away.

"Yes," he agreed, "it was easy toward the last, but we're far from clear. British whaleboats will search this river unless the Spanish governor sends a ship upstream on patrol."

He gave his full attention to his steering for a moment then commented further.

"One of the bad things is that we're short of supplies. There was no time to get them at the last. Another matter is that we're short-handed for a quick trip upriver."

Hugging the east bank of the river we passed the British town of Baton Rouge with no incident, and we all knew that we were making good time. Then, as the morning sun climbed, we saw a big ship coming upriver, closer and closer to us. We watched uneasily until we saw at the mast peak the gaudy ensign of Spain. Linn waved his hat.

"That gets us by, boys. She'll go all the way to Natchez."

We could not continue to travel at night because of the danger of floating snags, and we tied up for a supperless, fireless camp with sentries set to change each hour. We slept on board for there was plenty of room, our powder taking up less than a quarter of the bateau's capacity. Mcfail and I talked a while that night after he had asked to see Drough's knife. Passing it back to me, he spoke soberly.

"The boy's on my mind, Martin, for I urged him to join the Lambs and he was so proud of the service. Now he's dead and the colonel—"

He stopped suddenly and tapped the knife hilt.

"Don't let that blade get too hungry. Maybe if Eben had taken a bullet I wouldn't feel so bad, but a bayonet—"

He stopped again, and I felt there was more, much more beneath the surface. He would have known Gibson very well, and when he mentioned the man's name there was no respect or kindness in his tone.

Food became a problem at the close of the second day, so two of the men fished as we traveled and took some catfish. At our camp, we killed two rabbits and a coon, but considering the heavy labor, we needed hearty food. Linn explained to the men that there was supposed to be a store of corn for us at the mouth of the Arkansas, but some of us, at least, knew that place was a week's travel ahead.

Well above Natchez, we tied up for a day's hunting, and Hoadley killed a small bear. That night we feasted, the fatty meat being very welcome. All the men were more cheerful, but two of them, Beal and Burnett, were still weak from wounds taken in the tavern fight. Despite our light cargo, we did not have men enough. While we used the sail all we could, it was plain that we could not reach Pitt before winter gripped us and the river.

When the men had scattered into the woods, Linn looked curiously at me for a moment, then spoke slowly, choosing his words.

"Martin, you've been an officer; let me have your judgment."

He seemed to be considering carefully, as if marshaling his thoughts so what he said would be clear.

"First, my orders are to turn over all our cargo—mark you, the written order says 'all,'—to the commandant at Fort Pitt. Well, when I boarded the ship and signed for the kegs, a Frenchman who did not give his name was there. He came on down to the bateau with me and told me that, if I had any doubts about the cargo, I was to turn it 'all' over to the Fort Pitt commandant."

I nodded; here was another vague thing. Linn stood up from sitting on the gunwale.

"Come into the cabin with me."

The powder kegs were stowed carefully under sailcloth, which he lifted. At one end of the storage rack, separated from the others by one of the boat's braces, were ten kegs exactly like the ones we had loaded, excepting that close to the bung of each was set a small brass tack. Linn crossed to the other side of the boat and showed me ten more of the marked kegs. He replaced the cover and frowned. His voice showed how deeply puzzled he was.

"We loaded and you checked one hundred fifty-six kegs. Stored here are twenty more, nor do I know by whom or how they came aboard. The men say they were here when they started stowing the powder kegs; they stumbled over them in the dark. What does it mean?"

I thought of Mcfail, who had been about the boat almost from the time we had reached New Orleans, but he was the sort of man who would have promptly reported such a matter. Linn hurried on.

"I was busy, did not go into the cabin, but Mcfail says a dray came along the levee about when the men were assembling their gear. None of us was on the bateau then."

Evidently, our lieutenant had spoken to all the others before he came to me. I shrugged my shoulders; nothing about New Orleans could be regular and aboveboard.

"The kegs came down fast, I checked them, but once when I glanced into the cabin, it seemed pretty full. Linn, you and I are soldiers. Why bother? We'll obey orders and let the commandant figure things. Maybe somebody gave us extra measure."

Linn sniffed derisively. He did not seem satisfied with my attitude, but as he turned away he said, "No extra measure in New Orleans. Anyway, I wish those kegs were filled with cornmeal; we could use that."

Next evening, he assembled all of the men and talked to us. "Boys, we've got the powder but we're short of grub, and winter will catch us on the way upriver at the rate we travel. Now, I propose that, when we get to Walnut Bluffs, we send a man to Nashville to get those folks to send more men and provisions to Flour Island. Remember, we tied up there coming down. A man can cut across from the Walnut Bluffs and strike the trace in a day. The rest of us will keep the boat moving toward the island."

No one commented, and Linn continued after a glance around. "I was going to send Sergeant Mcfail, but he's the best riverman we have now that—"

He stopped, embarrassed. We all knew he had been going to mention Eben Drough. He cleared his throat noisily.

"So, if he'll go, I figure to send Martin. He's more at home on a trail than on a boat."

The Natchez Trace; six hundred miles of forest, canebrakes, loneliness, swamps, and rivers. A bloody road it was because travelers, returning from the south with proceeds from the sale of their boats and goods, were often robbed and killed by land pirates who waited for the unlucky traders in the laurel thickets. Men seldom took that road—alone. Indians in the hills, snakes in the swamps, dead men in the thickets; the trace had a most unsavory name. But Linn expected me to go. After all, there would be no problem of intrigue in doing it; no young woman who seemed both Tory and Patriot, no George Gibson to doubt.

The attitude of the men seemed to change after I was selected for the trip. While no one had ever mentioned it, losing the gold had not helped my status with these frontiersmen. Now they talked to me at every opportunity, passing along tips on wilderness travel.

One of our older men named Sims had once traveled north on the trace. He seemed to have no other name and was so entered on our roster.

"Martin," he said, "Mistress Mellin's Tavern is just about where you'll hit the trace going across from the bluffs. Watch out fer her; she'll feed you

like a king or slit your throat before breakfast. That woman, she's a heller."
He grinned broadly. "Anyway, it's a nice three weeks' walk to Nashville."

Early the following evening, we tied up at Walnut Bluffs, two great
humps of thinly forested red clay ground on the eastern side of the river.
Linn, with Sims commenting, drew a rough map of the route, while
Mcfail went over my gear carefully. Men tried to lend me things I might
need, and I did take young Hoadley's light blue blanket and two extra
pairs of moccasins but rejected Linn's offered loan of his pocket compass.
He would need it more than I would. In the gray of a misty morning, I
climbed the steep bluffs to a wide tableland stretching to the east.

Linn was about right in his calculations for, following a faint path,
by midafternoon I came out on what I knew must be the trace, here a
pretty good wagon road with ruts made by wheeled vehicles showing.
Soft places were bridged with the inevitable corduroy of the frontier. But
I did not see any signs of habitations until almost evening when I reached
the tavern about which Sims had told me.

It was a huge, sprawling building, looking as though each different
wing had been built to it as an afterthought. Originally it had been a
two-story cabin; now, a long porch tied both cabin and wings together. Benches along the wall invited loafers; back of the house chickens
scratched busily and the grunting of hogs could be heard. Beyond a
fringing of brush and a small brook were fields from which came the
tinkle of a cowbell, a sound that made me homesick for my own place
until suddenly I remembered that I no longer owned it. Above what
was probably the main doorway was a crudely lettered board, which announced that this was: "Last Chance, Mistress Mellin Prop."

As I walked up, a woman stepped out on the porch, standing there
with hands resting on ample hips and smiling. She removed one hand
and pointed at me.

"You're hungry, young man, and just in time."

I followed her into the house and set my gun and pack in the corner.
The big room was delightfully clean, as was the woman herself. A bit on
the stout side, she showed white teeth when she smiled and her print
dress, though worn, was very clean.

The usual bar was set across one corner with a door opening back from it; the floor was of well-smoothed puncheons and most of the chairs had woven rush bottoms. After the cramped quarters of the flatboat and bateau, this place looked huge and most comfortable. Gesturing toward a small table, my hostess left me to return in minutes laden with steaming dishes and followed by a black girl carrying more.

They fed me royally on boiled ham, potatoes, some sort of spicy greens, and chestnuts cooked as they do them in my country. It is doubtful if there is any better food than these nuts unless it be the breast of a young wild turkey.

"Mellin's my name," she told me as I ate. "My man's off to Nashville to pilot a flatboat down to Natchez. He makes a living that way, though I see little of him because of it. Mayhap you've seen him in your travels; a small man but wiry, with a shock of upstanding, near-gray hair."

There was an odd quality about this woman, as though back of the facade of real friendliness she was measuring me carefully. Curious about me, she was too shrewd to be blunt in her questioning. Now I noticed that she did not even wear the usual moccasins. Her soft kid shoes had silver buckles on them, and I caught the glint of golden earrings when she moved her head.

"No," I answered carefully, "I've not been on the river very long. I do not believe it has ever been my fortune to have seen him. My name is Martin Jon Richtier, and I carry a message to Nashville."

"Oh," she said, her eyes bright. "Belike your message is important. Mebbe it would be good to tell it so folks could pass it along if something happened to you on the trace, like a snakebite or such happening."

When she spread her palms on the table, I smiled.

"I would not know, mistress, since the message is sealed." Fumbling in my pouch, I found some silver and paid for my supper.

"Perhaps you could put me up some provisions for the trip ahead; I am well able to pay, and I shall have no time for hunting."

She was smiling, her chin resting on one hand so that the sleeve fell back showing her arm bare to the shoulder. With her other fingers, she poked the coins.

"You will stay the night, my young friend, and be rested to start your long journey. There is lively company for a tall man with red in his hair and a hungry look on his face."

She leaned far forward across the narrow table, and her eyes were bright and like deep pools.

"Tell me, Martin Jon, would she have none of you, this great lady? Couldn't you find amusement with lesser people but more friendly?"

I stared at her until she looked down at the table. Perhaps what she said was mere accident, but she was going on.

"News travels fast, young friend, news of a boat on the river that goes north, a boat that went south not long since. There are those who travel fast in canoes and who ride fast horses. But, you shall have a bed and sleep. No, our Indian lass with skin the color of buckskin will not bother you, even though you are a young buck with plenty of money in your pouch. Nor will Mamie, the toast of these parts and the apple of my eye. You will sleep; you are sleepy now.

It had grown dusk as I ate; a skimpily dressed young girl padded about the room, lighting candles. I had another deep draught of the spiced cider that went with the meal and was sleepy, desperately so. Across the table, the woman nodded to me.

"Sleepy, come; I'll find you a bed."

I stumbled after her up a steep stairway, and the bed in the narrow room was wide and deep. As I sat on the side of this couch loosening my moccasins, her fingers were at my throat, untying the laces of my hunting shirt. Presently I sprawled back on the bed and dropped into a black well of sleep.

What happened that night has never been clear to me, but for most of the time, I must have slept like a log. Yet sometime in those night hours I was not alone. There had been candlelight and soft fingers stroking my forehead, while a voice droned near my ear.

"You were on the boat, Martin Jon, on the boat with the kegs, but where was the French gold?"

The words sounded like the annoying singing of a mosquito until, in exasperation, I said, "There is no gold; only powder."

"You are a liar, Martin Jon." The voice was thin now and stopped after repeating the statement.

It could be that I dreamed the whole of it, but I could not understand, when I dressed in the morning, why I would have dreamed of
gold. I grinned to myself about the incident. A little later I learned that,
whatever her morals, the Mellin woman knew what a man needed on the
trail. First, there was a good breakfast and, piled on the table, a supply of
parched corn, dried meat, hard bread, maple sugar, and a small wooden
box of bacon drippings.

"I'll live well," I exclaimed when I saw what she had for me, and she
smiled.

"Yes, you will live, but what for? Martin Jon, you are too solemn. A
young buck with money and he sleeps alone." She chuckled deep in her
throat.

"Why, that Mamie; I have a hard time keeping that husband of mine
away from her."

I threw back my head and laughed at her dismay of me, then I took
out some money and divided it into three piles.

"This, mistress, is for you, that for the Indian who is like buckskin,
and the third pile is for this wondrous Mamie."

She cackled with laughter and put the silver in her pocket. When
I had slung on my pack and had shouldered my gun, she put her arms
about my neck and kissed me. For just a moment her fingers stroked my
forehead, and there was something familiar about the touch. Releasing
her, I went out on the porch, looked about, then struck off up the trace.

Back on the boat, I had told myself that this venture would be free
from problems, but the night at the Last Chance had brought its own.
It was easy to set the whole down as a dream, but I was awake when
the Mellin woman had kissed me and passed those fingers across my
forehead. Gold. Wayne had hinted about French financial help; Linn
had spoken of a Frenchman who wanted our cargo turned over to the
commandant at Pitt. In the night, there had been the question. Earlier,
the Mellin woman had asked me if some woman would have none of me.
No, the problems had not all been left behind in New Orleans. Shrugging my shoulders under the pack, I set myself to the task before me.

In a mile, the trace was no longer a wagon road but a wide horse path
that found the best grades up and down the small hills. This business
of forest travel was an old story to me; resting five minutes out of each

hour, eating the noon meal as I walked, and stopping before dark to cook meat and ash cake. When this was eaten, the first hour of darkness meant more walking until a friendly thicket gave me a place where I could sleep, curled up in Hoadley's blanket.

My days followed this pattern of walking from dawn until well after dark, and as I warmed to the work, there was time to note that the weather was pleasant and that I was traveling through an autumn wood, though in this southland there was not the rich splashing of color we expect farther north. Yet there was that in the air that told of nuts being ripe, of grapes hanging rich and fragrant in the thickets, and squirrels well fed and busy.

Linn had claimed he would have enjoyed the trip, and so I would have had I been able to forget the men out on the river, short of food and laboring desperately through the hours to bring their vital cargo through. Also, my mind kept turning to Hester Jordan with her courage, her disdain of me, and the question of whether she was really friend or foe. Often, too, when I was dropping off to sleep, I had to shut away the picture of Eben Drough with the steel through his throat. Sometimes I even speculated about Mistress Mellin. She had been the soul of hospitality, but I was sure that had she lived in Old New England they would have hanged her for a witch.

Eighteen days out of Walnut Bluffs I came to the first big river. Horses could have managed the ford, but a man would have been soaked; so, I found a dead tree a quarter of a mile upstream, cut it down, and, with a pole to help, crossed, getting wet only to the waist.

Once across, I changed moccasins, for I could not risk burning my feet. Too many depended on what they could do. As I bent over this task, my hat was ripped from my head and I heard the crash of the shot. Instantly, I dropped behind the log on which I was seated, primed my own rifle, and watched for the marksman to expose himself. The smell of burned powder hung in the air, but the forest was still. Even the small wild people were hushed. When nothing more happened, I circled the place, rifle ready, but did not even find a track. But the shot did me some good; I was more cautious about the thickets, and I crossed the hills more carefully.

The day following I found hard work because the watching added to the labor of walking. So it was that, after I had my evening meal, I did not go more than half a mile before I found a thicket and was so weary that I slept heavily.

The morning was misty. Working my legs loose in the blanket, I rolled over and looked straight into the barrels of a fowling piece held not ten feet away by a man who was seated on a rock. This first glance showed me that there were two other men, and one was small and wiry, with a shock of iron-gray hair. He did not wear a hat. The man who held the gun reminded me a bit of Linn because he was carefully dressed, his face cleanly shaven, his stock neat, and there were wind wrinkles at the corners of his eyes. But his lips were thin, too thin. When he spoke, he kept his voice down, but there was a grating quality about it.

"Tie him up, Bill."

Bill was the big fellow dressed in slovenly buckskins, not the man with the gray hair. He was rough about the business and used rawhide straps as the Indians do. Presently, I was tied to a beech tree with my head the only part of me that I could move.

The leader laid down his gun and came close to me.

"Now, my friend, some questions. You were one of a party that left Fort Pitt and went to New Orleans."

I did not reply and my questioner turned to Bill, who promptly slapped me in the face until my eyes ran. The rasping voice continued its questions.

"That party is coming upriver; where is it now?"

"I don't know," I gritted through teeth set in anger and pain.

The leader jerked his head at Bill, who loosened my bonds enough so he could tie me facing the bole of the tree. Then he beat me savagely with rods cut from a nearby thicket. There were more questions; why I had come overland, what time the boat was making. When I kept silent, Bill ripped off my shirt and began to cut my back into ribbons with limber rods.

"You went down for powder and French gold," the voice grated. "Did you get the gold?"

Too much hung on the success of this expedition for me to talk.

I remembered the Colbert attack, but then I was well fed and had company. This was different; no chance to fight back. The leader was standing close to me, and I did not turn my head even when his voice raised to a wild shriek. Bill began the beating again, then the world went mercifully black and I felt my body sag down in the cords.

They had captured me early in the morning, and the sun was high when I came back to consciousness to find myself unbound and lying at the base of the tree. There was no trace of my captors and, turning my head, I saw that all my gear, even my weapons, lay heaped close to me.

Moving at first seemed impossible, but I did manage to drag myself to the little brook close by where, rolling over, I managed to get my torn back into the cold water. After a half hour or so, I got on my feet and found strength coming back to me, strength I would need desperately. My whole back was an aching mass, but pain or not, word had to get through. So, carrying my things in my hands, I went forward doggedly.

At times I wanted to fling away my gun or the packsack of provisions, but I knew that probably meant death and the failure of my mission. Flies buzzed about, trying to get at the clotted blood on my back, and finally, I walked swathed in Hoadley's blanket. Before I lay down that night, I nibbled on a bit of Mistress Mellin's cornbread and fell into an uneasy sleep, for each time I turned, the smarting of my wounds wakened me.

But fortune was with me. By noon of the following day, I came out into a natural clearing that had been broadened by ax work, and there was a big cabin beyond which flowed a wide river over which ran a cable. From what the men had told me, this would be the ford of the Duck River.

He was a huge man with a forest of beard who saw me and came forward, then snatched my things from my hand and supported me until I sank down on the edge of his porch. My head was swimming with weakness and exertion.

"You be a Lamb!" he roared, pointing to the tuft of wool in my hat. "I was with them in Virginny."

He lifted the blanket clear and saw my back.

"God!" he cried. "Was it Injuns or what?"

But he did not press his questioning. Later he was to tell me he was Henry Mark and that he used to help with wounds. Lifting me easily, he put me inside the cabin on a good bed and anointed my lacerated back with some kind of cool ointment, after which he dosed me with whisky and I slept.

Mark had a good horse. When I was able to tell him my errand, he left me with his man and himself rode to Nashville where he said he would give my warning to Colonel John Neville. Two days later he returned, bringing three other horsemen with him, one a rather small man dressed neatly in town clothing but with his white shirt open at the throat. The others deferred to him as he came to my bed.

"I'm John Neville, Richtier. You'll feel better when I tell you we've already sent our patrol to the river. You see, we've a mounted volunteer company so we didn't need to lose any time."

This man, Neville, was a tremendously interesting person, sitting with me most of the time during the rest of that day and the next until they felt I would be in shape to ride in with them. He told me of the development of Nashville, of their boat building, of the improvements made, and their concern about the war. More than half of their able-bodied men would march with Clark once he got his expedition underway, and the blow would be struck at the British forts north of the Ohio.

"Destroy them and Nashville will be to the new United Colonies what Fort Pitt is now. The open river with a flow of trade to the gulf will be life."

I said nothing of the British ports at Natchez and Baton Rouge or how his boats were to pass them. The enthusiasm of the man was contagious. He was full of questions, and I told him of the fighting about New York, of Wayne and his love of the bayonet, and of Washington, moving down the Delaware to check Howe. "If His Excellency loses there," I said, "he may retreat inland." Neville gestured with his hand excitedly.

"Yes," he said. "Let the seaboard go. Washington's army in this great inland country can draw strength from the land. When we gain enough power, we can push the British armies into the sea." So we went on speculating and talking about the war, the importance of horse breeding, the quality of this western soil, and a hundred other things.

"When the war's over, Martin," he said, "you'll have to come out here to us and farm."

He was running on, but in my mind's eye, I was seeing my own small place with its stone house, its covered spring, the level fields, and the hills lifting back of it. Now that was gone. This western land might be productive, but it was not home. Bitterness welled in me; from the time Hester Jordan had looked at me so disdainfully back at Fort Pitt until now, misfortune had dogged me until here I sat in the Tennessee wilderness with an aching back. But in spite of what was in my mind and what showed on my face—for Neville was looking at me curiously—I could not forget the courage in her eyes and the fragrance that clung about her like the hint of a spring morning.

We rode slowly after Mark had set us over the river, refusing all pay for his hospitality.

"We be of the same flock, Martin," he said. "What would Sergeant Mcfail be saying if he knew Hen Mark had taken ought as pay from a fellow Lamb?" he had said, and I knew he watched us going, though my back was too stiff to allow me to look behind.

We passed through a country already being settled. There were 'deadenings' where trees had been girdled, then stump fields, then cleared ones. Cabins became more and more a part of the landscape until we reached the Cumberland and gazed across to Nashville town. Looking ahead, I knew that six hundred miles of that devilish trace lay behind me and that I had not failed, for men were on their way to help Linn.

The town itself was a mixture of log cabins and stone or clapboarded houses, and the people on the streets were like their dwellings. Here were those in hard shoes and cloth coats, others in tow cloth and buckskin, but all were friendly. There was even an Indian or so loafing in front of the stores.

Neville saw to it that I had quarters in their best tavern and insisted that I was the guest of the territory. But when he had seen to the accommodations, he insisted on my coming over to his place of business, the Western Lands Company, where we held a sort of open house. Word must have been passed around, for many gathered, and I had to tell of the expedition, of the powder that was coming, and of the trip. I told of Colbert's attack, of the British capture of the Lambs and how Linn had freed them, and I talked of New Orleans and the friendly governor. But I said nothing of Gibson remaining in the city or going with Pollock. Nor did I mention Hester Jordan or my own troubles. Later, Neville came to my room; he had picked up some news.

"The men who captured you were seen here," he said. "They came from above, likely Fort Pitt, and the leader was a man named Doak."

I thought of Mistress Mellin and her description of her husband. Neville shook his head when I mentioned him.

"No, I do not think one of the men was Mellin. But those taverns are in with the land pirates that follow the trace."

"Sir," I said, "what is this story of gold? Mistress Mellin spoke of it, as did these outlaws."

"That's a rumor," he answered. "It followed you down the river." He looked at me quizzically. "Is there gold, Martin?"

And I had to answer him as I did the men who had beaten me: "I don't know."

Neville had sent a second expedition to meet Linn, but I was taken on to Louisville where a doctor did some things for my back, which had been slow in healing. But I was well again when finally Linn and his men arrived with the precious bateau load of powder. All of them showed signs of the privations endured.

"No corn on the Arkansas," Linn told me. "We had to carry some of the men ashore because of their weakness. Then the Indians were good to us, and we killed a buffalo. Martin, we ate pemmican. It smells to high heaven, but it does stick to a man's ribs."

I told of my own trip, and his lips closed grimly when, at his request, I showed my back. Then I asked him about the gold, and he shook his head.

"You know all I know about it, Martin, but the kegs are there, twenty of them marked with those brass tacks."

He changed the subject.

"Mcfail's a different man, dour all the time and bitter against the colonel. He broods about young Drough; even thinks Gibson warned the British."

Linn and most of the rest of us Lambs went by horseback to Wheeling, the boat being in charge of and manned by men of the volunteer patrol companies along the way. Sergeant Mcfail remained with them.

At this small fort, we Lambs went aboard and continued there until we finally tied up at the wharf we had left so long before.

I do not believe Nashville, with all its claims, could have put on a welcome such as we received. Certainly, Philadelphia would not have dropped its dignity as the people of this place did. Here, powder was life, the only wall between homes and the red flood of British beasts. These folks were disposed to show us honor.

Corn whisky is a staple in these parts, but the others of our small company had more stomach for it than I had. I found time on the second day of our arrival to write a long letter to Wayne, and Breon dispatched it over the mountains. For myself, I was debating whether to follow the letter or to take my private feud down to Nashville and out onto the trace, for every twinge reminded me of those three outlaws, and I wanted to see the silver barleycorn sight of my rifle against the face of that man with the rasping voice.

General Leith, Commandant at Pitt, was the speaker at the celebration's final big dinner. I looked at him carefully as he rose to present us Lambs, one by one. A tall man, thin faced, he wore full regimentals, and his voice had a bit of rasp in it, unpleasantly reminding me of the outlaw, Doak.

I bowed, as did the others, when my name was called, and I thought there was an odd look on the general's face, but I set that down to the whisky. The guests applauded when I seated myself, but their hands seemed hard to manage from the amount of whisky they had consumed.

CHAPTER SIX

IT WAS A real relief to be back in Lon Breon's comfortable tavern after the speechmaking and the backslapping, together with the free-flowing whisky that had turned the good men with whom I had labored and fought into maudlin fools. Besides, though I had gone with the expedition and had tried to manage my own part, I felt a real bitterness about the loss of my farm and the unjust suspicion that had fallen on me because of the disappearance of the money. Certainly, I had guarded my charge well, but there was no way of proving my contention that the English pennies were already in the bag when it was turned over to me. Hester Jordan had voiced her fears, but I had distrusted her too much to profit by her suggestions.

"You'll have to learn the hard way," she had said scornfully, and I had, through the fighting on the river, the dangers in New Orleans, and the misfortunes I met on the Natchez Trace.

Breon and I had a long talk in my room. The innkeeper was a good listener and a keen commentator. I told him the entire story, leaving out Hester Jordan, whom he did not mention either.

"Martin," he said, "we're both Dutch and a little slow, but I never liked nor fully trusted Gibson. He's a great fighter and a hero, excepting to his creditors. It's said that his wife even sends him money from the little she makes at the mill down east."

He drew strongly on his pipe, which was filled with good Lancaster tobacco.

"Hartlin's another. The doctor has big interests in Philadelphia and out here. I know that he buys and sells tracts of land, heads a string of

Indian traders and is hand in glove with them—even speaks their languages. It's my opinion that he cares little who wins this war just so his interests are safe when a peace is signed." His pipe seemed to bother him; after he had tamped the bowl with his blunt finger, he held it up and I saw the ashes clinging to it.

"Hartlin, Gibson, and Pollock know each other and I know nothing, but I'll wager Hartlin has some hold on George Gibson. Maybe it's money loaned him; maybe something else."

Looking at the heavy face of my friend wreathed in tobacco smoke, and having heard his comments so far, I asked a question. "Lon, was that money ever in that buckskin bag?"

To my surprise, he nodded in affirmation.

"Yes, the money was raised mostly in Virginia, part about here, and I saw them put it in the bag—British sovereigns, French gold, Spanish dollars; all hard money. Martin . . ." He smiled, leaned forward, and changed the subject. "Forget about that little farm Pollock and they took from you. Settle out here and get on your feet trading. I'll lend you any money you need."

He roused in me that feeling of homesickness that is so strong in us who own farmland; the longing for brown fields, for split-rail fences, for the whisper of growing cornfields in the breeze, the sight of potato bloom. I turned toward the window and was silent for a long time. When I did look back at my friend, he was frowning.

"Tell me the story of this Carmichal business again. There's reason for my asking."

I shrugged my shoulders and helped myself from his tobacco pouch.

"Not much to it, Lon. I never liked the man. Carmichal is a captain who has friends in Congress and relatives like Gates and others. He knows his influence, struts about, and considers himself a great duelist. After my enlistment ran out while I was wounded, I came back to re-enlist. Wayne wanted to promote me. Well, at a dance I took a girl who was Carmichal's partner out on the dance floor too often, and the upshot was that he threw wine in my face and I knocked him down. When he challenged me, I said I wanted to fight with knives."

Breon chuckled.

"Knives, Martin; was that fair with your skill—"

"No, but swords would have been as bad for me, so when he got the opening that I was now a civilian, he declared that he could fight only gentlemen, not Dutch farmers. So I hunted him up, thrashed him well, and then nicked his ear—not much but so he will carry a scar."

Breon shaped his lips to whistle, then commented, "So the man went to his big friends; Wayne likely stood by you and sent you out here until the fuss died down."

I nodded; that was essentially the situation, though Wayne wanted me to use my time and status to learn about the situation around Fort Pitt.

"That's about it, Lon, but why ask about Carmichal?"

"Because the man was here while you were away. He was on some military mission to Commandant Leith, who is his cousin. It was the captain's regular tour of duty."

I frowned, remembering that Wayne told me Carmichal was to go south.

Breon had more to say. "The grapevine has it that Leith does not like Wayne because he thinks that general wants this western command. So a man who had served with Wayne is not welcome out here, and I do not think Carmichal improved your own status, Martin. Especially is that true since the loss of that money. Martin, if you were not a Lamb, you might have to be very careful."

There was plenty to think about in what my friend had told me.

If Carmichal had been here, trouble would raise its head at the first opening—and it did the following morning when two uniformed soldiers came to the tavern with the peremptory statement that I was to report to General Leith's headquarters at once. There was no explanation, just an order.

The commandant looked a little the worse for the carousing of the last few days, and a glass of spirits stood on the table beside the inkhorn and rack of quills. At another table, a young officer busied himself with papers spread before him. Leith's pale eyes studied me; his thin hand reached for the glass but then withdrew.

"Richtier, you were once an ensign in the army."

I nodded. He had simply made a statement, and he picked up a paper, reading from it.

"Ensign in a rifle company connected with the First Pennsylvania Line regiment. Served as a scout, was discharged while wounded, attempted to re-enlist but were refused, after which you came to this place as a trader."

Now he sipped from his glass and shuddered.

"You had charge of Colonel Gibson's funds during this expedition for powder.'"

I nodded. My temper was rising, but I remembered Wayne's caution about trouble. Surely I had had enough of that sort of thing by now.

"You lost this money."

When I did not reply, he snapped at me, "Answer my question!"

"The general is making statements."

He frowned, glanced at his paper, and did ask a direct question. "How many kegs of Spanish powder were loaded?"

"One hundred fifty-six, sir."

He raised his quill and pointed it at me like a pistol.

"There were one hundred seventy-six kegs, Richtier. Perhaps a score of them contained curved ingots of gold sent to Washington by French sympathizers. Curved ingots made of gold coins and jewelry to the amount of 200,000 Spanish dollars. Your General Wayne knew of it."

I stared at the man in utter surprise. Wayne had hinted about gold, but I was sure he had not been certain or he would have warned me. The Mellin woman and the dream had concerned gold; I had been beaten because of it; nor did I think Linn really knew about it, for he had said he knew no more than I did. Gibson had seemingly deserted us. Pollock—

Leith was speaking again, interrupting my thoughts.

"Those kegs, Richtier, were delivered with the powder. Last night, the twenty marked kegs disappeared from our warehouse. Two hundred thousand dollars sorely needed by our cause have disappeared. Your record is bad—you are a brawler, you have lost or taken money entrusted to you—"

"Sir," I interrupted, "I did not know of the gold. I did see more kegs about which Lieutenant Linn and I knew nothing. I left the expedition at Walnut Bluffs—"

"You're a civilian, Richtier, but I'm going to lock you up. Later, I shall consult with George Gibson, who is returning from the east. I should like to add, Richtier, that it gives me pleasure to put a man like you behind bars."

Stunned by the news that there really had been a gold shipment and that it was lost, I stood there scarcely hearing the vindictive words of the commandant. Probably we had not been informed so that none of us might be tempted by the presence of the treasure. A soldier plucked me by the arm and led me to a cell in the guardhouse where there was clean straw and a good army blanket.

They fed me well during the week I was imprisoned, but there were no visitors, and usually there was a sentry close outside, for I could hear him moving about. Thinking did me no good, for I seemed to be beyond unthreading the web of happenings that had brought me to this pass. My farm was gone; I was imprisoned as a thief. There was nothing to do but fall back on the soldier's habit of sleeping all I could.

It was not noise that awakened me that seventh night in General Leith's guardhouse, but a current of air fanning my face. As I sat up on my low bunk, there was a sharp whisper.

"Martin."

It came from the window, and when I crossed to it I saw the shutter had been pried away.

"It's Mcfail," the whisper went on. "Crawl out, and hurry."

Escape would indicate some confirmation of my guilt, but I was too discouraged to care much, and Mcfail was impatient.

"Hurry," he hissed. "You've no chance in there. Leith has lost that gold, and you're his whipping boy."

Five minutes later, I was out of the window and stealing away through the shadows until we were beyond the fort enclosure and on our way to Breon's tavern where we found Lon in his big kitchen with all the shutters closed and only a single candle for light. There was a small pile of stuff on the floor, and I recognized my gear wrapped in Hoadley's blue blanket.

"What kept you so long?" Lon demanded sharply of Mcfail, who shrugged his broad shoulders.

"Sentries, of course, then Martin seemed slow." Breon turned to me.

"Listen carefully, Martin. Things are bad for you. Leith knows he'll be broke for the loss of this gold and figures that you'd be the right sort of victim to blame things on. We both tried to get to see you and couldn't. I do believe the man would hang you if he could. He's beside himself."

I had looked into the commandant's face myself and probably knew better than either of my friends how vindictive he felt.

"But the gold?" I demanded. "What happened to it?"

Mcfail answered, "We figure it went upriver by canoe; maybe as far as the Kittanning country, then overland to the east somewhere. Gold ingots wouldn't be of any use out here. If a man turned up with one, he'd be nabbed at once. There are plenty of traders' pack horses up at Kittanning, and the trail runs east from there."

"East," I said softly, knowing that Pollock would be there somewhere. Pollock and Hester Jordan.

It was quite evident that both men wanted me out of the place as soon as possible. If men like they were apprehensive, it behooved me to move, so I slung on my gear. Breon, I found, had stuffed my pouches with food, and I was glad for Hoadley's blanket.

"They'll be hunting you in the morning," Breon said, "so don't tell us which way you'll take and we can say we don't know where you are."

I grinned at Lon; he was not often nervous.

"I'll be seeing Gibson when he comes," Mcfail promised, with close to a threat in his tone. "He'll do some talking—it may be I can persuade him."

Outside, I swung away along the road, a high feeling of recklessness in me. My rifle and pistol were primed, and Drough's blade was in my sheath. For those first few hours of travel under the thin light of a waning moon, it would not have been very healthy for any of Leith's soldiers to stop me.

Better sense came to me finally and I bore away to the north. Leith would send a mounted patrol along the highway and there was no sense in fighting. In the east, I must see General Wayne. The loss of the gold just about overbalanced our success with the powder. Wayne would help; what was more, I felt sure he would trust me when I told him about the loss of the powder money. When I found who it had been that had defrauded me, I promised myself the man would pay.

Ingots of gold. As I traveled, I thought of what hard money would have meant to Wayne and his men. A single coin meant affluence if it were gold, and even coppers were important money to the soldiers. Wayne had hinted that the war might turn out here in this country, and I did sense some ominous movement. I thought of Hartlin, of Gibson, and my mind flashed to Hester Jordan. If anyone had known of the gold, it seemed to me she would have been the person. To drive her out of my mind, I drove my body.

There was no time on my journey that I felt any danger of pursuit. A woodsman could lose himself in this vast land of forest and hills, and for three days and half of another, I traveled north of the east-and-west road and south of the old Kittanning Trail. About noon of this day, I came to the summit of a high hill. Bushes obstructed the view, but I stepped out on a jutting rock that overhung a brush-covered slope, which was almost steep enough to be called a cliff.

From this new vantage point, I looked down into a narrow, hemlock-shrouded valley through which a good-sized stream flowed. Beyond this was a low hill over which I caught glimpses of a wider valley. The stream flowed north, and occasionally there were flashes of sunlight on the moving water until a turning of the hill shut out all other view of the creek. Having seen enough, I stepped backward, and the sudden movement dislodged the rock so that I plunged downward in a small avalanche of ground and stones. Somewhere in the mad plunge, my head must have struck either a rock or a tree, and my senses left me.

When I came back to consciousness, I was as confused as I had been back there on the trace. My head throbbed abominably, and there was fire in one ankle. Unable to put weight on my foot, I experienced one of the severest perils of a man alone in the wilderness. The stream was close by, so I dragged myself there and bathed both my ankle and my head in the icy water. Breon had put some maple sugar in my pack, so, using my neckerchief, I contrived a bandage soaked in sugar and water for the swelling ankle.

That night I slept in a laurel thicket on the other side of the creek, and in the morning the ankle was certainly no better but my head was clearer. A forked stick served as a crutch, and I started onward. By noon I was descending the low hill and entering the wider valley I had observed when I heard a sound that stopped me more quickly, I believe, than a rifle shot would have done. Unmistakably, it was the sound one hears everywhere in the farmland rather than in a wilderness such as this—the tinkle of a cowbell.

She was a nice little red animal with big horns, and I came to her where she was placidly chewing her cud as she stood in a small natural meadow. It did me good just to stand and look at her, and she appeared so peaceful that I did not see the farmer approach until he was all but in front of me.

In this land, where one could be suddenly at the mercy of Natives or Simon Girty's wild rangers, my carelessness could have cost my life; but the man who stood looking gravely at me was a big, powerful-looking fellow wearing dark woolen trousers, a brown linen shirt, and a wide black hat. His face was hidden behind a thicket of beard.

"So," he said, smiling, "Sooky has found for herself a man."

I smiled back into the bearded face then carelessly rested my weight on the bad ankle and almost fell. He was beside me in an instant and eased me down to a seat on a rock. His big fingers deftly felt the injured ankle, then he looked up.

"The sugar and salt is all right, but the ankle must be in the liquid soaked."

I appreciated his strength when, half carrying me and with the red cow following like a dog, he led me forward through the woods, which presently thinned to show broad fields beyond which were three cabins. Likely more of them would be around the turn of the ridge. The man told me his name was John Claus and this was the Valley Creek Settlement of the River Brethren. He was delighted when I mentioned my own small farm down on the Schuylkill.

"But the land here is better," he said, "and, with wars, here is peace."

River Brethren were no strangers to me, and I remembered how they had lost many in the old wars with the Delaware Indians. Further, by their presence, I knew I had come to a place close to the Juniata.

They were very good to me, these farmers in this quiet, lonely valley. Claus was as proficient as many physicians; his rosy-cheeked wife fed me lavishly and seemed hurt when my appetite refused to respond further. In the evenings, the Claus home was a gathering place, and I talked, telling them of Fort Pitt and describing the great rivers and the Spanish city at the mouth of the Mississippi. Of course, I spoke mainly in the dialect, and these bearded men would nod their heads approvingly. It was plain they were pleased to have a stranger with them, and especially one who was Dutch.

But the ankle was slow in its mending until Claus made a salve of witch hazel bark and bloodroot fried out in lard, with which he anointed the injury and the bandages with which he wrapped it.

"She, the woman, says for us to try this," he told me.

In all, I was with these people ten days before I was strong enough to travel, and perhaps I was a bit slow because the peace of the place had taken hold of me. Here were no problems, no lost shipments of gold, no disdainful young women nor intriguing soldiers. Temptation was getting a grip on me. My military career was probably ended—why not stay here? Claus showed me a place where one might easily make a clearing.

"Stay with us," he said in that kindly voice of his. "There is trouble in your eyes; your back is scarred; it may be your heart is scarred by evil ones. Stay here, Martin Jon. We will work in season and sit on the porch to rest, smoking our pipes."

Nearly all of the men saw me off on my journey, and the women waved from cottage doors. The ankle was almost well, and I felt better in my mind. This stay among the Brethren had helped me. Once, that first morning, I caught myself whistling a tune. Nine more days of travel and I had passed Harris Ferry and was on the Lancaster Pike where I rode in the stagecoach, listening to heated talk about the war. Washington had lost several battles; the British were in Philadelphia. In connection with this last, I remembered Gibson's comment. From all I could hear, the army was still intact; Wayne was somewhere with the regiments that made up the Pennsylvania Line; one of the Patriot forts still thundered at the British down the bay, though its fall was imminent.

In Harris Ferry I had made discreet inquiries concerning canoes coming down the river, with no results. Nor from anyone could I pick up any news of a pack train bound east. My determination was to find Oliver Pollock and try to get some information from him.

"The war's far from over," a stage driver said to me. "Our Tony Wayne will yet win a great victory once His Excellency unleashes him."

As I neared the fighting front where I hoped to meet my general, I began to be a little uneasy. The delay while my ankle healed would have given time for the news about the gold to come east, and I was sure Leith would send word of my jailbreak. Wayne was a quick-tempered man; he had expected me to do something to justify his re-enlisting me. If he felt I had failed, I was in for an unpleasant time.

Presently, after I had taken to walking again, I met a farmer driving an empty wagon, and in answer to my inquiry, he had some information.

"Wayne's at the Paoli. I just took a load of grain to General Smallwood's division."

He held up his whip and looked knowingly at me.

"Something's brewing down in them woods and hills. They say Wayne lies as snug as one of the foxes he used to like to chase."

Wayne at the Paoli, apparently hidden—my blood quickened a little. That was like my general, planning a stroke, masking it, then striking with all the power he had; the prospect was exciting.

When I had left the army on the Delaware, things had not looked too good; now something exciting was brewing, and it would not be for the comfort of His Majesty's forces. Tramping along, I kept reviewing matters. Around Fort Pitt, things were as muddled as the commandant himself, and I was hoping that the powder we brought would be handled wisely. With men like Doctor Hartlin intriguing, with Simon Girty and his mixed crew in the forest, with British forces on the lakes, we needed another man out there like this Anthony Wayne.

CHAPTER SEVEN

THE CAMPAIGN of the summer had been march and counter-march, with His Excellency facing Lord Howe, who seemed to have little taste for giving battle to the man who had fought and won the brilliant little victory at Princeton. There was talk in the army that Howe might, as a matter of necessity, go to the aid of the sorely beset army of Burgoyne, near Saratoga. Our forces finally maneuvered the British commander and the guarding ships under Howe's brother into the shelter of New York town. Therefore, it had come as a shock when intelligence told us the British Lord had embarked his army onboard a ship, for there was only one place for him to go and that was Philadelphia.

Our bedraggled force had marched pretty slowly, with little in the line of transport for even our meager belongings. There had been trouble in Jersey, where former Patriots had turned coat and sworn a new allegiance to the British King. The soldiers would take whatever food they found and make the claim it had belonged to a Tory. Wayne's disciplined troops had been busy with police duty, and many were ahead, scouring the Delaware for boats. After we had crossed, the river served as a guard behind us, for no craft was left for any pursuing British force to use.

So on this march, when nerves were strained, my troubles had come, and I had gone to the west. Now I was returning to the country that was to become the cockpit of the war, the twenty-mile area west of Philadelphia, with its back to the Delaware and crossed by the Brandywine and Schuylkill.

A dozen miles from the little town of West Chester, I left the stage for two reasons, one being that my small store of money was dwindling and the other was to see the small farm on the river, even though it was lost to me. But as an afterthought, I gave up the idea of the visit; if Wayne was close by, I wanted to join him. Of course, I knew little of the progress of the campaign, but if my general was hiding somewhere in that low range of hills that runs south and west from the Schuylkill, there was something important in the air.

As I drew closer to the city I was struck by the entire absence of people and wagons on my route. When I became hungry, I left the road and walked up a wide lane toward a stone house, back of which was a huge timber barn. Knocking at the door brought no response, and it was not until I had walked around the building twice that I saw signs of life, an open crack in the back door, and the sound of a child's voice saying, "It ain't a Hesshun, Mom." The woman who opened the top part of the Dutch door looked bedraggled, and when I took off my hat and asked for food, she appeared even more distressed.

"The man," she explained, "is away. There was Hesshuns here day before yesterday and took the chickens, also the little beef." I stared at her and questioned, "Hessians? Is the British army up here?"

She nodded slowly.

"Was an awful battle with cannon shooting. The armies march back and forth. Mebbe if you could do with a little cornbread . . ."

I ate the meager fare while the child, an eager little girl, told of the soldiers in red coats and high caps and the ones with big black hats, the woman nodding at the descriptions. But when I told her about my farm on the river, she trusted me enough to say that I could sleep in the barn if I did no smoking.

In the morning, she had fresh cornbread and an egg for me. Evidently, some of the chickens had escaped the "Hesshuns." She had no further information. I spoke to her of the stage driver and his reference to "the Paoli," but she shook her head.

"The man mebbe would know; it's over in the woods."

Further questioning would be useless, so I gave the child two bright pennies, being rather glad to be rid of them since they reminded me of the scene in Ungaza's office. Then I walked down the lane. The child was standing back there, a coin gripped fast in each of her small hands.

I knew "the Paoli" as a region of low tangled hills, scrubby forest, and abandoned farms, but I had never been there. After leaving the frightened woman's place, I swung a bit northeast in the direction of the village of Malvern. Now that I was aware that trouble had visited this country, I was more alert. As on the day before, no one was in sight. No cattle grazed in the fenced fields, no farm work was being done, and houses were shuttered; only one watchdog challenged me. The cold grip of war had stilled all peacetime activities.

It was midafternoon, though, before I saw any sign of anything really military. Having seated myself under a wayside oak to rest, I caught a flash of reflected light on a nearby hill, then horsemen coming in my direction trotted into view. At the foot of this hill was a farmhouse; here the troop turned from the road into the lane and surrounded the house. It was too far to see very distinctly, but troopers ripped off a shutter and some of them crawled into the building through the windows, afterward opening doors for their companions. Three troopers held the horses; all the other men disappeared inside the place.

I had no mind to be caught by a British cavalry patrol or even one of our own before I saw and talked with General Wayne, so when the troop was again outside and mounted I hid carefully in a nearby brush row. They came up my hill at a walk, and I recognized British Light Horse, wearing plumed hats, green coats, and white breeches.

A full score of them, they rode excellent horses. Ahead was a tall, thin officer sitting his horse stiffly but unbending enough to glance back over the line of men occasionally. These soldiers were foragers with loot like hams and great slabs of bacon tied to their saddles. One man dangled a child's sunbonnet from his fingers as he rode. It looked as though they had ransacked the house down there.

If British patrols rode this far west, things must be bad for us down below; that was my main thought, though I would also have liked to crease the man with the sunbonnet, using a good heavy bullet. Also I wondered if Pollock's powder ship had come up in time to help His Excellency.

The farms thinned out as I neared the wooded hill country, and the side road I followed dwindled to a mere cart track that I thought might lead me to Wayne's pickets. This area could well be a part of the loose term, "the Paoli."

But I was not allowed to move forward until I encountered a regular picket. Instead, I was ambushed by a half dozen rough-looking fellows who came at me from a thicket, muskets only too ready. None of them wore more than pieces of uniform, and their clothing was a travesty of what soldiers should wear. But their weapons looked well tended. A burly, red-faced fellow about my own age was the leader, and he poked my chest with a dirty forefinger.

"Where to, my hearty, this close to evening?"

I studied for a moment. These men could be Tory partisans, but I doubted it. In my best officer's manner, I snapped at him. "Take me to General Wayne's camp. I have a message."

He grinned at me and his men.

"Talks big now don't he, though? Wonder if he don't find that gun too heavy since he carries all that message. Might be hard on his back."

It was evident that I might be in real trouble, and I did not want to take a chance of losing time trying to placate them. Instead, I stepped forward, pushed the astonished leader to one side, and yelled, "Sentry!"

We were even closer to pickets than I had hoped. From up the hillside came a rustling noise, and two uniformed soldiers came down the cart track. I stepped up to them.

"Message for the general; take me to him."

These men were better disciplined, though they took no chances with me. A hundred yards up in the forest, they turned me over to a sergeant, and he, in turn, to an ensign whose hair was graying at his temples. He looked me over carefully and questioned sharply: "You have the password?"

"No," I answered. "My message is from Fort Pitt. Listen, I was an ensign in the First Pennsylvania."

"Who was your colonel?" he demanded.

"Wilson," I snapped back. "Craig Bierly was the other ensign in my company."

He grinned.

"It's captain now; Bierly and the First are just up the hill to your right, a little beyond the artillery park. Go on up, but watch your step; the men are touchy. Stop quick when they challenge."

Leaving the ensign, I went through a fringe of trees, wondering at what I had seen. The squad that picked me up could have been scouts, and the sentries were a scant thirty yards from each other in a double line.

It was dusk before I came out into what had been an old farm, abandoned long enough for scrub pines to stud the place. The guns were there, a long row of them, set neatly side by side with caissons hooked up, and the horses, fully harnessed but for bridles, were tethered to long chain tie-ups. Just now, they were eating their grain from the ground. Those cannons were ready to be swung into action in a few minutes. To the right of the park in the open field stretched the camp for a force that must have amounted to a regiment. From this eminence, I could see to the east that there were other encampments. This was the hiding place of an army.

Sentries passed me from man to man, and the first officer I encountered was my friend and boyhood playmate, Craig Bierly. He wore the insignia of a captain, and he was glad to see me, pumping my hand and striking me on the back, a bit of enthusiasm that was hard on shoulders too recently healed.

"Captain," I said, smiling at him. "You've come up."

He grinned ruefully. "After Brandywine, promotion came fast. Of the thousand lost, nigh a third were officers."

He led me down to his tent where a small fire glowed and there found me a camp stool, after which he shared his supper with me when I told him I had not eaten.

"Now tell me, Martin, what brought you here? Carmichal was west but he's safely south now. You've come to re-enlist?"

I shook my head. Bierly was a man I could trust, and I recounted my whole story, all but a mention of Hester Jordan. The fire burned low but he did not move until it was all told.

"So, Craig, I failed. The powder came through but the gold is lost and I'm a fugitive. Wayne would never accept me, even as a private in the line."

Bierly frowned. "Martin, the powder stroke was a great one. Gibson has become a sort of hero and has gone west again. But I do know the general has received two letters about you, for I was in his headquarters and heard him swearing and railing about a man named Hartlin and George Gibson. He finished by taking General Leith apart, for he never did love that officer."

He shook his head a bit ruefully.

"General Wayne is a stickler for military etiquette, as you know. Your escape is bad; he just might send you back to Leith."

I filled my pipe slowly and carefully to gain a little time. Craig Bierly was a good man, steady and with good judgment.

"Craig, I didn't tell you everything. I've come here to go into Philadelphia for an accounting with Pollock, if he's there. If Wayne wants to stop me, I'll stand on the fact that I'm a civilian."

Bierly did not answer at once, but when he spoke again, he told me, in outline, the progress of the campaign.

"From where you left us, Martin, it has been march and counter-march. Howe landed at the head of the Chesapeake; we met him at Brandywine and took a real licking; then it was fall back to West Chester, across the Schuylkill, then back again. Washington just led Howe about as a fox does the hunter. The bulk of his stores was at Pottstown. Well, the armies faced each other for an all-out battle at Warren's Tavern, but a heavy wind and rainstorm drenched powder for both armies. Then it was back and forth along the Schuylkill. Of course, the British occupied Philadelphia, but it was gutted of provisions and war supplies before they got in. Pollock delivered his powder all right."

He stopped, then I asked him point-blank, "Can you tell me what this business means, Wayne hiding here in the hills?"

"Yes, Martin, I'll trust you with it. Howe pulled back toward the city. Wayne's business is to intercept his wagon train. How you missed being picked up, coming in from the west, I don't know, for the whole British army is less than ten miles from here at Howelton. We're lying here, hidden with double sentries set. If Lord Howe knew where we were, he'd get between us and Washington."

We talked on, each asking and answering questions.

"If only Wayne had command out at Pitt," I said, but Craig had a quick objection.

"He couldn't be spared here, he and his eight state regiments. They're the heart of the army. By the way, Wayne is training the Fourth with the bayonet. Our old riflemen of the First have their rifles taken away. You should have heard the howl when they had to use muskets; now they like them. Of course, some of the best shots still have rifles to keep down British officers."

He stretched his long legs preparatory to rising.

"It was good, my friend, when we had nothing to do but go without pay, eat what we could, and load and shoot a rifle when we were told. Who the hell wants to be an officer?"

Standing up, he laid a hand on my shoulder.

"Be at home about here. The password's 'Coventry.' I'll bet every damned Tory in Chester County knows it by now since we've had it two days. Got to make the rounds."

The little fire had burned down to a fine bed of coals and around everywhere were the sounds of an army getting to bed. There were no bugle calls and the glow of fires to the right of this section of the camp had dulled. On the tie-up, the horses still munched at their grain. Once I heard a ringing sound when the metal butt of a sentry's musket cracked against a fieldpiece. I sat there studying, for what Craig had said made an impression.

It was true, Wayne might send me back to Leith, but it was also equally true that he would want me to use every effort to recover the lost gold. The two letters from the west bothered me, though one could have come from Breon. Yet, Carmichal had been out there.

I half rose when I thought of him and what he had cost me through our quarrel. True, I had marked him, but in my turn, I was marked both in body and spirit by the succession of things through which I had gone.

Hester Jordan! I seemed to see her face in the coals, with disdain on her lips, scorn in her voice.

"You'll have to learn the hard way."

There was no doubt in my mind that she had been right. Here in this camp, with the military stir and the business of war all about, I wished that I had curbed my wild temper. Then I would never have encountered her. But I thought of her slim white neck and how the strength had run from my arms and hands as they clutched her.

Captain Bierly did not return, and I finally stood to relieve my cramped muscles. Some native caution made me take up my short rifle and reprime it by the dim light of the fire. Then I slung the piece over my shoulder and checked my pistol also. The day had not been too clear, with a light shower in the morning. Now, while there was good starshine, there was just a hint of fog up here in the hills; about us was the dense darkness of the woodland where the sentries were. The thought of their presence in double lines made me feel tense; ten miles away lay ten times our number, yet I knew General Anthony Wayne's skill in making the most of any chance, even though it was slim. My uneasiness was a matter of nerves, not judgment.

The sentry at the corner of the artillery park stopped me, and I muttered the word, "Coventry."

"Past ten o'clock," he commented, then, as I turned to face him more directly, he chuckled and added, "and all's well."

A thin moon climbed slowly, but the mist still hung in the trees. From a little beyond the sentry post the pattern of the whole camp could be made out. Evidently, the old fields made a sort of arc to the south and east of the artillery park and the camp of the First Pennsylvania. One could see an occasional glow down there from the coals of campfires, and it was surprising how quiet everything had become. Captain Bierly had spoken of eight regiments commanded by General Wayne, but I was sure they were not all here in "the Paoli"; the camping ground was not extensive enough for an army of that size.

Ten miles north and west there would be the British if they were in the village of Howelton, and as I looked that way through the darkness, the uneasiness felt earlier returned. Surely scouting parties must have located Wayne's hiding place. I remembered also that there were Tory sympathizers about this country as there were at Fort Pitt.

Far down the wooded slope of this hill, I caught the sound of brush breaking, then silence. But there would be two lines of sentries there; some of them must be moving. After listening a few minutes longer, I had just turned to go back to Bierly's tent when a musket crashed down there; then another and another until a scattered line of reports outlined the entire system of sentry posts. The attackers were clever; the alarmed sentries gave away the whole position of Wayne's army by their fire.

Not one of us ever quite understood how they did it, but the British General Gray, the man they called "No Flint," brought two men for every one we had against us that night, and they came out of the darkness as Indians would have done; this, in spite of the sentries set about our camps. We learned afterward from prisoners that every soldier in the attacking force of grenadiers and Hessians had his musket flint removed so no chance shot could give Gray's force away until they were among us.

The second line of sentries let go its scattered fire, then we heard the first man scream out in the dusk under the trees as a bayonet ripped away his life. I felt a weakness in the pit of my stomach at the sound, and I remembered Drough's staring eyes. The bayonet is a devilish weapon in broad day; at night it is doubly so, and our men were close to panic, all but those who had pulled away the guns. Wayne's force was made up of veterans, but the rushing sound of thousands of men, coming up through the dark woods like some awful destroying flood, came close to demoralizing them entirely.

Captain Bierly and the other officers were at work. At their quiet orders, the man had hooked up the already harnessed gun teams.

"Bear right, bear right," the officers told the drivers, and the quiet voices brought some measure of sanity to the situation. The artillery had moved off as though this very scene had been rehearsed, but the camps were in confusion below us.

The full force of the attack had not yet broken upon this First Pennsylvania, for we were well to the left of the line. Nevertheless, we could see by the light of blazing tents some of the horror among the other regiments. There had been smoldering campfires, and the attackers tore down the canvas and hurled it onto the coals to have more light for their butchery.

Without orders and without thinking much about it, I moved toward the edge of the field, back of where the artillery had been parked, and others went with me. Ahead of us came the sound of brush chafing against cloth and of heavy breathing, then the huge, cocked hat of a Hessian appeared, silhouetted for a moment. Two stabs of fire came from us, and the hat went down. Then we were firing at will and I remembered that these First Pennsylvanians were made up of the rifle companies. With muskets, their speed of fire was startling. Others of our men came running up in the darkness. The smell of powder was strong because the fog held the smoke down, and there was a continuous slashing of the muskets. Somehow we managed to hold. Our men began to cheer; some of them wanted to run forward into the woods, but a sergeant stopped them.

"Keep back!" he yelled. "D'ye want them hellions to spit you in the dark?"

We turned our attention to what was going on below. A fourteen-pound musket will send a triangular bayonet through a man at a lunge, and the soldiers seemed to be everywhere, yelling, stabbing, overturning tents, and driving steel into men still swathed in blankets. It was a bitter irony that this bayonet attack should be launched at the only portion of the Patriot army that never used the weapon. The men of Wayne's First Regiment were to learn this night by bitter experience that there is little defense against steel in the darkness.

Squads of us trotted toward the fighting, led by sergeants, ensigns, and some individual soldiers. As we dashed through a shallow ravine and came up to the main camps, I saw Wayne. He was mounted, a great cape flowing from his shoulders. Standing in his stirrups, he yelled, his voice sounding above the clamor.

"Muskets, men! Load and fire!"

Officers took up his cry, moving among the men, and resistance started to stiffen. Our own companies were firing whenever there was a clear chance at the enemy. Then, by the light of a blazing tent, I saw a huge Hessian whip up his musket to plunge his steel into Wayne. Someone from the darkness threw a camp ax, and the would-be killer went down in a tangle of arms and legs.

Another officer, mounted on a gray horse, had joined our general, and they had ridden to the edge of the field. Then I saw this second man stand in his stirrups, swing his hat into the air, and yell. Immediately there was the skirl of fifes from the shadows, then the heavy rhythmic tread of soldiers and they came into the open—a long line of our own men. Later, I was to learn this was Wayne's Fourth regiment, the one he had been drilling with the bayonet. Wayne at one end of it, the officer on the gray at the other, they brought this steel-tipped line forward, and before it, the blood-glutted attackers broke. Soldiers who had been demoralized joined the charge, some swinging axes, some tent poles, some muskets by the barrels.

We were told afterward how few of the attacking army had fallen that night, but we who had witnessed the action smiled, for we had seen the firing, had seen that magnificent charge of the Fourth regiment. We, too, had seen the redcoats and the Hessians break back into the darkness from which they had come.

Some of us began scouting the fringe of woodland down through which the enemy had disappeared. I had gone only a short way when I heard a man running ahead of me and tangling himself in the brush. Finally, he tripped and I overtook him as he came to his feet. In the half-light, I saw the shine of his sword, which I fended off with my rifle barrel, then leaped upon him. He was a strong man and fought hard, even desperately, but I had him down and whacked his head against the ground until I knocked the fight out of him, after which I dragged him back to the field where some of the men had started a fire. My prisoner was a civilian. Some of Bierly's men saw him, and a roar of anger went up.

"That's a Tory—lives just down the road!" one cried and pointed to a white band on the fellow's arm.

"British guide," two or three yelled, then they rushed forward, brushing me aside, and took the cringing man. There was nothing I could do, and Bierly was busy elsewhere. These men had heard the screams of their comrades killed in their blankets; there was no holding them, and they used their musket butts savagely.

The artillery had a good start, but in an hour or so Wayne's whole force was moving across country. Bierly walked with me for a while and told me that every gun and every pound of cannon powder had been saved. The main loss was in tents, blankets, and personal equipment of the men. There were few wounded; the bayonets had done a thorough job.

Battle is an exhausting thing, and we moved wearily south and east. This was Wayne's home country; he had hunted foxes over much of it.

This night, he led us to where the British had been a few days before. By midafternoon, we filed through the little village of White Horse and went into camp. Wayne still had a mobile army; the massacre in those Paoli hills had been bad, but it had neither wrecked this army nor lowered its morale. Before nightfall, we were told that the British army was moving back to Philadelphia. Evidently, it had had enough of the game of hare and hounds in a country Washington and Wayne knew so well.

Now that the battle was over, my own private business challenged me, and I tried to see General Wayne, who had taken up headquarters in the home of a friend. The place was called Larchmount. There was no seeing our commander until the afternoon of the second day following the attack on us. When a sentry admitted me, the general was busy at his desk, and I was struck by the neatness of the man. Certainly, he did not look like a man who had just been through a hazardous campaign and who had saved an army from a savage night attack that could well have destroyed it.

He stopped writing and looked up, his sharp eyes boring into mine, his strong face grim.

"Martin—Martin Jon Richtier," he said softly. "I've been waiting for you, now that the bad penny is back."

There was another officer in the room, but I had not noticed him until now. My glance told me it was the man who had ridden the gray horse during the charge at Paoli. He had been reading a book over by a window, and he put this down to watch and listen. Wayne drew a long breath.

"I sent you west to clear yourself of fighting and carving up my officers with that damned knife of yours. Yes, I know you had no official mission, but I thought you'd see things. I know the whole story, from the dead bear to your arrest by that skimmed-milk, white-livered Leith. You did well, to a point; you did get powder, but you let a man named Hartlin and that big ass, Gibson, make a fool of you. Now you're a military fugitive; my duty is to return you to Leith, You've lost your property, you—"

"Sir," I interrupted, but he scowled.

"God knows how much our cause needs that lost French gold. It meant sacrifice to our friends who sent it, danger to the ones who secured it. Now it's gone. That gold was as good as a victory." He leaped to feet, came round the desk, and we stood almost toe to toe.

"Martin, get back west; find that gold if you have to use that damned knife of yours on every stinking Tory in Fort Pitt."

"Yes, sir," I said meekly. "Does the general want me to start at once?"

Suddenly, he put back that handsome head and roared with laughter, then he caught my hand and shook it vigorously.

"The general has spoken, Martin. After all, you're a civilian. Let's talk like neighbors. General Greene, let me present my neighbor, Martin Jon Richtier, late ensign in the First."

The big man with the book smiled and nodded. He was a hard, tough-looking person until the smile lightened his features.

"Have him tell his story, General," he suggested. "I've heard a part of it but want it all for His Excellency."

So I had to tell the whole account, and it was not easy, for both men would interrupt with questions. This time I mentioned that Hester Jordan had warned me on the boat about the money, and I noticed the two officers glanced at each other. When I finished, they sat back and watched me until I shifted in the chair. Then Wayne spoke.

"Leith's charge has been quashed, Martin. I want you out there again."

"Sir," I remonstrated. "Breon, Mcfail, and I felt the gold had come east somewhere. I want to get into Philadelphia and see Pollock. Is he there?"

Wayne nodded.

"Yes, he delivered the powder in time. Now, he's in the city, playing the part of a good Tory, I suppose. By the way, Martin, I understand Gibson got title to your farm from Pollock."

"Gibson?" I interrupted. "Gibson?"

Wayne's steady eyes met mine squarely, and I noted every line of his face, the eagle beak of a nose, the high forehead. The man's features resembled those of a portrait on a Roman coin, and Anthony Wayne could speak to you without words.

"Sir," I said, "let me get into the city and see Pollock. Then I'll go west and wring Gibson dry."

Greene smiled; Wayne frowned and spoke.

"You're a rough customer, neighbor, but I believe His Excellency would approve a little wringing of friend Gibson, even if it were his now popular neck."

I stood up, ready to leave, and then asked another question. I had mentioned her being on the boat, so perhaps I could get more information.

"General Wayne, who and what is Hester Jordan?"

Wayne was always a ladies' man; he straightened his stock, flourished his well-tended hand.

"She is a very clever young woman who owns a lot of property here and there and wishes to take care of it. She is a niece of Oliver Pollock, dances well, and holds an estimable place in society."

He had evaded my question very skillfully, then he ended the interview by reminding me that if I went into Philadelphia, it was at my own risk—yet promised that when I went west, letters would be sent with me to expedite anything I might attempt. Greene stood up as I was leaving, his heavy face sober.

"The gold, Ensign Martin; don't forget it would be lifeblood to our cause. His Excellency needs it desperately."

CHAPTER EIGHT

ORDINARILY, Brigadier General Anthony Wayne was not so garrulous, certainly not before a third party. Therefore, I assumed there was much back of what he said. General Washington did not trust George Gibson; Hartlin was an important factor in matters about Fort Pitt. Wayne had spoken freely before a man whom I knew to be one of His Excellency's most trusted officers. There were other things I could gather, but Wayne had carefully and skillfully refrained from giving me any real hint concerning the girl, Hester Jordan, and her part in the whole affair. Why would a woman of means travel all the long way down the rivers on a flatboat, then sail up the Atlantic to get to Philadelphia, when she might have gone overland along the old Forbes Road?

Captain Craig Bierly was not busy and was most eager to help when I told him I was going into the city to see Pollock. He knew the merchant's place of business but not where he lived, though he was sure it was in Germantown, somewhere south of the Lower Burying Ground. He clapped me on the back.

"We'll find it, Martin. Between us, we could find anything, from Lord Howe's latest lady friend to a lost reputation."

"No, Craig. It won't do for you to go, for you're an officer. You couldn't get in wearing a uniform; without it, they'd hang you as a spy. Now I'm a civilian; the worst that could happen to me is a night in jail, if they picked me up."

Bierly grumbled, but he did see the sense in my point of view. Probably he knew Wayne would refuse his consent also, so he busied himself getting together some clothing for me in place of my buckskins. When I set out, I wore a good brown coat and a fine cocked hat. My own leather breeches had to serve, but I had really good woolen stockings and shoes that felt stiff and awkward after so many months of wearing moccasins. Weapons seemed out of place, but I did take Eben Drough's knife, its scabbard fastened up under my arm so that I could reach it easily by thrusting my hand into the waistcoat. I did not tell Craig that it was my determination not to be handled by British soldiers, hence the knife.

Lower Germantown was less than a score of miles from our present encampment. It was generally known that the greater part of the occupying British force was quartered to the north of the city in the locality to which I must go. However, since Tories were common and farmers must come in and out of the city during the day, I felt no misgivings about avoiding trouble.

The country through which I passed and the roads seemed deserted. Shutters were closed on the houses, and I saw little signs of life. Here and there was a burned building, usually a barn or a storehouse. Foraging parties from both armies had swept the area clean; even the usual straw stacks in barnyards were gone. On both the Lancaster and Chester Pikes I saw the litter left by passing troops, for both Howe and Washington had used these roads.

I crossed the Schuylkill at the Matson ford because it is a lonely place. Here I removed shoes and stockings to wade the stream and rejoiced at the coolness of the water on my feet tormented by the stiff shoes. A mile beyond the crossing I struck the Ridge Road, followed it to Barren Hill, and then went over to the Germantown Pike. Now, to my right was the wooded ravine of the Wissahickon and on the left small farms, some no larger than big gardens. At early dusk, I came into the outskirts of Germantown and stopped for supper at a tavern called Drovers' Inn.

Heavily laden wagons were drawn up in front of the place, and there were long pole racks on which were piled the packsaddles of horse trains. Men stood or sat about on the long, wide porch, and the room where I ate was thronged with carters, drovers, pack train men, and soldiers in fatigue uniform. One of these last was particularly noticeable, for he sat at a table all by himself and ate prodigiously.

The man to whom I paid my reckoning for the excellent meal apologized for not knowing where Oliver Pollock lived. Like Craig Bierly, he was familiar with the merchant's place of business downtown but not with his residence. However, he was certain it was below the Burying Ground, and when he mentioned that place, he shook his head a little and glanced round the room, particularly toward the sergeant whom we could see through the doorway and who was still eating.

"A bad neighborhood, the Burying Ground," he cautioned in a whisper. "It's drunken soldiers; they hang out down there."

I smiled my thanks for his warning, and he looked sharply at me; his eyes were level with mine, for we were both big men.

"At that," he added with some conviction, "you just might be able to take care of yourself."

The dusk of the town through which I passed was broken by only a few widely spaced street lamps, and the stone and brick houses were set so close to the curb that they seemed to crowd me into the street. It has often puzzled me why people will build houses so close together when there is so much unused land about.

Eager now to find Pollock, I walked fast, paying more attention to making time than to my surroundings. The houses thinned out, and I was passing the huge bulks of mansions set well back in parklike grounds. There were many black patches of shadow from the trees and almost no street lamps. Out of one of these patches, a half dozen big men suddenly emerged with the reek of liquor and onions strong upon them. From their guttural voices, I knew they were Hessians.

"*Geld*," demanded the big fellow who stood close in front of me. "*Gebt uns schnell.*"

I understood his garbled German well enough, and my mind flashed back to the Paoli hills and men in black cocked hats, hunting victims by the light of burning tents. This man did not expect any resistance, therefore he did not even attempt to parry the sharp blow I drove just under his ear.

When I plunged forward, one of them tripped me, but I rolled and brought the big knife clear. The man who grabbed for me took the wicked edge across his palm. Certainly, it would be a long time before he handled a gun or bayonet again, if ever. He screamed.

"Gebt acht—er steckt!"

Those rough Boston days had been hard schooling for a man little more than a boy, but here again, they stood me in good stead. I rolled over twice, slashing at legs close to me, then gained my feet and ran in among what proved to be the gravestones of the burying ground.

The Hessians who had attacked might have been drunk, but not too much to give over their attack, so I had to double in and out like a rabbit, damning my stiff shoes as I did so. When I thought I had eluded them, I reentered the street where the light was better. Coming from the direction of the city was a squad of marching soldiers, the little light from the streetlamps glinting on the tips of bayonets. At a sharp word from their officer, they stretched across the roadway and stopped me.

"Friend," the officer in charge greeted me, "you've been running; what's up?"

There was sharp authority in his voice. He seemed too old for the usual British subaltern. Likely, he was a sergeant.

"You're right. I've been running," I answered. "Some of them damned Hessians jumped me. I got loose."

Abruptly, he pushed me aside and snapped a word to his squad, then I turned and saw my pursuers coming down the street like a pack of hounds.

The British soldier is sometimes a phlegmatic person, but he is often brutally efficient. So it was here; the sergeant spoke softly to his men.

"Use the butts."

The Hessians were too close to get away; they were caught in the ring the soldiers flung round them. They were beaten down savagely and ruthlessly with the butts of those Brown Bess muskets, which could strike like the kick of a mule. Then one soldier opened his lanthorn and looked over the groaning men on the ground.

"One here's got a cut hand, Sergeant."

The non-commissioned officer took the light, shone it on the wounded Hessian, then back on me.

"Likely the fellow fell on broken glass. Get them on their feet, men; we'll turn the swine over to the patrol."

When they were all on their feet, the sergeant walked along the line of Hessians, holding up his light by which he inspected them. One man was retching; probably he had taken a blow in the stomach from a musket butt. The sergeant roughly pulled his head up and back, looked into his eyes for a moment, and then released him.

"Sour-smelling beast," he commented and turned to me. "Is there something we can do for you?"

"No," I answered, "unless you can tell me where the merchant Oliver Pollock lives."

"Not too sure," he answered civilly, "but look for a gray brick house three or four blocks below here."

With a quick salute to me, he put his squad in motion, taking with them my late attackers who stumbled along, utterly beaten. Evidently, the British occupation believed in properly policing the city they had taken.

I found the house easily; gray, square, two-storied, with one of those common little stoops over which a light shone down across the dark panels of the door, which was ornamented with a heavy brass knocker. All the shutters were tightly closed; no life showed; nothing but that light.

I thought of many things that had happened, from the time I had killed the bear until now. Inside this house would be the man who had grimly taken my property from me because of the fraud about the money bag. Now, technically, I might be considered a military fugitive, and I stood in a city held by hostile forces, waiting outside a front door. One by one, I thought of the men: Gibson, who had tricked me somehow, of that I was sure; this Pollock, with his neat brown clothes; General Leith, whose vindictiveness had made me so much trouble. Then Hester Jordan was in my mind, the fragrance of her, the life in her eyes, the slender throat. Somehow, she had tied my hands, but I did not feel toward her as I did toward the men who had used me.

The knocker made a loud banging in the quiet of the street. Light footsteps sounded inside, and the door swung open to show a wide hallway from which I could look through to a second open doorway and a lighted room at the right. She was standing there, Hester Jordan, one hand still on the doorknob, the other raised to her lips, parted in surprise. She could see me plainly enough for I stood under the stoop light.

"You," she said. "You—what are you doing here?"

In spite of my surprise, I remembered this was almost exactly what I had said to her months before: "That's what I said to you on the flatboat," I answered.

I could not deny the joy I felt at seeing her, no matter what she had done to cozen me. But just then, over her shoulder, I saw a man in the lighted room and remembered his face. He was not in uniform now, but I recognized the British officer I had seen with this girl before me, in New Orleans.

With a quick jerk, she closed the outer door after I had stepped inside and turned my back to the other open doorway. She took one step and opened the second hall doorway to the left, motioning me to enter. There she faced me.

"Martin Jon Richtier, did you come here to be hanged?"

"No," I answered, exultant because I caught a note of real apprehension in her voice and because she was certainly more disturbed than I was. For once, with her, I was master of the situation.

"No," I repeated calmly. "I've come to see Pollock. Between him and you, my affairs are in a sad tangle. Also, there is the matter of some lost gold belonging to the colonies."

Her breath was coming faster, and I looked at her lovely neck, at the rich hair piled high, and her small hand raised to the lace at her breast. She stepped closer and laid a hand on my sleeve where I noticed it was soiled from my trouble with the Hessians.

"Martin Jon, British officers are quartered right on this block. The lieutenant who tried to trap you Lambs in New Orleans is in the city and will visit this house later in the evening. Get out of the town before they take you and hang you."

I shook my head, and temper flamed in her eyes; she stamped her small foot.

"You stubborn, stubborn—" Her small teeth seemed to cut off what she would say as she set them together. "You almost deserve to hang."

I reached out my big hand and touched her shoulder gently, certainly not as I had done that night in the Spanish city. Then I spoke back to her the words she had used on the flatboat: "One man could watch one woman spy. Surely you could—"

She left me, and with a swirl of skirts, almost ran from the room into which came, a few minutes later, the man I sought, Oliver Pollock, dressed as usual in sober brown with lace at his throat and silver buckles on his shoes.

"My niece said there was a stubborn young man here," he said evenly, coming forward with hand outstretched. "So it is you, Martin Jon Richtier, come to see me."

He took me into a back room furnished as an office, found a chair for me, and poured two glasses of wine. I drank mine thirstily.

"You have questions, friend?" he said, settling himself carefully in an armchair and then placing the tips of the fingers of one hand against those of the other.

"Yes," I answered shortly. "Why were we not told about the gold?"

He frowned and seemed to consider.

"It took a lot of getting, Martin, and we smuggled it aboard your boat almost at the last moment. We thought that you would have enough trouble thinking about powder. Gold would have made things worse for all of you. It might have tempted some of your men."

"The Lambs are not thieves, sir, as were those who stole it in Fort Pitt." I leaned forward. "We believe the gold came east; do you know anything about it?"

He shook his head.

"No, Martin, you are all wrong. The gold has not come east, but it may, once the war is over. It is somewhere in the wilderness, waiting. Then those who took it will bring it forth for themselves."

His face seemed to stiffen, his hands fell apart, and he dropped his languid air as one would a coat.

"Here in Philadelphia, they think me just an amiable merchant, interested in making a penny with no particular care as to who wins the war. But I'm in touch with Wayne almost every day, and I know all your story, Martin, even to the scars on your back. The gold is not here; get back to the Allegheny. Find Gibson, find Hartlin, do everything to get that gold. It's life to our cause life, I say."

He flung out an arm.

"Make Gibson talk. God, I wish Wayne were out there! The new commandant, Colonel Brodhead, is good, but he does not have iron in his blood as does Wayne."

I half sneered.

"But you gave my bill of sale of the farm to Gibson."

The merchant struck the arm of his chair smartly with his palm.

"Martin, if we do not win this war, it will not matter what you or I or Hester Jordan owns. I used that property of yours like a playing card. Gibson owed Hartlin, who had expressed a wish for a place in this area, a quiet one where he could rest. So I took Gibson's deed to his gristmill in Lancaster County and gave him your bill of sale to transfer to Hartlin. Mark you, that man has not committed an overt act against our cause. I think, Martin, that he got the gold and that he will try to bring it to your farm somehow, but I am not sure."

He paused and was silent so long it was as though he had forgotten I was there. When he did speak, it was in a musing tone.

"Hartlin and I meet on the ground that neither of us cares who wins so long as we make our profits. It is so with others I know in New York, even in Montreal. My course is not a plain one—someday I shall make a slip—"

He grinned but there was no mirth in it.

"The British have excellent ropes."

The man's earnestness convinced me that his statement about the gold was right; that I had followed a wild-goose chase east, but what he said about my small farm was startling. I saw clearly the scene on the trail that morning, the discouraged-looking company. Then Hartlin and I had talked of the farm.

Pollock was speaking again.

"Martin, you have done well with the powder. God knows what His Excellency would have done without it in this campaign. Now I fear you do not realize how much responsibility is yours about the gold. Linn has gone west with Clark into the Illinois country; Gibson is not to be trusted. The gold now is more than powder; I fear you are the only man placed so he can recover it."

I looked at him with something of a frown on my face, then I rose.

"Gibson—" I said, and he interrupted.

"Yes, Gibson may be the key. He journeyed home at ease while his men fought weariness, cold, and famine. I fear our tall friend plays both ends against the middle. It is possible that our Patriot cause could spare George Gibson—all of him."

I wanted to say and ask more, but Pollock's thoughts seemed to be far away. Suddenly, to me, he looked old and weary, so I left him and he did not appear to notice my going.

Hester was again in the hallway when I went out, and for a brief moment, we were alone. She looked into my eyes and there was just the hint of a smile in hers and about her full lips.

"It may be, my stubborn friend, that you will grow old and gray instead of—" She broke off, again sober, urgent. "Oh, hurry, Martin Jon, get out of the city."

My hand grasped the doorknob, exultation singing in my veins. My life really meant something to her, therefore it was worth more to me. As I stepped outside, she touched my shoulder lightly, and going up the street, I felt I had received an accolade.

For years I had followed forest paths as surely as a hound keeps a trail; now, my head was in the stars and I had gone a full city block before I realized I was walking in the wrong direction. Since I did not wish to pass the Pollock house again, I took another street that proved to be little more than a lane and very muddy; so much so that at one place, on rounding a corner, I found boards laid over a puddle for a walk.

Absorbed in balancing myself carefully on this plank, I all but collided with a British officer who carried a lanthorn. He backed up immediately and so I saw him clearly enough to note his regimentals.

"A moment, friend," he called civilly. "I'll find a place to turn out."

There was a faint familiarity about the high nasal voice. He did find a wider place, and as I stepped forward to pass, he held up his light to help me.

For a long moment, we looked into each other's faces. Hester had just told me the man was in the city. Here was the officer who had handled the trap for our Lambs at Crane Haven. His men had killed Drough.

"God," he said softly, his free hand reaching for his sword. "Powder runner, I'll spit you first, then we'll hang what's left."

He had made the mistake of talking too much, which men often do but should never try when their hands are full. I snatched away the lanthorn, feeling the satisfaction that it was a heavy one, and smashed it across his face so that he was knocked sprawling into the mud.

With my knife out, I watched him writhe there for a little. This man had as truly killed my friend as though he himself had driven the bayonet. Mcfail or any other Lamb would have killed him without a thought of mercy. But I could not knife a helpless man so I ran away into the darkness.

There might have been some sort of hue and cry for me that night, but I was fairly certain it would not come until that officer had cleaned away some of the mud. Then sheer bravado made me spend the night in the Drovers' Inn, even though there were four other men to share the same room and all of them smelling strongly of horses and rum. I was down early in the morning for a good breakfast of sausages and cornmeal mush. The tall landlord passed while I was eating.

"Eat hearty, young man. Had you a good time and did you find friend Pollock last night?"

"Yes," I answered, and as I finished my meal, it seemed the same answer applied to both questions.

Retracing my way, I met a number of squads of British soldiers, some of them mounted; but they did not stop me, although they did look me over carefully. In my sober coat and hat, I was quite an ordinary-looking person, which has its advantages at times. Late that afternoon, I reached Wayne's new encampment, a few miles closer to the city and northward toward the Schuylkill. There I found Craig Bierly, who was anxious to know what had happened on my trip inside the British lines.

He listened carefully to all I had to tell about Pollock, of my encounter with the Hessians, and the run-in with the British officer.

"Hard to lose your land," he commented, "but property means nothing if we lose." He smiled suddenly and went on.

"But, of course, we'll win. His Excellency will not lose his army, so British occupation of towns means nothing."

"How about the militia?" I inquired, which question had been the bone of contention among officers from the opening of the war. "You know, Craig, they won't fight and they run away."

To my surprise, he bridled.

"You did not see the militia fight at Brandywine. Also, if these men do go home after each campaign, they are alive and ready to come into the army again. Martin, the enemy cannot destroy our power to fight, so long as we have the militia."

He was very much in earnest, and I clapped him on the back and went on down the village street to find General Wayne's headquarters. If the gold had not come east, I wanted to go west at once, but I felt I needed Wayne's approval first.

The new headquarters house was the last on one side of the street and stood a little distance from its nearest neighbor. As I walked up to the front door, two sentries presented their carbines smartly, but they neither challenged nor stopped me. They wore the leather horsetail-trimmed caps, the olive coats, and the dangling sabers of the dragoons. Ordinarily, Wayne used one sentry, and that man was always an infantryman. The orderly just inside the door was a man I knew.

"General Wayne has just stepped out, sir," he explained, "but you are expected. Go right in."

"Expected?" I asked, and he smiled a little.

"Yes, sir; a messenger was sent to find you less than a half hour ago. Step right in, sir."

Puzzled, I walked through an open door into a wide inner room. There was only one man there, and he stood looking out the window. For a long moment, I stared at the tall figure in his correct, beautifully fitting uniform, at the massive head, the powerful hands linked behind his back. There was no mistaking him; I felt a catch in my throat. Then, George Washington, commander-in-chief, slowly turned while I stood stiffly at salute and stammered, "The general sent for me, sir."

The sober lines and planes of the great man's face relaxed into the hint of a smile.

"Oh, yes, you will be Martin Jon Richtier. General Wayne has told me much of you, and I believe I have seen you before."

He glanced at my hair and clothing, and I colored like a schoolgirl. This time he really smiled.

"Martin," he continued in his sober voice, "the powder enterprise was most fortunate for us here in the east and out there at Fort Pitt. I'm most sorry you lost your property through it. Yet most of us have lost something, and we'll agree that liberty is worth its price." He half smiled again, and as his eyes searched mine, I wondered at the steady gaze of the man. There was nothing cold there; only a kindly weighing of my feelings. Perhaps he had expected me to be bitter.

"Oliver Pollock is a hard bargainer; he once bought tobacco from me in peaceful days. If he seems to have used you hard it is because he worked a hard bargain for himself as well."

The general spoke slowly, with frequent pauses.

"Martin, that lost gold at Fort Pitt is life to our cause. It can buy the same thing won in a victory—the confidence of our people. It could make folks see our paper money has value with gold back of it; it would loosen up sources of supply we cannot touch without hard money. I sent for you because both General Wayne and I think you are the one man who can find the thieves who stole the French gold from Leith. You will go out there and find it—for me and—your country."

His gray eyes clouded; the lines of his face were suddenly sharp and deep.

"There will be one more battle, young man, then winter quarters. If, in the spring, I do not have the treasure you seek, only God knows what may happen to our cause."

Abruptly, his great hand came out and clasped mine. The strong fingers closed warmly.

"Forget all personal things, Martin. Remember only the cause we serve. You will not fail me, Martin; that I see in your eyes."

"Yes, sir," I stammered when I meant "No, sir," and the general was smiling as I saluted and went out. Walking up the street, I felt that I could march into Philadelphia and chuck Lord Howe under his third chin, for General George Washington depended upon me, Martin Jon Richtier, in good behavior, of the First Regiment, Pennsylvania Line.

CHAPTER NINE

GENERAL WAYNE may have "stepped out," as the orderly said, but he was gone for two days, during which I was so impatient that I felt like starting west without further word with him. Inaction gave me too many things to think about. Above all, Hester Jordan was in my mind and the fact that she had been fearful for me.

I tried to think through some plan for finding the gold. Evidently, it had gone upriver, hence the rumor that, reaching Breon and Mcfail, had sent me east. But, above and to the east of Pitt was vast forest land larger than many European countries. Here were mountains and small rivers that no white man had seen as yet. And in it were the Natives who found attacking wayward travelers easier and more profitable than trapping beavers. Further, we were not sure the gold had not been handed over directly to the British, for they and their Tory friends would have plenty of pack animals for transport.

Late the second afternoon, a peremptory summons reached me to report to Wayne's headquarters. There was a knot of officers on the porch showing the buff and blue of the Line, the blue and red of the artillery, and the plumes of the dragoons. Among these last was Captain Clow, a hard rider and a good friend. He winked at me brazenly and gestured toward the house.

With Wayne, who was seated at a desk in the first room, were two colonels to whom he presented me.

"Colonels Stewart and Wilson, this is Martin Jon Richtier about whom I have told you. He was in the city recently."

Both officers responded civilly but I thought they watched me closely.

"Martin, our friend Lafayette is in trouble or is about to get into it. Remember, his letters and influence had much to do with getting the gold you Lambs brought upriver so Leith could lose it. We owe the marquis a debt that must be paid."

He glanced at the colonels, and I was sure that Stewart had been smiling before he looked down discreetly at the floor. Wayne continued.

"Lafayette has about twenty-four hundred men north of the Schuylkill, somewhere close to Barren Hill. His left is likely on the Wissahickon, the right on the Ridge Road. Does that sound correct?"

I nodded, while his eyes bored into mine. He cleared his throat.

"A reliable messenger has come to us from the city with the word that Howe is about to trap our young friend. He has seized all the Schuylkill fords, a column of five thousand men is moving around Lafayette from the north, and another big body of troops is marching straight out of the city to meet him head-on. While I know you have urgent reason to leave for the west, I'm asking you to go with Captain Bierly to the marquis with the news. Then, act as guides and try to get him out of his trap."

"Yes, sir," I answered. "I'll go find Captain Bierly. We'll leave at once."

Wayne smiled.

"Perhaps you'd like to see and talk with the messenger?"

That had not occurred to me, but I could see some advantage in doing it. Wayne rose and opened the door through which I had gone to meet His Excellency. I stared, incredulous. Dressed like a forest running boy, as I had seen her first, was Hester Jordan!

"Mistress Jordan, here is the man we will send to the marquis with your message. I believe you know him."

There was a faint edge of irony in the general's voice, but the girl bowed so that a strand of her loose hair touched her flushed cheek.

"Yes, Martin Jon and I sailed down the Mississippi not so long past."

I managed my best bow; my heart was hammering as though I had been running. She was looking directly into my eyes, and there seemed to be some message she was sending, but whether warning, challenge, or amusement, I had not wit enough to know. So she had taken the risk of riding directly into the American lines in daylight, even though a few nights past she had been entertaining British officers in her uncle's home. I bowed again.

"I think there is nothing I need ask the messenger. If I have the general's permission, I shall find Captain Bierly."

Wayne nodded; I had turned to leave when he stopped me.

"By the way, Martin. Last night Captain Clow raided the city. He took several prisoners, one some sort of British paymaster who had lately been on the lakes. The man declares that no gold has been brought into their posts. When you return, your letters will be ready. You can then leave for the west. I shall take the responsibility for your delay."

As I left the house, Stewart was close to the door and touched my shoulder.

"Good luck; take good care of our precious marquis."

Craig Bierly had known of our mission and had the horses ready and waiting. We followed the route I had taken before, both of us noting again the desertion of the countryside.

"Can't blame the people," Craig said. "I'd move away from a war, too, if I were able."

It was possible that the British held all the fords on the Schuylkill, but I had a feeling they would miss the Matson because it was not used a great deal. The bottom there is uneven and the steep pitch up the hill on the north bank is hard for a team and wagon to climb. Yet Craig and I approached with almost an excess of caution. Half a mile from the river we left the road and followed it on either side, dismounting and leading our horses. When we came together again, neither of us had seen anything larger than a rabbit. Even so, we kept up the caution; I covered Craig with my rifle while he crossed, then he, from the far bank, covered me, for both of us knew how helpless a man in the water can be.

Now we hurried. If this ford was open, there would be a chance for the young Frenchman to cross his army. Twenty minutes after we left the water we cantered through the little village of Barren Hill, swung southeastward, and in another mile met our first challenge from the pickets. These men had a lanthorn and noted Craig's uniform.

"Messenger for the marquis," Craig said, and we were promptly passed along until a sergeant took us in charge.

Troops thronged the road on either side, and all were at ease. We saw dark forms stretched out on the grass, knots of men gathered about small fires, and we passed gun teams harnessed to caissons and ammunition wagons. There were two miles of this; Lafayette's army was here. Presently we saw a larger fire under a big tree and a group of officers clustered there about one man who sat on a field chair while just back of him an orderly held a saddled horse.

"Messenger for the marquis," our guard told an officer, and the group opened promptly so that we stood directly before the man in the chair— Lafayette, who had come so far to aid us.

The firelight shone brightly upon him and the man looked slight to me, but that was probably because all of us near him were big men. His cocked hat rested on one knee, and his powdered wig was cut so short at the sides and back that it looked like his own hair. He was not a handsome man, for his nose was too large and inclined to turn up, but his face was a pleasant one and his manner courteous. Craig saluted properly, and I managed a good bow, then the captain delivered Wayne's message and the marquis turned to an officer.

"Colonel Clinton, how about our advance outposts?"

That officer stepped closer and replied, "The riflemen are in the Wissahickon ravine, and there's a small body of our militia well down the Ridge Road."

Lafayette muttered something to himself in French. It seemed to me he was impatient about the militia.

"Colonel," he ordered, "get some cavalry down that road well past the militia's post. See if our friends from the city are coming." While we waited, the group of officers melted away, all but two lieutenants and the orderly. The marquis turned to us.

"Gentlemen, you will tell your general that I am most grateful. Captain Bierly, I think I have met you, have I not?"

Craig nodded, well pleased.

"Yes, sir, and this is Martin Jon Richtier."

The boyish face brightened.

"That name is also familiar. You are one of those Lambs who brought powder up the Mississippi, powder and the gold bars in their small kegs. I trust it will get to General Washington in due time."

I bowed to cover my surprise and because I did not know what to say. Then I remembered that Wayne had told me this man had been instrumental in our getting the treasure. I could not tell him the gold was lost.

"Yes, sir, and we are indebted for your help. The gold will be brought east in due time."

He eased himself about in his chair and smiled ruefully.

"You will pardon my restlessness; I have a slight wound that bothers me when I am still too long. Now, if you are not tired, I would appreciate your riding after Colonel Clinton and bringing me word if he makes contact with the enemy."

Our horses had been ridden carefully and were still fresh; both of us knew the road, and Clinton had only a few minutes the start of us. A mile of riding and we met a straggling knot of militia coming back toward the main force. They told us Colonel Clinton had sent them back. A few more minutes passed and we heard a rifle crack, then another, followed by a popping sound.

"British cavalry over there, running into our pickets," Craig declared. "Let's get back."

Lafayette was mounted, and we told him our news. He nodded. "I might have known that General Wayne would send me reliable news. But you say all the fords are guarded?"

"Sir," I spoke so quickly that I half feared I was interrupting him, "the Matson was clear about a half hour ago when we crossed."

It should be said for the young French marquis that he acted quickly. In minutes, he had given his orders to the officers who went to work on the hard job of turning an army around in the darkness. Lafayette was everywhere on his big horse, speaking in that pleasant, unworried voice, and presently we were on our way toward Barren Hill and the ford beyond.

"Gentlemen," the marquis said to his officers, "we'll follow our guides."

I thought he would send a detachment of horsemen with us, but he did not seem to think of it. However, in a few minutes, some riflemen trotted up and past us, fanning out to cover the advance. When we reached the river, these same men formed along the crest of the hill overlooking the ford while I rode slowly down, urged my horse into the water, and began to feel the nervousness felt by every soldier when he knows himself to be an excellent target. Craig was close behind me, but I motioned him to wait until I was over. While it was night, there was still enough light to make a shot with a musket a fairly sure thing.

The bottom was evidently rocky, for my horse stumbled badly several times. We were two-thirds of the way over when a gun cracked somewhere in the brush up above and my hat was knocked from my head. Instantly I clapped heels into my horse's ribs and finished the crossing, while the riflemen back of me searched the darkness ahead with rifle fire.

There was no one on the bank to stop me nor any sign of a force of the enemy. Ensign Bletz, in charge of the riflemen, joined me in a minute and called to his squad, "Fan out, men. Up- and downstream."

No time was wasted; the man who had fired at me might have been a scout; we must get over before any considerable force gathered to stop us, so the ford was soon full of men, horses, and wagons in orderly confusion.

The enemy did come at us, but by then most of Lafayette's army was across. There was one ammunition wagon in the water and the last company of infantry was moving down the bluff when the British cavalry rode up, approaching from the direction we had just taken. The foot soldiers must have felt themselves trapped; they ran down the bank and plunged recklessly into the water while the enemy poured a hot fire onto them. One of the horses pulling a wagon was killed, and the ford became a confusion of rearing animals, frantic men, and spray kicked up in the excitement. Then Lafayette saved the day by forming a company along our bank to pitch a covering fire toward the bluff until the attackers were forced back.

We were finally thoroughly dispersed, though there were dead men and two horses back there where the action had taken place. But the army had been saved. It had crossed just in time, for if the British had guarded the place, we would have had that terrible business of forcing a crossing in the darkness.

Craig and I paid our final respects to the marquis at a little inn when we were about to leave in the morning. He was mounted, and his face looked tired in the gray morning light.

"My obligations to you, gentlemen," he said courteously. "I shall speak of you to General Washington, who remembers good service bravely done."

He reached down and touched my arm with his small hand.

"Good luck to you, sir, with the gold. It is sorely needed and would be a victory in itself."

By noon, I had my letters from one of Wayne's orderlies and started west, trying to look as unmilitary as possible. My rifle was wrapped in sacking and the other weapons were placed in my war bag, which also contained emergency rations of dried meat and parched corn. Six miles from Wayne's post, I took the stagecoach running toward Lancaster and York.

The vehicle was so crowded that the occupants made room for me grudgingly. Merchants on their way to see Congress now fled to York. There were a number of soldiers, evidently on leave, and several women. We were packed in tightly, wedged against one another.

At first, we rolled through a deserted country where the only moving wagons were en route west, some of them loaded with household gear. Then, after we crossed a low mountain, the land was normal again with livestock showing about the barns and corn shocks like Indian tepees dotting the fields.

The man against whom I was pressed shifted a bit and pointed to a scar on my hand.

"You were a soldier and wounded?" he said inquiringly.

I glanced at the scar and knew, of course, that I could not tell him that was where Carmichal had nicked me with his sword before I took it from him.

"Yes," I answered shortly, "but that nick I took from a farm sickle while cutting grain."

The man looked out the window for a while then spoke thoughtfully.

"Farms; this war would die were it not for these fruitful fields. If the enemy moved in here, our cause would be finished."

I thought of my own farm not too far from here and remembered His Excellency's words about the price of liberty. Yet, somehow, I had the feeling that in the fortunes of war, I might own it again.

York was more crowded than the stagecoach that ran into it. There were no rooms for travelers, but I wanted none, for I was bound west. Five miles out on the road to Shippensburg I was picked up by a man who said his name was Steck and who drove a six-horse team drawing an immense wagon. Each team had its yoke from which bells jingled, making a most cheerful sound. When I told Steck I was bound for Pitt, he cracked his whip out above the horses' backs and said, "George Gibson from our parts is out there. He's a big fellow in mind and body."

"Yes," I said. "I know Gibson."

The driver shook his head.

"He's got a fine wife and a son. She labors to keep the little mill she owns going, while he hunts glory in untamed parts. The story is that he brought powder and gold up the rivers, but I'll wager he brought no gold to his family. George was always in trouble of a money kind."

"Gold?" I said. "Where did he get gold?"

"Just a tale, I guess," was his answer. "I would not know where or how he would come by it. Now if I had a coin or two of that yellow stuff, I'd sit by the fire of a winter evening and just look at it."

He cracked the long whip over his team, not touching the sleek side of a horse as he did it, and I sat wondering how far and fast this gold story had traveled.

After passing through Carlisle and Bedford, I saw no travelers of any kind. In this hill country, I no longer carried my weapons under their covers but out where I could use them. Here, along this road, was good hunting for fearsome Delawares, wandering Shawnees, and an occasional band of Wyandottes, who found fighting white men to be pleasant and profitable.

The road was rough, with stumps hacked low to permit a wagon axle to go over them. The steep hills were managed by a system of switchbacks such as one sees in a hilly pasture where the cows make their paths. It was incredibly lonely. The wilderness, with no sign of man's occupancy, is seldom lonely; that feeling comes when there is a sign that men have been there but have gone away. At night, I used my little fire for quick cooking but always slept far from any sign of my camping. Hoadley's blue blanket was pretty thin, but I preferred to be a bit cold rather than risk the warmth by a fire. Lying alone in these high hills with the stars so close, I had plenty of time to think.

George Gibson was my key. He had been genuine enough in launching the expedition for the powder, but I felt sure there was something haunting the man. He was like somebody who has done an evil deed and so must watch over his shoulder for any sign of being followed. My conclusion was that his trouble was about money, and I was almost sure it was he who had tricked me with the bag of pennies. Somehow I must make the man talk, and Pollock and Wayne had hinted broadly about using any method necessary for doing this.

Beyond Ligonier, the crooked roadway followed the stream, and I came to a lonely looking house set right at the edge of the wagon tracks. There was no one in sight until I walked back of the building, then I found an old man in buckskins coming out of the brush. He carried a rifle taller than himself.

"Was looking for you," he explained gleefully, grinning so the stumps of his teeth showed.

"For me?" I said in surprise, and he nodded emphatically.

"Yes, for a fellow called by the good Dutch name of Richtier. He was to be tallish with kind of red hair and a peppery temper."

The description was not too flattering, but it seemed to satisfy the old man. He took out a twist of tobacco and worried off a huge chew.

"I was to tell this Richtier man he should hurry and see a man named Breon."

That was all I could get from him, though I tried persuasions, which he rejected, and a coin, which he refused.

"Nope," he declared, "I got little use for money; besides, I'm in a hurry. There's turkeys over that ridge, and I'm a wasting time with you."

At the close of my fourteenth day on the road, I went down the ravine through which runs the Forbes or Kings Road, whichever one wishes to call it, but which should awaken no pride in the dead Forbes or the living British King. Before me was the great "V" of the rivers, holding in its point the fort, looking like a toy from this distance. About the enclosure clustered the widely spaced houses that made the town itself. Down there somewhere lay the answer to my problem. Gibson had come here, and I would make him talk.

"You will not fail me." I heard the words in my mind and thought of the lined face and the understanding eyes of our great leader.

Breon was so glad to see me that he became effusive, pounding me on the back and then taking me to the kitchen where he fed me lavishly and gave me cider because I did not like the fiery raw whisky of these parts. As I ate, we talked. He knew nothing of the old man who had accosted me, but after an hour's visit, I found Breon was well informed as to things in the east and satisfied that Pollock was right that the gold had not yet moved eastward.

"But, Lon, I'll see Gibson. There are ways to make the man talk. It will be Gibson for me tomorrow morning," I said grimly.

Breon shook his head.

"Not that soon, Martin," he said ruefully. "Your colonel marched with Colonel Crawford against the Wyandottes weeks ago."

In exasperation, I slapped the table. Here was further delay and already months had passed since I lay in Leith's jail, months during which the stolen gold might have been taken anywhere, even to coastal cities, though Pollock did not believe that had been done. My mind ranged over the problem; Hartlin owned my small farm; what did the man want of it? Certainly, he was not a person to find the narrow limits of husbandry satisfying.

"Lon," I asked, "what about Hartlin?"

Breon nodded.

"The doctor has been seen about here a couple of times, though Leith would not arrest the man. The new commandant, Brodhead, has had some trouble taming down his officers. We cleared you before Leith in a couple of days by showing you had an alibi. Then we learned that two big canoes had gone up the Allegheny that selfsame night. They were big canoes and had plenty of paddlers. We accounted for all the Lambs. There were no black sheep in your outfit."

He busied himself putting out more food, particularly the pickled cabbage that he knew I liked.

"It's right to start with Gibson, Martin, but I feel Hartlin's the man. It's my notion he has George fast in some way, for the man is always in debt. Hartlin lends, Gibson spends. But—"

He set the dish down with a bump.

"Gibson won't come back!"

I half rose in my excitement, and Breon stepped to the door, opened it, and made sure there were no listeners.

"It's Mcfail, dour and dangerous as we both know, a good friend and a deadly enemy. He had a sister that made a common mistake and had a child by a man Mcfail did not know, and she would not tell, even when she died a few years later, leaving a boy whom she named Eben Drough."

This explained the big sergeant's grief at the death of the young man. But Breon had not finished.

"Crawford took several Lambs with him, but Mcfail wouldn't go for some reason. Then, after the expedition left, an old emigrant from Mcfail's home country showed up on his way to Kentucky. Mcfail went to work on the man; probably he had an idea the old fellow knew something. Well, he got his answer; the man who fathered Mcfail's sister's child, Eben Drough, was George Gibson, and he had deserted her, for even then he was a married man." Lon allowed the story to sink in. Both of us, knowing Mcfail, understood what would happen if it had not done so already. Finally, he nodded, replaced the spoon in the cabbage, and spoke.

"The sergeant left to join Crawford just a few days ago. What odds would you give Gibson to come back?"

My own course appeared plain; it was to get to that expedition wherever it was in the wilderness and see Gibson in time, or else to stop Mcfail before things were too late to remedy. Early in the morning, riding a horse Breon had found for me and accompanying two dispatch riders, I rode west. The men grumbled at the pace I set, but we had to keep together; this was Indian country where stragglers met unpleasant ends. I felt I must get to Gibson first—perhaps, after that, I would not have too much concern about what happened to the colonel of the Lambs.

CHAPTER TEN

A THIN, cold rain was falling in the late afternoon of our fourth day out of Pitt when we reached the encampment of Colonel Crawford's expedition. My companions on the way had explained that its purpose was to strike the Wyandottes in their home villages on the Sandusky and that the colonel had nearly five hundred men, with Williamson as second in command. Crawford, I knew, had been a lawyer; he had participated in some fighting in the east under Washington, and I had seen him once, a tall, sober-looking man given to fits of silence.

This officer received the messengers, took their letters, and though I stood with them, he completely ignored me. Nor was he overly polite to the men who had ridden so far to reach him. As we walked back through the encampment, I noted the poor fires and the disgruntled appearance of the men who seemed to be all frontier militia with no stiffening of regular soldiers. Near a tent larger than the others were some officers, among whom I recognized George Gibson from his great size. He saw me in the same instant, waved his hand, but made no sign that I should come over to join him. It was Mcfail who, moments later, gave me a real welcome and led me to his own place.

Here were Hoadley, Selin Frye, and Orton Weigh, who had been with us on the river. They had made a big lean-to of their shelter tents before which they had a good fire going, and all were effusive and noisy in their welcome, which they also extended to my two wet and cold companions, the dispatch bearers.

"We've got some venison we were holding back," Weigh announced, producing it from under the browse of his bed. So we sat about the fire, roasting the meat, and I added to the meal a bottle of Breon's good cider, brought with me in my saddlebags. Mcfail seemed his old self, garrulous, noisy, pleasant. His questions tumbled out faster than I could answer them, and I told much of Wayne, of Lafayette, and the campaign down east.

"Me," he said with conviction, "I'd like to get back close to Harris Ferry where I was born, and I'd like to see big armies march and fight. I'm kinda tired of these crummy little wars."

Shrugging his heavy shoulders, he made a gesture toward the rest of the camp and the militiamen.

"They'd all run after the first couple of shots—if there was a place to run to. Crawford's got a bellyache most of the time, and yet he won't let Williamson do a thing on his own."

Only once during the entire evening did Mcfail show any sign of what was moving him. Then he leaned over and half drew the knife from my sheath. It was Drough's blade, the one I had offered him several times but which he had declined. I wondered now if I should make another offer but did not.

The army got underway slowly the following morning in the distinctly unpleasant fall weather. Most of the leaves were down, the sky was overcast, and we all knew that miles of this same drab country stretched ahead of us. The timber was mostly hardwood with many dense thickets and an occasional rocky place.

Close to nine o'clock, while I lingered about Mcfail's lean-to, an orderly found me with the word that I was to report immediately to Colonel Crawford. He was seated as he had been the night before, just inside his tent fly. Most of the other tents were down and packed, giving the prospect before us that wrecked look common to military camps packing to march.

The man's thin face was stern, his light gray eyes accusing.

"Richtier, what are you doing in my camp?"

It had never occurred to me that I might be asked such a question, and there was no very definite answer I could give him. Therefore, I suppose I showed some confusion. Certainly, I could not tell a man like Crawford my real mission.

"I came to see friends and perhaps to volunteer for the campaign," I managed to say finally, and he shook his head and frowned.

"You were under arrest at the fort, charged with taking that French gold."

This time I simply stared at him, with anger choking me. In my pockets were letters that would reduce this arrogant man to his proper place, but I would not use them. He picked up his quill, examined the point, then laid it down again.

"True, charges against you were withdrawn. It was a sort of Scotch verdict—not proven."

It was hard to tell what was disturbing this man. Surely it was undignified to call someone before him and then cast aspersions as he had done. The colonel suddenly reminded me of both Leith and Carmichal. He cleared his throat noisily.

"Naturally, I cannot send you back, for this is Indian country. But keep away from my officers. If you fraternize with Sergeant Mcfail and his crew, you'll be birds of a feather. That's all."

I leaned forward and took one fling at him.

"You forget that the powder in the horns of your men was brought upriver by this Mcfail and others."

He could not meet this truth very well, and I walked away after deliberately turning my back on him. With a man like that as a leader, almost anything could happen.

Mcfail was waiting and grinned when he saw me.

"Your face talks, Martin. You have had a going over by our illustrious colonel and belong to our order now. We got ours by making suggestions about scouting ahead and to the flanks of our column. You know, war might be nice if it wasn't for the generals and colonels."

Used as I was to Wayne's handling of troops, this force shocked me by the way it straggled along in a line sometimes two miles from the advance to the rear. Men moved as they wished, sat down and rested when they wanted to, left their own groups and visited with others. But even in this confusion, I could not get to talk with Gibson, for he was always riding with Crawford.

Colonel Williamson was a soldier and the direct opposite of his commander. He was everywhere on the march, checking equipment and seeing to it that nothing was thrown away, as is the habit of militia. Once I saw him form a short column and march it along with real snap, but after a half hour of it, an orderly came to him with a note. Williamson read it, shut his lips grimly, and walked away from the men.

Late in the afternoon, we learned that two stragglers at our rear had been tomahawked and scalped. There had been no sound or uproar; Hoadley, who had taken a private swing back of our column, found the bleeding bodies. Instead of burying these men where they fell, Crawford insisted on bringing up the bodies and interring them "decently and in order," as he said. But each man of that raw militia had a chance to look on and think until he felt jittery. We were a long way from home in a forest; the enemy could be anywhere, ready to strike like this with no warning.

We talked late that night in front of our lean-to. Mcfail was sure the enemy was close about us, simply waiting for a good chance to make their attack. Wyandottes, Shawnees, Delawares, and Mingoes haunted these forests, and it was rumored that Brant, the great Mohawk chief, was out here, for the Mingoes are, after all, Iroquois.

Next day we did not make quite ten miles, and we lost three men. One of these had been under arrest for drunkenness and, escaping his guard, he ran into the woods. Those who followed heard him scream, but they were too late to do anything except bury him. A scout up front was shot but not scalped, and a straggler did not return. Our toll of losses was now five, and Crawford ordered Mcfail up front with the scouts on the following day. Since the other Lambs were up there as well, I was left to my own devices.

It was that night we heard them around us in the brush, just sly rustlings we were meant to hear. One of the scouts claimed there was a big village only a mile or so up front. Our pickets were posted two rods apart, for Crawford was getting nervous. The little movements out in the dark and the night-bird calls too often repeated made the pickets fidgety.

"Martin," Mcfail said to me, "let's you and I and Hoadley get ourselves some collateral."

We made our way unobtrusively to the edge of the camp where Mcfail knew the sentry.

"Just let us pass, Frank: we want a prisoner."

Away from the fires, we lay in a thicket until we could see better. Mcfail explained his plan, and I was elected to be the bait.

"You were a Lamb," he chuckled, "now you'll be the sheep bait for these wolves."

A couple of hundred yards out from the camp, I stood up and blundered around like a man hunting a latrine. I didn't make much noise, but it was enough to cover what little disturbance was made by the two Lambs in the bushes. My hand was on the buckhorn haft of Drough's heavy knife, and I kept eyes and ears busy, wishing that I could smell as an Indian can.

Our plan worked so quickly that it came near to being the end of me. He was upon me before I had heard a thing, a warrior with his body greased so that I could get no hold on him. He tried to use his war ax but made the mistake of coming so close that I tripped him.

We went down in the thicket, clawing at each other. The big knife came free, and I slashed at him every time I could. There was blood on my hands. Neither of us made a sound but, in the end, I had him under me. Then I raised the heavy blade, trying to strike with it as one does with a light ax. My antagonist went limp, and Hoadley pulled me clear.

The three of us carried our victim into camp, passing the sentry, who swore softly. In the light, we saw the warrior was just a big boy, and my heavy blade had struck him back of the ear, stunning him. His body was twitching now, and he was bleeding badly from knife cuts.

"John," I said to Mcfail, "I'm glad you're going up front with the scouts. Any more of your plans and I'll lose my hair."

The Indian was attempting to sit up. Mcfail squatted before him, balancing his tomahawk in one hand. The boy saw it. We tried to make him talk, but even the threat wouldn't loosen his lips. "We'll take him to Crawford," Mcfail at last declared.

Hoadley and Mcfail led the young warrior away, for I wanted none of Crawford. They had been gone the greater part of an hour when I heard yelling, then some shots. When the two woodsmen returned, I had to ask questions to get any information.

"They tried to pump him," Hoadley said. "But either he couldn't understand English or he was stubborn. He perked up a bit when Gibson used French. They asked him about the Wyandotte villages, and he just waved his hands. By and by they got careless, and the Indian made a break for the woods."

I swore softly. There did not seem to be a thing I did which was not bungled later, and I had taken the risk of getting this captive now—"Did he get clear?"

"Hell no," Mcfail grunted. "Gibson killed him with a pistol after two guards had crippled him with musket shots."

I do not think many of the men slept soundly that night, for they had heard and seen too much; their own dead, the dark forest, and now this rumpus kicked up with our prisoner. The morning brought little cheer, for it was overcast. While no rain was falling, it threatened to do so at any minute. Breakfast, for most, was a sketchy meal, but we Lambs did pretty well. Weigh was a good cook. Having eaten, we tied up our gear quickly into tight, easily managed packs.

The four Lambs—Hoadley, Frye, Weigh, and Mcfail—went up front to report to Crawford. The colonel was no longer taking chances about scouting. Williamson had charge of the rear, and we started through an open hardwood forest with occasional thickets of witch hazel and high laurel.

After perhaps two hours of marching, the advance body, consisting of about sixty men with Crawford and most of his officers, was drawing away from the main army, which was moving slowly, as usual. Finally, they were so far from us that we lost sight of them, and Williamson and the sergeants were keeping the rear closed up. Somewhere up front there was a good-sized creek, and we could hear a loud splashing, which meant the men were fording it.

Williamson gave orders to step more lively, and as the woods thinned, we caught sight of the advance far up and across the creek. Then it happened, sounding as though this silent wood had been storing up this racket since the oaks were acorns. There were yells, shrieks, and musket fire. Through the smoke, we could see hundreds of warriors closing in on the company, which was cut off from us by distance and the water. Then came the screams of tortured wounded and the shouts of fighting men.

Williamson and his sergeants knew their business. At first, the men, in sudden terror, had tried to bunch, but the officers, with blows of swords and fists, forced them into a line so that we could advance in the shape of a half-moon. No one wanted to be alone; there was no hanging back, and men moved shoulder to shoulder.

"No quarter!" Williamson barked. "They'd give us none."

We drove forward like a released spring, and I saw several warriors caught in the rush before they could get over the water. These were beaten down with musket butts and finished with war axes. Then we splashed through the creek, muskets held high to keep the priming dry.

The Indian attack had been so beautifully timed and executed that, even with our quick advance, we were too late. The open woodland was littered with the mutilated corpses of our men. At spots, they lay in piles, a few of them horribly mutilated with axes; all were scalped. If there had been any wounded, they had been finished with tomahawks.

We did get some of the enemy, warriors so drunken with their success that there were actually small knots of them that charged our whole force. There was no restraining the militia now; they surrounded and butchered these attackers, and I question if any of their number got away. One Indian, seeing he had little chance, ran for it. Three militiamen signaled to each other, then dropped to their knees; one counted, "One, two, three," then they all fired and their victim went down, rolling like a ball. A fourth man nearby ran up and finished the job with a blow of his hatchet.

We hunted through our dead, trying to identify the slain, but we did not find Crawford, the surgeon, or Gibson. It was Williamson's opinion that perhaps a half dozen had been taken prisoner. My own search for my friends led me to Weigh's body. He had been shot three times, brained with an ax, and scalped. There was no trace of the other three Lambs: Mcfail, Hoadley, and Frye.

Squads went to work burying the dead, and I dug a grave for Weigh near the creek. When he was buried, I covered the mound with the biggest stones I could lift so the wolves would not dig him up. Having used all in reach, I went up the creek, searching for a few more. A big stone was in my hands when I heard a groan in the thicket, and there I found the man I wanted—George Gibson.

There was recognition on his face as I eased him out into the open and placed a pillow made of my coat under his head.

"Too late, Martin," he muttered.

He had been shot several times in the body; his breath came in gasps, and there was a little bloody froth about his lips. Some of the other men approached, and he noticed this.

"Keep them back," he whispered.

I motioned to them and bent over the dying man.

"Martin, Hartlin—I owed him money. He got the powder money; took it from my place and I did not dare tell. He has your bill of sale. I gambled—he always won—"

His hand came up and caught my shirt.

"The French gold—he's got it somewhere in the woods. Get Hartlin, Martin, make him tell. He ruined me—"

I tried to pour into his mouth some of the whisky from the flask I had taken from Weigh's pocket, but he pushed it away.

"Mcfail," he whispered. "I got what I deserved—"

He was still, his eyes glazed; then his body writhed, his fingers clawed at my shirt.

"The gold—take it to—"

He was dead and we buried him there close to Weigh, whom he had once commanded during the good days when he led the Lambs in many a hard-fought skirmish from Tidewater Virginia to the land along the Allegheny. The man had been moved by great impulses and ideas but he lacked the strength to keep out of reach of those who tricked him about money. He had cheated me, had failed others, but now George Gibson was dead and buried.

"Mcfail," he had said. It was very likely that the sergeant had seen his chance and shot his former leader. The battle load of a Lamb would be a bullet and two buckshot; likely Gibson's life had been snuffed out by such a charge.

Williamson gave us little time. After Gibson was buried, he tied up the officer's belongings in a neckerchief, then he ordered us forward. We struck the first Indian village before night, and our men went into it like hunters flushing game. It was nearly deserted, but in five minutes nothing alive was left there, even the dogs being shot. Then we set the torch to the place and watched the bark and reed houses burn and the corn stored in willow baskets being consumed slowly like coal.

We destroyed four villages in as many days. In the last, we found a wounded warrior who boasted that they had taken six prisoners, that they had burned Crawford and another officer. They would burn the others later. Williamson stood by, looking at the Indian who now started a low humming. The commander raised his eyebrows.

"What's that?"

"Death song," a soldier answered.

"Well," Williamson said dryly, "don't let him waste it."

A half dozen hatchets finished the business.

We came back to Fort Pitt by forced marches. Our mission had been to destroy the villages and that had been accomplished, but our news shocked the entire countryside, for Crawford was well known and had been in a place of authority for a long time. Out here most people knew what an Indian burning was like.

But even more than Crawford, the place mourned George Gibson. His powder exploit had made a great man of him, and he had patrolled the rivers, had held back the Indians. Now, he was dead with none to take his place. Linn had gone to Kentucky, the Lambs were scattered; some had died with Clark, some had dispersed elsewhere. They had finished their days of service.

When I saw Breon, his first word was, "Mcfail?"

I nodded, my heart heavy. I kept wondering if my friend would burn at a Wyandotte torture post.

CHAPTER ELEVEN

NOW THAT Gibson was dead, I was possessed with a feeling of futility, for I had counted on getting from him some direction or hint, whether he wished to give it or not. Now, that hope had vanished. True, he had told me things as he lay dying, had insisted that Hartlin had the gold "somewhere in the woods." That, of course, meant that Gibson felt sure Hartlin had not turned the treasure over to the British, and also that it had not been taken east, confirming both what Pollock had told me and what General Wayne had learned from the captured officer taken by Clow's dragoons. Hundreds of square miles spread about this Fort Pitt; to the east, to the north, to the west and south; all was woodland. But of one thing I did feel fairly sure; if the gold had been taken upriver in canoes, it would be hidden south of the Iroquois country, since even Hartlin could not move as he pleased in the land of the People of the Long House.

Hartlin; the man had seemed quiet, cultured, and fair when I had my only meeting with him, which had been on the trail that morning so long ago. He had mentioned troubled times and had given me advice. Since then, others had built up a different sort of man to me—a ruthless person, capable of cruelty and desperate deeds. And this man now owned my small farm on the Schuylkill.

Breon had an idea, and the landlord was always a good thinker, though he reached his conclusions slowly.

"Money is Hartlin's god, Martin. His concern in this war is to stay on the side that will allow him a profit in his dealings with Indians and settlers. If he took the gold, it would not be turned over to the British. The man does not love a distant English King as he does clinking gold coins. I believe he hid the gold bars until such time that it would be safe for him to get the stuff to the seaboard and turn it into cash. You just can't take a slab of gold and plank it down on a counter like it was a coin."

Twenty little kegs, each with a single brass tack set in it for a marker; I had seen them under the tarpaulin on the bateau and had looked at Linn's puzzled face as he pointed them out to me. A half ton of gold bars meant pack horses, big canoes or bateaux; and if, as my friends thought, the stolen treasure had gone by canoes, it could not be at too great a distance. One cannot hide a canoe on open water. Somewhere, not too far from Fort Pitt, I would find it. His Excellency had said I would not fail him.

"Lon," I said to my friend, "I must find Hartlin. It's easier to find a man than small kegs in a great wilderness."

I spent another day about town and the fort, much of it standing on the battlements, looking north and south over the rivers that come together here, each of them, beyond the clearings, losing itself in dark bars of woodland. It was a vast land to search, too vast even for an army. When I did get back to the tavern, Lon was mysterious, and further, was dressed in his best blue coat. For once, his stockings were in order and his shoe buckles shone.

"There's a visitor, Martin. Your shaving tackle is ready and your best clothes. Those buckskins are quite badly stained."

He was so serious that I humored him to the extent of shaving and donning the better clothing. Lon stayed by me until he was satisfied that I looked my poor best, then he led me out of my room and down the hallway.

Over the common room was the largest of the upstairs chambers, one that faced north and west. Breon tapped at the door, opened it, and stepped aside so I could enter first, which I did, frowning at all this mummery.

But Lon did not follow me in; the door closed at my back, and I heard a faint click as the latch dropped into place. I stood, staring.

She was here, over by the window, dressed in a flowered gown that fell in deep folds to the floor where the tips of polished slippers showed.

There was lace at her throat and wrists. Her hair was piled high on her head, and the sunlight touched it with brightness.

"Martin," she said softly, "I have come here to talk with you."

All my impatience with Breon vanished and with it any natural assurance I might have possessed. I tried to say something but mumbled it. The only thing perfectly clear to me was that I was so very glad to see her. She came forward, and for a moment I held her small hand in mine, my fingers stained by the outdoors contrasting with hers, which were so white.

"You are glad to see me, Martin Jon, though you'd like to say you are not."

She seemed to read my mind. Gesturing toward the west window, she walked over there and we took chairs facing each other. To a man who has lived so much in camps and the wilderness, a chair is an awkward thing; so this one seemed.

"It's high time, friend Martin, that we should understand each other," she announced firmly. "General Wayne was going to explain things to you, but I asked for the privilege of doing it; I was coming out here ahead of you and would meet you when you arrived."

Abruptly, I had something to say and blurted it out. "Did you leave a message for me on the Loyalhanna?"

She laughed. "Yes; while I knew you would make good time, the old man there had so little to occupy his mind that I gave him the message so he'd feel important as he watched the road. I thought you'd guess that I had come that way."

Her fingers went down to a pocket in her skirt and came out with a small piece of paper well sealed. I took it and broke the wax.

"That, Martin," she said softly, "will explain things."

> *Dear Martin:*
>
> *Hester Jordan, as you should have guessed long ago, is an agent for our cause. She has been under His Excellency's and my orders not to divulge this to anyone which is why she could not tell you. Throw out your foolish suspicions and work for her and with her so that more good will be accomplished. She went with Gibson to New Orleans to help her uncle, Oliver Pollock, in the*

*deal for the French gold; she kept us advised about Philadelphia
while the British were there. Also, if you have lost property, she
has forfeited a hundredfold more.*

—*Anthony Wayne*

My ears seemed to be ringing as I looked down at the bit of paper
torn from a field notebook. The general had not even signed his military title; it was simply a note from one friend to another to clear away
confusion.

"Now, Martin, you understand."

I felt my face coloring as I remembered her warning about the money, which would have saved me much pain; the news of the trapped
Lambs; the message that had prevented a disaster to Lafayette's troops.
Slowly, my eyes lifted until they met hers and found there only kindness
and understanding. Clumsily, I began an apology, but she reached out
and touched my sleeve.

"Don't, Martin, you have been an honest man, and they seem a bit
scarce these troubled days. Now, we do not have much time and I have a
great deal to tell you."

There, in Breon's upper room, while the sun at the windows slowly
faded, she told me a remarkable story, proving what Wayne had said
about her losses. Her father, a wealthy landowner in Philadelphia, had
also acquired holdings in western Pennsylvania. The man I knew as Doctor Hartlin had managed real estate deals for Jordan and had finally been
given power of attorney, which permitted him to handle Jordan's property as though it belonged to him. After Hester's father died, she was suspicious of Hartlin, but he refused to yield his authority. She had come west,
had found him an active Tory, and had learned that her losses, through
him, were great. The commandant, Leith, had profited through some of
Hartlin's deals and so was lenient with him. That morning when I had
sold the bear meat to the fleeing Tories, Hester had followed Hartlin for
a last chance to get an accounting.

The new commandant, Brodhead, had promised help, and Hester,
with Philadelphia now dangerous to her because of her warning brought

to Wayne, had come west again in the hope of finding Hartlin and getting his power of attorney from him.

She had gone to New Orleans with Gibson on Wayne's orders and because she had influential French friends down there. In Philadelphia, she posed as a Royalist sympathizer.

After she finished, and at her urging, I told of the visit to Washington and how I had come west to locate Gibson, of Mcfail's feud with his colonel, and what the dying leader of the Lambs had told me.

"So, Hester, I must get through to Detroit and find Hartlin."

She shook her head and spoke doubtfully.

"You do not know the man as I do. He is cold and so set that nothing can be had from him. If you go to Detroit he would turn you over to the British as a spy and they'd cheerfully hang you to please him."

She rose abruptly and I realized the room was dusky.

"Mr. Breon has horses waiting to take me up to the fort, Martin. Colonel Brodhead will be back tomorrow and we'll talk with him."

I came to my feet, wanting to say I would escort her, but I was too awkward. Every time I met this girl I had left her in some sort of chagrin; this time it was because of social awkwardness. But I held her slim fingers in mine again, felt the warmth of them; then, she went out.

Yet the room was not entirely empty, for the faint fragrance of her perfume lingered. She had been sitting in that chair and the sun, filtering through the small diamond panes of the window, had touched her hair. I told myself that I was growing maudlin. Here I was, a small farmer, now owning no land at all, and she was a very great lady. My possessions were limited to this town suit of mine, my worn buckskins, and the weapons I owned. Further, I had been so deluded that I had thought her a spy when she was truly a great Patriot. I kicked the chair on which I had been sitting. Hester Jordan and I had as much in common as a blue jay and a groundhog.

Restless the next morning, since I had to wait for Brodhead's arrival, I walked out from Breon's tavern in the direction of Grant's hill, coming finally to a smithy set a little off the main road. It was a long, low stone building roofed with good shingles, and a wide open door led into the main shop. But there was a forge and an anvil outside, at which the smith, Joe Gayle, who had shod my packhorse and who remembered me, worked. He stood now, with strong hands resting on his hips and a smudge across his face, and seemed to be studying something.

"Richtier, there was a man here this morning early, looking for you."

I made no immediate reply for he seemed to want to say more.

"I was wondering how you'd take it—this man, I mean. Mebbe you'd get ideas."

I grinned at him.

"Trot out your man any time, Joe, then I'll figure how to take it."

Gayle jerked his shoulder toward the open door.

"He was going down to your tavern; he's in there now. Suppose you talk with him."

I walked through the open doorway and found it pretty dark inside, but my eyes adjusted themselves in a few moments so that I saw a man seated close by the forge. Dressed in buckskins and wearing a fur cap, he seemed rather short but powerfully built about the shoulders. Another thing in frontier country that one becomes accustomed to is men carrying rifles, but this man rested his piece across his knees, and the muzzle was trained on me. He did not move but spoke presently.

"Gayle sent you in."

He got up slowly, still holding his weapon across his body, and I could see he wore a neatly clipped beard, and he was not a short man for his eyes were level with mine. They were as cold as rifle fire. His hands on the gun were long-fingered and strong, and on one shoulder of his hunting shirt was some sort of military insignia that looked like a bit of ribbon. I stared back at him.

"If you want to talk to me, put that rifle down."

My voice was as cold as I could make it, for I did not relish this business of being told to go in and face a man with a weapon. His lips twitched and he glanced from me to the lock of his rifle.

"My name is Gerdes," he said softly. "Simon Gerdes."

It took me a minute before I understood the pronunciation of the name Gerdes, for one seldom heard it pronounced that way, nor was it often spelled that way. I was facing Simon Girty, whose name was anathema in all this country and for whom a reward would be paid at the fort less than five miles from this place.

"Crawford," I snapped at him, and he frowned. The line on his lips went straight and his eyes grew a bit colder, if that were possible.

"Yes," he answered, "I'll be carrying that to my grave along with many things for which I am not to blame. No, I hated the man. Richtier, did you ever sit at a Wyandotte council fire or that of a Delaware or a Shawnee?" He shook his head as a negation for me and continued. "Remember, I am a British partisan officer." He touched the ribbon on his shoulder. "I lead partisans and Indians. Crawford saw to it that I did not get a commission with the colonies. Pike blackened Crawford's face that night, not I. Any damned fool would know there was naught I could do. My best was to get Mcfail, Hoadley, and Frye sent on to Detroit."

"They're safe?" I cried, and he nodded.

"Safe as men can be in prison barracks with winter coming." He set his rifle against the anvil block, seated himself carefully, and pointed to a box for me.

"Richtier, I didn't come here to risk my neck talking about why I'm with the British. I'm a fighting man, same as you, only I'm on the side where they pay wages." He pointed his finger.

"You brought gold upriver, gold and powder. Clark's giving us hell in the Illinois country with some of the powder, but the gold's gone. Is that right?"

What he asked was common knowledge, so I nodded, but excitement was stirring in me. I faced possibly the most daring man on our frontiers on either side of this war, one capable of anything, and he was about to talk.

"Richtier, Hartlin, four Senecas, and I took your gold. We simply walked into your storehouse past two drunken guards and carried it out. We took the kegs marked with brass nails about which there had been loose talk at the unloading of your boat. Hartlin had brought me written orders from the British commandant in these parts to assist him in getting powder away from you folks, and I was subject to his orders. You were all so busy celebrating that it was easy to move those kegs up the Allegheny."

Excitement must have shown on my face for he grinned before he continued.

"The word's out around here that you're after those kegs Leith locked you up for stealing."

He seemed in a hurry for he gave me no chance to reply.

"We stopped those canoes at the mouth of the Mahoning Creek, the crookedest bit of shallow water in these hills. The Shamokin Path goes up that way. It was then Hartlin told me we had gold, not powder. He planned to send the Senecas up to their country for horses and then pack the treasure to Niagara, not Detroit. While he waited for transport, of course, I had to get back to Detroit. My orders ran that way."

He took out a laurelwood pipe on which was carved an odd, obscene symbol, filled and lighted it, and did not speak again until he had smoked for a few minutes. Then he waved the pipe, making an arc of smoke.

"Months later, this Hartlin showed up at Detroit with the story that his Senecas did not come with the horses and that a band of about twenty of your own partisans jumped him, killed his single Indian companion, and made off with the gold. Richtier, that report went with the British because they owe Hartlin so much, but it don't talk to me. He may have influence with them, but I'd have killed the man—"

"You want the gold," I interrupted bluntly, and he nodded promptly.

"Yes, that's why I'm here. Hartlin has it somewhere in the hills, but it can't be found without him, Richtier. Now, I grew up on the Susquehanna, and I'm getting tired of wars and raids, of scalpings and burnings, and of sitting round with a lot of hair-triggers. I want to go home, but down there they'd stretch my neck if I did. There's been a power of lying about me by folks that need a whipping. But I've friends. George Washington knows me well for we campaigned together under Braddock, and I helped him survey land."

He had grown so earnest that his pipe had gone out and he was leaning toward me.

"This is my plan: I'll throw in with you and we'll kidnap Hartlin out of Detroit and make him show us where the gold is. I've been with the Indians long enough to know just how to make a man talk, even Hartlin who's as cold as a snake. Then we'll take the gold down the Susquehanna and you'll get a pardon from Congress for me. All I want is that and what one of them kegs holds."

My mind was racing; after all, it was a tempting scheme, all but the possible torture of Hartlin. Yet I had claimed I would make the man talk, had said that to Hester. The whole scheme was feasible, even to the pardon that Congress, put to it to find money, might grant. Yet the gold was not mine, nor could I guarantee this outlaw anything. He was talking again, half to himself.

"There's a place down there halfway between Harris Ferry and Fort Augusta where the hills crowd the water and there's a rock the shape of a man's head. I can take salmon in the fast water and the deer come down to the old fields every evening. Partridges drum on the dead logs and I know where to find mountain tea on the ridges. It's the only place that'll ever be home to me—"

"Gerdes," I said, "Congress won't listen to me, and I couldn't guarantee the bargain if I made it."

"George Washington sent you out here, and you say that!" he cried, coming to his feet in a flash, and I thought he was angry, but when I rose, he was smiling, showing white teeth.

"Was afraid of that," he declared. "You're like the rest of the Dutch—honest but slow on the uptake. Some would have made the deal and left me to hold the bag."

We were shaking hands, his fingers steely strong, his eyes looking directly into mine.

"I'd liked to have worked with you, Richtier. They say you're a good man with a knife or on the trail. I'll go after that gold myself, and there's a gang of hellions I can pick up to help me. If I can't buy that blood-drained Congress of yours, once I have twenty kegs of gold bars, I'll be—"

He had turned and was halfway out of the shed when he stopped and returned to shake hands the second time.

"Here's how, Richtier. Next time we look at each other mebbe it'll be over a rifle barrel. Who knows which one of us will float down the Susquehanna on boats loaded with gold? Let's play hard, Richtier."

He dropped my hand and walked out of the smithy; paying no attention to Gayle, he marched off into the forest as a casual hunter might go. At no time did the man seem nervous for his own safety, even though he must have realized what would happen to him if he were taken in this locality.

Gayle looked at me and gestured toward the disappearing man.

"Not so bloody as he's made out to be. It's a case of give a dog a bad name. I knowed Simon a long time and he's had a hard life; held back by men that thought themselves his betters, men like Crawford. Don't you believe too much of this scalping stuff, for he's saved a good many; some of your friends from what I've been told."

Then I remembered; I had not thanked Girty even though I was certain it was his influence that had saved the Lambs from the torture post. Surely I owed the renegade a debt for that. But my concern had been about the gold. After all, His Excellency had said I was not to be concerned about personal matters.

CHAPTER TWELVE

WHEN LON told me I was to report to Colonel Brodhead's headquarters, I felt differently than I would have had the direction come from his predecessor. While I had never met or seen the colonel, I knew he came from Northampton County, which is close to my home country; that he was a veteran of the old wars and was known for a reckless courage like that of Colonel John Kelly, General Hugh Mercer, or our own Anthony Wayne. He had participated in many engagements and was one of the three Pennsylvania colonels in charge of state troops. Further, he had had a vast experience with Indians, both in handling and fighting them.

It was sharp, bracing weather as I walked down the King's road, entering the fort by what we call the Covered Way, which got its name from the bar placed over the gate. Mcfail would have approved, for there was a sentry on duty who looked me over carefully and another at the Grenadier bastion when I had passed through the second gate. Turning left there, I approached the long, familiar building we call Officers' Quarters, where I was told to find the commandant.

This time it was not an empty room with a single man back of a desk and a secretary like another piece of furniture close by. The place was an orderly litter of military equipment with each sort on a separate pile. Everything was here, from a pack saddle to a swivel gun complete with its mount. In the midst of the confusion moved a short, powerfully built man in the blue coat and light breeches of the Light Infantry and with the insignia of a Line colonel on his shoulder. He carried a piece of paper on which he was making check marks.

"The colonel sent for me, sir," I said, trying to be military but forgetting to salute.

Brodhead laid down the paper he had been examining and turned to me with a smile on his heavy, sunburned face. He was an older man than I had expected, but there was vigor in every line of his features.

"Yes," he said. "It's Richtier, is it not?"

He gestured toward the clutter on the floor.

"I've been looking over some of our equipment; for this western work, we may need to make some changes from what we used down east. You were with Crawford and, while I have Williamson's report, I'd like to hear what you saw."

I took the indicated chair while he straddled the seat of another as though it were a horse, placing his arms along the back of it as though that might be the pommel of a saddle. Like Wayne and other able men, he listened well, almost without interruption. Even after I finished, he was silent for a moment.

"Poor Crawford; what a way to die."

Then he looked up, his eyes boring into mine.

"How did you learn that Mcfail and the other Lambs were taken to Detroit?"

I had been careless and was off balance in my thinking, but there was no help for it; the encounter with Girty must come out.

"Simon Girty told me."

Brodhead was off that chair like a man leaps from a horse; then he crossed to his desk and back like a person who needs action in order to curb his temper. His eyes, I saw, were gray and hard.

"Richtier, I had not meant to speak of this. General Wayne has much confidence in you and expects you to make a name for yourself. But he says you have a faculty for getting into trouble—and out of it."

"Born to trouble," I said grimly, interrupting him. I was angry clear through. The same thing had happened before with George Gibson. But Brodhead sat down, his impatience gone.

"Don't get that Dutch back up, Richtier. General Wayne needs you. His Excellency depends on you in this gold matter. Tell me of this man Simon Gerdes, or Girty."

He had broken the rising tide of my anger largely because, with his last words, he smiled. So I told him of the interview at the smithy, of Girty's nostalgia, and of his scheme. Brodhead nodded.

"Not a bad scheme, Richtier. It might be the best thing that could be done. Congress just might pardon him, but again that august body might throw the book at you. 'If thou hast stricken thy hand with a stranger, thou art snared with the words of thy mouth.'"

Daniel Brodhead, Colonel of the Eighth Pennsylvania Light Infantry, did not seem the sort of person to be quoting Scripture, but he had certainly picked an apt sentence.

"Poor Girty, think how it would be to a man never to come home again. He was born down there—" He stopped and held up his hand. "My apologies; they took your land from you, I am told. I did not think in time."

"Colonel Brodhead, if I meet this man, Hartlin, I think I shall have my farm again."

His lips twitched; probably my statement seemed like a boast to him.

"I do not doubt that. At any rate, I can help you to see the man if he is in Detroit. I do believe any real search for the gold must begin with this Doctor Hartlin. He should have been placed under arrest before he left here. The British hold close to two hundred of our people as prisoners in Detroit, and I am about to send several of my officers up there to negotiate for an exchange. Some of this number are women and children; the winter may be hard on them if we cannot get them home. Richtier, if you want to take the risk of being recognized as a Lamb, you can go up there with my mission."

I may have seemed too eager, for he held up his hand in a warning gesture.

"Remember, you are going under a military flag. Nothing may be done to aid prisoners to escape or to otherwise violate the terms under which my officers travel. Have I your assurance not to commit an overt act?"

"Yes," I promised. At any rate, I could look about the British post and make further plans. It might be that I should encounter Hartlin or even see Mcfail. Certainly, it would be better to go up there than to blunder about Fort Pitt to no purpose.

The next two days were busy ones while we prepared to go to Detroit. Lieutenant Greene, a young fellow full of spirits, had charge; his companion was a much older man, a seasoned borderer, Ensign Brady. The plan was to go first to Presque Isle by horses, then on to Detroit in a boat that would be provided. Somewhere between Fort Pitt and Lake Erie, a British party would meet and take us to Presque Isle.

Brady had managed to get some fair horses, and we camped the first night across the river from bloody Kittanning, where Armstrong had attacked the Delawares under Shingas. The place still looked grim to us, with high hills pitching up about it to shut out the sunlight. I could imagine I saw where that terrible torture post had stood.

Most of the river tributaries came into the Allegheny from the east, but it was the Mahoning that I wanted to see most after hearing Girty tell that that was where Hartlin had stopped with the gold. We did see a stream meandering back into the hills, which seemed to answer the description, but a better look at it meant fording the river and, after all, our mission was to get to the lakes, so we rode on.

A dozen miles farther north, where there were wide natural meadows, we were picked up by our escort, a hard-looking crowd of three scruffy-looking Indians and two white men. The leader was a cross-eyed little man, inclined to be surly and who made no effort to hide his contempt for rebels. The second white man was a silent, watchful sort of person who did not seem to trust his own people, much less us.

We rode slowly because this leader, who gave his name as Ensign Kahle, did not push his men. He seemed to take delight in the fact that the slow progress irritated us, and when we camped, none of them helped toward making us comfortable. We prepared our own meals over our own fire and slept some little distance from the escort, which suited Greene.

"They smell as though there was something dead in the British army," he said to me in a low voice, and when I laughed, the two white men looked at us suspiciously, as if levity was some broach of the articles of war.

On our second day's march, we crossed a hill and looked into a valley through which ran a well-defined trail, but before we reached it, Kahle stopped us, and the reason was apparent in a few minutes. A long file of

Indians was coming along the path from the east. We sat there on our horses, though Kahle and one of the Indians did ride down closer to the trail. The hackles on my neck rose as I watched.

There were probably a hundred warriors and they had come a long way, judging from broken moccasins and torn leggings. But the few scalps I saw dangling from belts looked old and dried. They passed at a sort of dogtrot, glancing our way in such a manner that the whites of their eyes showed, but they did not pause or pay any further attention to us. One thing that struck me was that all carried good muskets, which would be British issue, and their sidearms looked serviceable.

Greene, Brady, and I sat still until the last warrior had passed, then we rode down to Kahle.

"What tribe?" Greene asked the man, but he shrugged his shoulders and answered insolently, "Dunno; jest Injuns, I expect."

One of the tribesmen with us looked at him soberly then back to his horse's ears, after which he dug his moccasined heels into the animal's ribs. I did not think this Indian wasted any affection or respect on the ensign.

Greene was a good-natured man, but at our last camp, Kahle went too far. This time he spat tobacco juice into the officer's fire, and Greene leaped to his feet and stood over the man.

"Don't ever do that again, Kahle. You've been nasty all the way. If you were in my company down home, I'd give you a taste of the cat."

Kahle stepped away from the angry lieutenant, and for a moment I thought he was going to repeat his act. One of the Indians loosened his tomahawk. Finally, Kahle sneered and walked away, but we heard him mutter, "Mebbe we'll be down for your scalps one of these days."

Presque Isle was different and a relief. While the regular soldiers treated us coolly, they were decent about it and polite. The garrison was small, but an escorted boat was ready and waiting for us.

It was a small boat that carried us, and it pitched and rolled a great deal on the way up the lakes to Detroit River; I found myself a poor sailor, to the amusement of the British sergeant in charge of us, so I was glad and relieved when we entered the broad river at the upper end of which the fort was built.

Men have explained that Detroit was a much more important post in the days of the old French wars than in the Revolution, but I was surprised to find such a small stockade, and the town built about it was not nearly so extensive as that about Fort Pitt. The streets were wide, the buildings far apart, and there was a small river back of the main fort and town, beyond which, on a low hill, was a second fort. There was a good moat about the palisades and a narrow firing zone cleared and plowed. I looked it over carefully, thinking of the old days and the bitter fighting that had occurred here.

Inside the fort was the typical neatness of the British army. There was smoothly clipped grass about the gun embrasures, and the brass pieces in sight were polished until they shone. Neat piles of round shot were placed beside the gun carriages, and there were racks for muskets. Barracks, officers' quarters, and storehouses preserved the air of cleanness and efficiency. Mentally I noted that our Colonel Clark would find this a harder nut to crack than the slovenly forts in the Illinois country.

We were served a good meal in the officers' quarters, and that evening we were escorted to the commandant.

Colonel Hamilton received us with stiff military courtesy when the lieutenant who had brought us in introduced each one of us carefully. Then, at Hamilton's suggestion, we took seats. No other officers were present, but there had been a sentry just outside the door.

This man to whom we presented Colonel Brodhead's letter was very different from the mental picture I had of him, a picture created by his nickname "Hair Buyer," given him on our frontier, where it symbolized every horror of Indian warfare. I had looked for a hard-swearing, blustering brute; this man was a tall, slim soldier, immaculately dressed in the uniform of his rank. His face, however, remained blank and cold as he read our colonel's letter.

"Gentlemen," he said when he had finished, "I shall hold an officers' council tomorrow morning to which I shall present the letter just brought to me. Then I shall be able to give you some word to carry back with you."

The interview had not taken a full ten minutes, and after Hamilton rose, the lieutenant took us back to a barracks building where we were given a room furnished with bunks, chairs, and a table. There was also a big open fire, most welcome in the sharp weather. After we had been alone for some time, Brady opened the door we had entered and was promptly confronted by a sentry.

"Sorry," the man said. "Orders are that you stay inside."

Brady bristled at the thought that we were prisoners, but Greene reasoned with him.

"We wouldn't let British officers run loose about Pitt or give them keys to the powder magazines."

In a way I was glad about the sentry because I was tempted to go out and search for either Doctor Hartlin or my friends, supposed to be prisoners here.

After the noon meal the following day, our lieutenant, whose name was George, advised us that the negotiations for the release of prisoners had been placed in the hands of a Major Creede, who was also adjutant of the post, and we were taken to his office.

This Creede was a fastidious person, even to the way he wore his uniform, and he looked dry, as if he had been sitting too long in a chimney-corner. However, he affected an affability that was as irritating as was his mannerism of rubbing his hands together.

"Gentlemen," he said pompously, "you have come about the prisoners. Your interest in them shows your humanity."

Greene bowed, Brady stared, and I looked out the window, trying to cover a sudden amusement.

"We have over two hundred of them, as you know. Many are women and children that we ransomed from your Indian neighbors." Brady grunted, and Creede shot him a sharp glance before he continued.

"The women and children are quartered about the village, where most of them are employed in domestic service. Some of the younger males work on wood-cutting crews and other labor that arises. Of course, wages are quite low."

He consulted his notes, cleared his throat, and gave his hands another careful rubbing together.

"The list shows close to one hundred men taken in action, including a number of questionable characters suspected of spying on His Majesty's military dispositions. These men are being investigated."

I wanted to ask if he meant Mcfail, Hoadley, or Frye, but Greene was tense, Brady angry, and I remembered Brodhead's careful direction. Creede pushed himself well back in his chair and rolled a quill about in his fingers.

"These men figure in a long story that has to do with an incident on the Mississippi when some of our soldiers were killed."

Brady half turned, thought better of it, and looked straight ahead. I felt my muscles stiffen. Greene took this veiled gibing best of all.

"Some powder was brought up the river and some gold in the form of ingots, which were contained in kegs. This gold was taken from your storehouse by some daring fellows and borne well up the Allegheny, where the men who had it, while waiting for transport, were set upon by some of your partisans and the gold taken."

Creede was having the time of his life, baiting us while he knew we were helpless. He moistened his lips with the tip of a very red tongue and shot his bombshell.

"Colonel Hamilton directs me to make this offer to your colonel. We will turn over to him every prisoner in our post here at Detroit when Colonel Brodhead turns over to us the twenty kegs of gold."

Unable to be silent longer, I broke in.

"Sir, we do not have the gold, but your man Hartlin does—"

Creede almost giggled, he was so pleased with himself, as he interrupted me.

"Doctor Hartlin is a most estimable person. If he said the gold was taken from him, then it was. There is no reason to doubt a man of his patriotic devotion to His Majesty's interests. You have Colonel Hamilton's final terms."

Greene's voice was choked with anger. "You propose the impossible. Your Tory doctor has his stolen treasure well hidden."

Creede paid no attention to what the lieutenant was saying but rose from his seat.

"You will be quartered here another night, after which you will be taken back to Presque Isle. Of course, we will prepare a letter that will contain the terms offered by Colonel Hamilton."

We had reached the door when Creede cleared his throat again and exploded his second bombshell.

"You will understand that those leaving will be Lieutenant Greene and Ensign Brady. This man Richtier is a notorious person, and a military mission does not offer him sanctuary. He will be detained here and investigated thoroughly until we are sure of what was done on the river and elsewhere. It's the old powder business, my friend. I am afraid my colonel would like to hang you."

He had addressed his final words directly to me, but now Greene whirled back into the room and stood up to Creede.

"Quiet, you moldy beast. Keep this man and Colonel Brodhead will lock up every Tory about Fort Pitt. Harm this man and I'll personally string up a half dozen Tories or soldiers who wear the red coat."

Creede merely bowed, then tapped the table with his inkhorn. Immediately, a file of soldiers appeared in the hallway and hustled us across the parade ground to our quarters. On our way, we could see at the far end of the open space beyond the drill ground a log building with grating on the windows and with just a single chimney.

The three of us sat about and argued until our candle burned out and until we had used the last of our firewood. Then we crawled into our bunks to keep warm under the blankets.

"He'll hold us to the terms," I kept saying. "You two quit fussing about it and get home. That damned gold will hang us all if we're not careful."

Greene was grumbling in the dark when I dropped off to sleep, and in the morning I delivered my final opinion.

"Friends, Hartlin's here in Detroit and the secret I want is with him. The more I hear, the more I think he has the gold hidden in the hills, waiting for peacetime. Mcfail's here somewhere. If I went back with you, I'd just have to return here to get a start. The gold is needed—I'll stay here."

Some of Greene's anger had drained away in the night. He was not satisfied with my reasoning but could see some sense in it. Besides, he was helpless.

"Martin, Brodhead has some friends here either in Detroit or Presque Isle. I don't know them, but the colonel will get in touch with you somehow. I think one of the men is a boatman, but I'm not sure."

I took off my equipment and gave it to these friends.

"Take care of that knife; it was Drough's; that and this pistol. It throws a ball a little high. Don't worry; if Mcfail and I can get together, we'll get out of Detroit whenever we have a mind."

That was straight, big talk for I had no idea where or how I would be confined, nor was I sure that Mcfail was here. But I wanted to reassure these men, and I was satisfied with the chance that lay before me. I would find that gold somehow. The only bit of equipment I did keep was a small clasp-knife, which I tucked into the top of my moccasin.

Greene and Brady left me with protestations as to what they would do. I liked these men; they really meant the big things they said. An hour after they had gone, two soldiers escorted me to the building I had seen across the parade ground. With no further word, they unlocked the door and shoved me inside. The first man I saw in the interior was Mcfail, and back of him, wearing a beard, was Hoadley.

CHAPTER THIRTEEN

THE BUILDING had a roofed-over entryway through which I had been pushed; there was but one long room with bunks set along either side and a huge fireplace taking up nearly all the space of the far end. The floor was covered with puncheons and the log walls carefully chinked with marsh grass. Three small windows opened on one side between tiers of bunks. To me, the place was little warmer than the outside, and the half-hundred men housed there evidently wore all the clothing they owned. When my friends greeted me they all flocked about us, hungry for whatever news I brought.

It seemed Mcfail would never let go of my hand, which he pumped vigorously at intervals, and Hoadley thumped me on my back while Frye stood by wearing the friendly grin so characteristic of him.

"Men," the sergeant shouted, "here's another Lamb, the one who went up the Natchez Trace for help. He's been east and can tell us of the fighting there."

They found an old keg to serve as a stool for me, and I told how I had gone east after the powder expedition. I explained how I had been delayed by an injury and of the time spent among the peaceful Brethren. Then my story went on with the Paoli massacre and Lafayette's close shave.

They interrupted me at will, trying to get the picture clearly in their minds.

"God," one bearded giant muttered, "I'd like to fight in them parts where you need look only one way and no sneakin' critter can slip up behind after your hair."

"There was to be another big battle," I added, thinking of what Washington had mentioned to me. "Then it will be winter quarters somewhere. Maybe we'll all be down there again by the time the robins come."

It was hard to satisfy these men who were starved for news. I was to learn that some had been here more than a year; some had served with Clark, some with Lochry, and nearly a dozen with Crawford. They had information for me about the fighting in the west, and a man whose name was Allen told me more than I knew of the fight in which Crawford was trapped.

"We was too eager," he declared. "Crawford never saw the need of keeping his folks together. Our colonel didn't seem to know that Indians in bulk can outfight white men."

It seemed odd to me that there was no dissent to this remark. We talked of the possibility of escape, and Mcfail sniffled loudly. "The prison don't hold us. There's not over two hundred fifty Britishers in the place. But getting through the Indian nations is the trick. With no arms or provisions, those boys would pick us off and sell our scalps right back here to Hamilton—eight dollars a head."

At evening, two soldiers bore in a big steaming kettle of corn and beans boiled with a little meat for flavor. Four of the prisoners took the kettle and carried it over to our fireplace to reheat the contents. Then each received a small bowl and filed past while the stew was served in equal portions by a man using a long-handled copper ladle. With this went a square of hard bread brought in by a third soldier who carried it in a large basket. We ate with our fingers, sopping the bread in the stew.

A small piece of meat remained in the bottom of the now empty pot, and the man who had served us called out:

"Jenkins, Harkens!"

Two men shambled forward. Both had thin faces and walked with shuffling feet and bowed shoulders; each received half of the meat, which was divided for them.

"Sick," Hoadley explained. "We hold back the strengthening stuff for them that needs it most."

An odd and touching performance was put on shortly after dark when it had grown cold in the room. The men formed a circle so that four or five could stand before the fireplace for a few minutes while we counted to fifty. Then the circle moved, giving a chance for five more men, and so on. We kept this up for what seemed an hour before scuttling to our bunks. In very real kindness, I had been assigned a bunk by the fire, and I wrapped myself in the blanket left for me by the guard.

The long room filled with the sound of men sleeping. Many snored, some groaned, one talked softly to himself, scarcely sounding the words. Then Mcfail roused me and we went to the fireplace, where it was Hoadley's job to keep the heat going the first half of the night.

"Martin," Mcfail said, "you didn't mention the gold in your story, but Hartlin's here. I've seen him, and his house is the big one at the edge of town with its back to the little river. There's but one way to get the gold and that's to kidnap Hartlin and make him take us to it. There's lots of talk about gold among the men, and the guards try to pump us sometimes. They even had me and Frye in before the Hair Buyer himself. Martin, if you was to scratch than man, he'd bleed water or skim milk."

I told these friends about the scene with Creede and about my interview with Washington.

"You will not fail me." His words, as I repeated them here in this British prison, seemed unduly solemn. Mcfail nodded his bearded head in the faint firelight.

"No," he said with conviction, "of course you can't fail him, and we'll see that you're helped."

Then I said that Wayne thought the gold was as valuable as a victory. This time, Hoadley spoke thoughtfully: "Me, I guess I never saw a real victory, but I'd be willing to buy one—if I was able and had that gold."

His remark reminded me that I had probably never seen a clear-cut victory except in skirmishes. But two hundred thousand dollars would buy the services of more than two thousand men for a year; good men, too, like those of the Pennsylvania Line.

"Martin," Mcfail said cautiously, "we get in and out of here most every night, and we throw lots to see who goes. Sometimes a man gets out and finds extra food, a piece of a blanket, or something we can use. We've got some friends in the village that kinda pity us. Once, we got a whole peck of turnips."

In the firelight, I saw that the sergeant's hair was graying. He glanced along the row of bunks.

"Drough's knife—did they take it from you?"

He seemed tremendously relieved when I explained that my weapons had gone back with Greene and Brady.

"You knew that I got Gibson?" he questioned, and I nodded. "Yes, John, I got to him before he died and he talked a little."

Mcfail swore softly, then told what had happened.

"Gibson never used to be afraid. When those Indians jumped us, we was pretty busy. I saw him edge over toward the creek and was hoping the Red Sticks would save me the trouble. I guess they did wound him, but I let him have it just as he looked across at me, and he knew why I was shooting. Then he got hit again and I was pretty busy."

Hoadley broke in.

"We've got to be careful what we tell these men. They're all right, but a hungry man might sell out for tobacco or something. They know the rumor about the gold, but not your part in getting it back, Martin. The Gibson story is on the quiet, too."

"We've got to get out together," Mcfail declared, "and that's hard because we cast lots. And we can't tell them how important it is for you to look about, Martin. Maybe, though, we can fix things. I could make Hartlin talk, once we had him out of here—Detroit, I mean."

There was some stirring in the bunks, and we went to our places. We had broken the rules in using the fire more than our share. After I had begun to doze, I heard the firewatchers change places.

During the following days, I was initiated into the monotony of prison life. Most of the men tried to keep busy. Every third day there was a woodcutting detail, and the men who went on it were given the warmest clothing available. Each man looked forward to this labor, though it sometimes meant frosted hands or feet. Oddly, most of the prisoners had clasp-knives, and whittling was the most common diversion. Wooden chains were festooned on the wall, wooden fans were placed above bunks; there were knives, scissors, bears, all carved of wood and some of them blackened with soot as a finish.

The British issued a small quantity of woolen yarn on occasion, and this was knitted into socks by using wooden needles. Two of the men could do this work well, and they also repaired holes in stockings and breaks in clothing.

One of the strangest things about this prison was the fine way the men got along with each other. Confinement usually results in irritations that find an outlet in quarreling, but there seemed to be none of that here. The place was well organized; each man had his duties and his privileges and no deviation was allowed. Lots were cast for any advantage one might get over another, such as leaving the building at night or for a seat close to the fire because of illness or worn clothing. Fifty beans were placed in a leather sack; if, for example, five men were to be chosen, then five colored beans were placed in the sack. Each of us would draw a bean, and those who got the colored ones received the privilege.

The authorities seemed to have forgotten that I was to be investigated, and no further attention was given me, but in the third week of my imprisonment, I managed to make a small contribution to the general good. Twelve of us were selected to go down to the wharf and, under guard, unload a small sloop that had just come in, laden with provisions. The stuff was heavy; great wooden boxes, kegs, and sides of beef frozen hard as bone.

Things came along well enough. The sailors would break out the stuff for us, balancing whatever they had on the end of the unloading planks until we could take hold. We had nearly finished when up came a quarter of beef, weighing perhaps ten stone. It was frozen solid and awkward to handle. Suddenly, there was a yell; the meat had slipped from the sailors' fingers and dropped into twenty feet of icy water. One of the officers with the guard swore, and his companion joined him in looking into the water. He shook his head.

"It's gone; goodbye to His Majesty's beef."

We looked on wistfully; they were going to allow this fine piece of good food to remain down there in the water when we were hungry. I looked at the lieutenant.

"Sir, would the lieutenant let us have that meat if we get it?" He looked me up and down, then shook his head.

"Man," he said, "that water's icy. We've no grappling poles long enough. You could have it, but—"

I did not wait but began to tear off my clothing as fast as possible, the wind stinging my bare hide. One of my fellows understood and snatched up a light rope, which he fastened under my arms. Then, at my gesture, he made a second noosed line and I held its loop in my teeth. The water would be bad, I knew, but I was not yet weakened by confinement as were my companions; therefore, I'd try it.

Luck was with me, and the water was not as bad as the wind had been. I went down, slipped the one noose over the beef leg, made it tight, and they drew up me and the beef promptly.

"Get the man to quarters," the lieutenant snapped, "or he'll freeze."

They ran me naked to our prison and, inside, rushed me before the fire, where they took turns in slapping and rubbing me until I felt all right once more and then put on my heated clothing. The officer in charge of the unloading sent down a small keg of rum that evening and an extra portion of bread, so we had a feast, each man having a piece of meat to roast. We ate, drank, howled, and sang.

"Regular damned blowout," Allen declared. "We drink to a Lamb turned duck."

The men did not forget the incident, and the first thing it gained for me was the privilege of going outside with Mcfail when the lots gave him his turn. But that privilege did not come until I was there another month and had lived through cold made more bitter because of our lean rations. But I do not believe we fared much worse than the garrison, for supply boats could not come through the gales and the lake ice. The local people had scarcely enough to keep themselves and their families and sold little to the garrison.

Through occasional work on the woodcutting crews, I came to have a good idea of the post. Our work and the ox teams went north and east, following the curve of the river toward Lake Saint Claire as far as the old camping ground of the great Pontiac, and southward until we could see the point of the Great Island. It was mostly level ground over which French, English, and Indians had fought and camped and planned.

Mcfail's turn came early in March. We were never closely guarded, for the authorities knew the difficulties of real escape and that only a most desperate man would undertake to cross the Indian lands. We slipped out one of the windows at about nine o'clock. The guards usually kept out of sight in the shelter of the small anteroom of our building. There a fire was usually kept burning.

Mcfail did not forget his duty to the men inside. When we had passed the stockade, we kept to the denser shadows. Our destination was a farmhouse some distance from the fort. There, candlelight showed at a window, and a bent-looking man with big hands opened the door to Mcfail's rap.

"Turnips, Mr. Rivers; can you spare a few tonight?"

"Yes," he answered, "just opened my ground cellar. I can spare you a peck of turnips and a few large onions."

He saw me and pointed.

"Is that the feller that dived for the meat?"

I nodded and laughed, after which he chuckled.

"Mebbe you better dive under the ice and get some fish."

Mcfail paid over a few coppers taken from our treasury, and we took the provisions back to the break in the palisade. Mcfail went through the opening, and I handed the sack to him. He was gone such a long time that I was uneasy, then he returned so quietly that I did not hear him until he dropped into the snow beside me.

"Couldn't take chances," he said a bit breathlessly. "Had to take the stuff to the prison; tossed it through the window. Come on now, we'll have a look at Hartlin's house."

The Savoyard River is the small one that runs back of Detroit town and fort and it is little more than a good-sized creek. About two miles from its mouth, set a little distance from other houses, was a big, two-storied clapboard and log structure, its back almost on the river, the clattering of which covered any sound we might have made approaching. Mcfail tried the rear door, turned to me, and said, "Unbarred."

The shutters on the lower floor were in place, but through chinks we could see that lights burned inside. Using my small knife, I opened a crack in a shutter so we could look in. Mcfail took the first turn and dropped back to me almost at once.

"Great God of the Mountains, Martin, look what's going on!"

It was a large room into which I looked, well-lighted and with a cheerful fire burning in a huge stone fireplace. There were fine tables and chairs, together with some bookshelves along the wall. It was a gracious, well-furnished room. Beside a table sat Hartlin; there was no mistaking the calm features and the professional manner of the man. He was dressed in moleskin trousers and a white shirt; his long fingers rested on the arms of the chair. But, before him, with his back to the kitchen door through which he had probably entered, was Simon Girty. His face was convulsed with anger, and in one hand he held a wide-bladed knife that glittered evilly. We could hear perfectly what he was saying, for he did not lower his voice.

"So, Hartlin, you double-crossed me. First it was powder, then it was gold for the British. All the while you planned to take it to the seacoast, get the gold bars abroad, and turn them into money."

The man in the chair said nothing, nor did he move. Girty tested his blade with a thumb.

"Now, my good doctor, you'll talk. You took the gold somewhere up the Shamokin Path that runs along the Mahoning. Don't ask me to swallow the yarn that the Americans got it. Those damned fools never saw it after Leith lost it. Talk—I'm Simon Gerdes!"

He came closer, raising the knife a little.

"The Shawnees have some little tricks with a blade that I'm going to show you. If you don't talk, I'll leave some Injun marks on you and slip out, after which gold won't matter to you anymore, either in your pockets or in kegs."

Hartlin's eyes may have widened a little, but he made no motion of his hands or body. We had seen enough. With Mcfail leading, we ran round the house and pushed open the kitchen door, our moccasins making no noise as we passed through and then into the room where Girty now stood over his victim. The point of the knife was well up along the doctor's nose where it could be thrust into the corner of his eye.

My diving leap forward was quick, and my outflung hand sent the keen blade flying. Girty sprang back, snatching at his belted hatchet, then Mcfail had him about the body. Girty was a powerful man, probably versed in all the lore of frontier rough-and-tumble fighting, but I have never seen a man who could handle Mcfail if the sergeant was really in earnest. A moment of struggle and Girty was flung backward on the floor, his head striking the puncheons with great force. Before he could gather his strength, Mcfail had tied his hands with a bell-pull snatched from the wall.

"That was good bear meat, Richtier."

Hartlin's voice and words were as matter-of-fact as though we had just met on the street the day after our deal. The man startled me, but I pulled my wits together.

"But pork's better," I said.

Mcfail stood up; he had Girty's weapons—the knife, ax, and a pistol. He gestured toward the trussed man and looked at Hartlin.

"What will you do with him?"

The doctor rose, crossed to Girty, and looked down at him for a little before he turned to us again.

"Did you hear what he wanted?" he asked, and his eyes were oddly alight when we both nodded. He made a contemptuous gesture toward the man on the floor.

"I was careless this evening. Now just throw him out."

Mcfail opened a window, dragged the tied man to it, and dumped him outside. After he had closed the window, he spoke emphatically. "You'd better have killed him."

Hartlin nodded.

"Yes, Mcfail. The man may be a valuable servant of His Majesty, but he becomes crude at times. You men are prisoners; such men are always hungry."

He took us into the kitchen, lighted some candles, and set bread, cold meat, and wine before us. We ate ravenously, after which he gave us tobacco and long clay pipes so that, for the first time in months, we had the full satisfaction that comes from good food and tobacco. Hartlin seemed to be thinking deeply until we finished.

"Men, I am a man with little sentiment in him. You saved me from something I always feared—blindness. Girty is an expert at that sort of business. When anger is upon him, he becomes a raving fiend. It's partly anger, partly his disease, a mild form of epilepsy. You see, I know the man well; perhaps too well."

The lines of his severe face softened into a smile.

"It's my notion that you men will escape one day; you are out of your quarters now. Martin Jon Richtier will be trying for that lost gold. You, John Mcfail, shot Gibson. Likely, you cannot go home."

"I paid a debt," the sergeant said through closed teeth, and Hartlin nodded.

"George Gibson was a weak man except in fighting. His weakness made him a danger to your cause. He could not and would not pay his debts; I pay mine."

He went to his writing desk, fumbled among the papers, and returned to us, extending one of them to me.

"Richtier, I thought at one time to establish a residence down near Philadelphia. Your small farm would have served well, so I made Gibson get it for me. The place is of no use to me; you have served me this evening. This paper makes you once more a landowner."

I stared at the paper. Hours before, I had been a captive in a log jail. Outside of a few coins, I had nothing. Now I was back to where I was that morning when I sold this dour man some bear meat for powder.

Hartlin took Mcfail's hand, turned over the palm, and placed some gold pieces in it.

"You'll need money when your chance comes. Some boatmen are for hire to either side."

His face sobered, became cold again, and so were his next words. "Now, gentlemen, a patrol stops here about this hour. I suggest you get back to the quarters where you belong, and I would forget all that happened here this evening."

We went out the back door, but not until Hartlin had filled a sack with maple sugar, the whole of a large fruit cake, and what was left of the cold meat. As an afterthought, he put in a bottle of rum, all of which we shared with our fellow prisoners in the morning when we boasted of robbing an officer's cellar on our night's prowl.

CHAPTER FOURTEEN

DURING THE following days, I was both exultant and depressed. Washington and others had urged that a man should forget his personal gains or losses in this great struggle, but I loved my small acreage, and to know it was mine again after I had thought it lost thrilled me. However, the season was advancing, and presently armies would be marching and fighting. There must be no more delay about finding the gold. Then, one morning before dawn, we heard a monstrous cracking sound like that of cannon fire, followed by a great rumbling and vibration of the earth. All the men piled out of their bunks.

"Ice is going out of the river," Allen assured us. He stood beside me, shivering a little in the thin morning light.

"Wisht I was back home or in some reg'lar army," he muttered. "I'm tired of these colonel armies that ride out a piece way, fire a few shots, and run home in time for elections. Or you can get trapped, like Crawford done for us."

Later he said, "Boats will be coming in over the lakes, now the ice is gone."

"Boats," I half echoed his word, remembering vividly Hartlin's remark to Mcfail that night: "Boatmen for hire."

Suddenly I felt the grip of this confinement and a tremendous desire to be footloose and free, to feel forest paths under my moccasins, to sniff the air on hilltops and see the sun go down over the notched horizons of mountain country. I wanted to see Hester as I remembered the sound of her light laughter that night on the flatboat when I fell into the water, and with better feeling, the touch of her hand that afternoon in Breon's tavern.

"Allen," I said, "I'm getting out of here."

He laughed.

"Down below us the Pottawatomies are sharpening their hatchets on pieces of gritty stone, using a little stinking bear oil to make the grit work better. Ottawas are tuning up good trade muskets. Delawares are making big speeches in their lodges on the Ohio, and the Shawnees— hell, Martin, them Shawnees don't know how to stay put. Anyway, with scalps at eight dollars, Hamilton's Native brethren ain't going to be keen about beaver trapping."

It was a long speech for Allen, and he spat out the wad of willow bark he had been using as a substitute for tobacco.

"Boats," I said to him. "With boats, we could slip down the lakes, cross the divide to the Allegheny—"

He shook his head slowly. "A few could do it, maybe, if they had a boat. But if our whole crew here got loose, the British would make a campaign of it." That day, Mcfail, Hoadley, Frye, and I were taken to the office where Creede worked. The bloodless man looked us over carefully and moistened his lips with that unholy red tongue of his.

"Well, well, here we have our small flock together; a bit of a wicked crew, all told. You are called here because we have word that all of you passed through our lines, out of uniform, and did carry out actions hurt-ful to the interests of His British Majesty. You are to be hanged, the four of you, promptly on the arrival of confirmation from Quebec."

His tone of voice was unctuous, and it was easy to see he was enjoy-ing his grisly pronouncement. He spoke again.

"So my suggestion is for you to make your peace, since you probably have little more than a week to live."

None of us had moved, and we waited for a moment longer, then Mcfail slowly crouched and started forward, his long arms outspread. I watched, fascinated. There were guards outside the door, and I wondered if the big sergeant would wring the man's neck before they rushed in and bayonetted him. With his tangled beard, the wildness in his eyes, and those huge hands with the fingers hooked, Mcfail was a terrifying spectacle. Creede cowered back in his chair, pushed himself half erect, and then suddenly he screamed twice. Mcfail stopped, body and hands relaxed.

"Well," he said softly, "the damned thing is alive after all. I thought him some kind of spirit, but they don't yell."

This time the guards were rough with us. Running in, they clubbed us from the room with musket butts and ran us across the parade ground at the points of their bayonets before they locked us in our prison. By mutual agreement, we did not tell the others what had happened, only that we had been questioned.

It was Hoadley's night outside, and he was back in an hour with a haunch of venison and an excitement he could scarcely master. He explained to the group that a boatman had given him the meat, then, after the usual feast and the other men were asleep, we Lambs got together to hear his story.

"I dropped outside the palisade and he was there. I'd have pulled a knife if I'd had one, he scared me so; just a little fellow with an awful dark face. He explained to me, after I saw he wasn't some kind of guard, that he had a message for a man named Richtier, a message from Brodhead. Tomorrow night, at early moonrise, Martin's to be at the place of the Quiet People. Where's that?'"

"Graveyard," Mcfail grunted.

The lines in our prison had now been drawn so hard and fast that we knew we must take the others into our confidence, so in the morning we called them together and Mcfail did the talking.

"Men," he said, "the Hair Buyer's going to hang us four Lambs. Martin, here, is an agent for Washington himself, sent to hunt that lost gold. Last night, Hoadley bumped into a man from Brodhead. If we're to save our necks, we'll have to escape, take chances with the Indians. We want you to let us go and come at night until we can see what to do."

These men had been imprisoned for a long time, and getting home was their dream, but I have never seen a more generous group. There was no dissenting voice when they told us they'd help all they could. One of the sick men even suggested that we slip out and burn the town.

"All right, then. Martin goes out tonight, but it ain't his turn."

"It's mine," Allen said. "He can have it and welcome."

The cemetery was across the Savoyard, but there were a half dozen pole bridges across the stream so I had no trouble getting over without observation, for I had gone out in the early darkness. Waiting there was eerie business; sometimes a single dog, far up the river, barked mournfully; the stream close by murmured and then seemed still. Huddled close to a big wooden grave marker, I waited and listened.

When the signal came, just as the edge of the moon was showing, it was the sound of a cricket, one of the big black ones that like houses. He was a little man, and he emerged from the darkness so quietly I would not have known he was coming had it not been that the chirp of the insect had made me more alert.

"Richtier," I whispered. "Martin Jon Richtier. Who are you?" The musky smell of an Indian clung about the man as he shook hands with me.

"I'm Cady, Simeon Cady. The Native folks call me the Cricket. Brodhead brought me from down east to get you out of this." Squatting Indian fashion on his haunches, he explained his plans most carefully. For two nights more, a boat would wait for us a little distance up from the mouth of the Rogue, at a place called Outpost. Only five men could be taken, and Brodhead wanted the others to know he was arranging with Sir Guy Carleton, the British commander in Canada, for their exchange.

Cady explained further that he would have some weapons for us but that there must be no trouble lest it break up the prisoner exchange proceedings. The boat would land us so we could go overland to the Allegheny River.

"The colonel figures you Lambs must get out; they'd never exchange you. It could be that they'd hang you for spies."

I grunted and told him what Creede had announced, but that did not surprise him. He went on making me repeat the directions. A sudden idea occurred to me.

"Could we take a sixth man?"

"Who?" he demanded, and I said, "Hartlin."

He breathed a soft, low whistle then made the sound of a cricket again. After that, he placed a hand on my knee.

"I think I know what is in your mind, Richtier. It will be risky, but Brodhead explained to me about the gold and your job."

He stood up; now that the moon was higher, I saw he was dressed in buckskins. Once more he took my hand in his.

"Tyce is the name of the boatman; big fellow, noisy but good. Till the Mahoning then."

He was gone as quietly as he had come, leaving behind him that scent of old, much-used leather. In another half hour, I was back inside our prison building, explaining that our escape must be made the next night. However, I did not mention Hartlin to the whole company, but later I did to the men who would go with me.

"We can take a fifth man," I announced to the prisoners. "Who will it be?"

Jenkins, one of the sick men, made the suggestion.

"Cast lots."

We all watched while the correct number of beans was counted into the bag and saw to it that there was one red one. Presently all had drawn with the exception of us four Lambs. The men looked at each other quizzically, wondering who had won the red bean.

"Who has it?" a rough voice finally queried, and Jenkins slowly opened his hand. On his palm rested the red bean.

Again the odd look appeared on the faces of the men. Jenkins had been desperately ill. Now he was just a bag of bones and feebleness; a venture such as we were about to make would kill the man; certainly, he would slow us down. Then Jenkins walked forward and laid his lucky piece in Allen's big palm.

"You go, Allen. You're so damned big you eat more than your share here," the sick man said.

It was a brave thing for any man to do and especially for one whose chance of ever seeing his home grew slimmer each day. I saw a number of our fellow prisoners slap the sick man gently between his thin shoulders. As for Allen, he scarcely knew what to say. He tried but could only muster clumsy thanks.

The day dragged through hours that seemed endless. Those of us who would make the break had a little chance to talk, but not for long.

However, I did manage to tell Mcfail I wanted to kidnap Hartlin. When the hour came, we had shaken hands all round with these men with whom we had shared captivity for so long. They had given us messages, which we had carefully set down so we would not forget to pass them correctly to the home folks. One by one, we crawled through the window and passed across the strip of parade ground to the fence. Allen, next to last, had a hard job getting his big body through the window, but my boost helped him.

When we were together, Mcfail wanted to set a fire somewhere about the fort to draw attention from us, but I urged that any damage we did might be held against our fellow prisoners when it came to an exchange. Now I realized that Cady, while he said he had weapons, had not given them to me. Our arms then were those taken from Girty—one knife, one pistol, and one war ax.

"Hoadley, Frye, and Allen, get down to the boat," I directed and gave them the same directions I had received. When they had disappeared, Mcfail and I started to the Hartlin house, taking Girty's weapons with us.

This time, the back door was not open and we had to use the knife to force it. The man we sought sat in his living room, reading a book, which he laid down calmly when we leaped into the room. I stepped up to him.

"Doctor Hartlin, we're taking you with us."

He made no reply and I turned to the sergeant.

"Get some clothes for him."

Mcfail disappeared into a bedroom and came out with a bundle of clothing from which Hartlin took what he wanted. Then he pointed to the remainder of the garments and spoke disdainfully.

"Make the thing complete and take some clothes for yourselves; you look like tramps. Even a rebel should look respectable."

The sergeant picked up a scarf and a conservative-looking tow cloth hunting shirt, but I shook my head when he was about to hand me a similar garment. Hartlin's lips twisted into something like a sneer.

"Squeamish," he said, then he walked over to a small desk where he picked up his huge gold watch to which was attached a string of fobs. This he put in his pocket, and as he stood by the desk, I crossed to him.

"Give me the Jordan power of attorney; I'll take it to the owner."

He smiled.

"You are a little late, my chivalrous friend, just a little late. But there's still enough left for one maid; more than enough."

His fingers moved into the desk, took out a paper at which I glanced then thrust deep into my pocket. The man was quick; I was looking at the paper, Mcfail was hunting for something in the pile of clothing. In that instant, Hartlin snatched out a small pistol, presented it at me, and snapped the trigger. Only bad priming saved me, and Mcfail struck the weapon from the man's hand.

I kept my voice steady.

"Why did you do that, Hartlin? Mcfail would have killed you for it."

"Perhaps," he answered evenly. "But it's you, Richtier, who wants the gold. The others would not have bothered taking me with them."

"Come on, Martin, let's take him and go—or shall I shoot him now?" Mcfail growled roughly. He was standing there with Girty's pistol shoved against the man.

I felt a little better for the attempt on my life; not that I enjoyed taking a chance like that, but because now the amenities were destroyed and I needed no longer think of the return of my farm or of the food Hartlin had given us that evening.

Once outside, we gagged our victim with his own neckerchief, remembering his word about the patrol. At that, we nearly did run into it near the bridge, but we had time to slip back of a shed, pressing Hartlin between us, until it passed with a jingle of accoutrements.

The whole escapade was almost alarmingly easy, so much so that we could scarcely believe it. Pushing through the village, we crossed one of the pole bridges, then continued down the stream until we reached brushland where the woodcutters had worked and ascended a low hill from which we could see the few lights burning in the town and fort. Everything was still; even the dog upriver that loved to bark was silent this night.

The smell of water was fresh upon us as we descended the hill. At its bottom, our three companions stepped out and stood in the path.

"There's a boat just below," Hoadley told us, "and I heard somebody moving."

Another hundred yards and we could see a darker mass at the riverside, and against the skyline the tip of a mast. Mcfail whistled the cry of a sleepy bird and was answered by a flash of light as the door of a lanthorn was opened. A gruff voice challenged: "Who's there?"

"Friends of Cady," I answered, then Mcfail cut in with a whisper that carried almost as well as a shout.

"Jim—Jim Tyce, so it's you we're hunting."

A loud grunt from the boat answered; the craft swung closer to the bank, and a huge figure leaped to the shore.

"So it's you, John Mcfail, with trouble in your lap as usual."

The two men shook hands with each other and slapped each other's backs; then Tyce stepped clear.

"Get in, boys, we can't be all night."

We shoved our captive aboard. The rest of us crowded onto the small craft, and when Tyce leaped from the shore, the boat lurched sharply. Mcfail whispered to me.

"Knew the man long ago; recognized his voice. Jim Tyce will get us through."

"Got to get around Point Sable come dawn," the boatman told us. "After that, we'll try for open water."

There seemed to be some other cargo on the boat besides its human freight. Our host sat in the stern, managing the tiller with one hand and the sheets of his single sail with the other. At times, he leaned over and put the tiller under his armpit. After a quiet half hour or so, he began talking.

"You know, men, I can't understand me. I'm Jim Tyce, loyal servant of the King, God bless him. But this damned boat keeps getting me into messes like tonight. Here I am with a load of good buckskins for Presque Isle, and I find myself linked up with people like John Mcfail."

He snorted loudly as though he had gone underwater and had just come up for air.

"Along comes this Cady man that once fixed up my wife's rheumatism—"

"Which wife?" Mcfail interrupted rudely.

"John," Tyce's voice was gentle, "don't give these people wrong ideas; there's things about you like that girl down back of Old Town. It was my third wife that had the rheumatism." No one spoke for a time; only the sergeant was chuckling quietly as if to himself. Then Tyce spoke again.

"There's something about that damned Cady and his herbs. He kinda comes out of nowhere; no wonder the Indians call him Cricket. Well, he sits in your house and talks. Pretty soon you think of sweet fern on a hill or the taste of sassafras or mebbe goldenrod tea that grows on a high gravel hill. Someday I'm going to sell this here boat and dig ginseng for a living."

"Jim," the sergeant said, "you remember the march with Forbes and how you were a litter man?"

Again the snort came out of the dimness of the stern.

"Don't be reminding me of old days, John Mcfail. This little flier tonight'll cost you just as much as if I'd never seen hair nor hide of Cady or a suspicious-looking party of tramps, one with his mouth tied shut. And you always have money; if I'd shake you, likely you'd jingle."

It was my notion that Tyce kept up the flood of talk to keep our minds off the fact that occasionally we shipped water over the low sides, for we were deeply laden. Back of us, we could see the dim glow from the lights of the fort, and that was growing fainter; all about us was the choppy water that meant we were out of the river and on the lake. We tried to stretch our cramped legs for more comfort, and when the sun finally showed, our host stopped talking altogether and gave his full attention to his little craft.

We were a hard-looking crew in this early light. Hoadley had taken the neckerchief away from our prisoner's mouth; Mcfail was sleeping soundly, sitting up with his back to a bundle of hides. Tyce showed himself to be a huge man with a heavy beard trimmed off squarely. His hands looked easily twice the size of mine. On his shock of hair was a stocking cap of brilliant red. For the rest of his garb, he wore a blue shirt open at a hairy chest and woolen trousers cut off at his calves and belted with a short length of small rope. His huge feet were bare, but a pair of moccasins rested beside him on the thwart.

Once, during the forenoon, our boatman moved rapidly. Our sail was down in a jiffy, and at his gesture, Frye and I put out the oars, shipped neatly alongside, and rowed hard, keeping steerageway. Presently, Tyce pointed.

Far out over the stretch of little waves, I could see what had alarmed him; the sails of a ship, and I realized that any large craft here on this lake would belong to the British.

"Sun's on the waves so they won't see us," Tyce explained.

Several times during the long day we had a little dried meat and a drink from a huge bottle of cider that passed from man to man, even Hartlin taking some, though he only nibbled at his piece of meat. We shifted about on the odorous cargo, trying for comfort, and in midafternoon Mcfail spelled off Tyce, who promptly curled up like a huge dog and slept.

Darkness relieved our eyes from looking over this watery wilderness; then Tyce woke and took over once more. After the first dark hours, the moon was well up, and we changed course sharply, going at right angles to the thin path of moonlight on the choppy water.

"For me," I said, "I'll settle for no more boat rides."

Tyce answered with a chuckle.

"That's what I thought once; then my feet got sore from tramping over them damned hills, and here I am, lugging stinky hides across this big drink of water."

So far, Allen, our big man, had said little or nothing, but at the mention of feet, he cut into the conversation.

"Feet, now, there's just one way. You take a piece of good woolen cloth and lap it careful around your foot, and then you dip your hand in melted tallow that's not too hot and grease the cloth real good. The tallow makes the foot slip in the shoe without rubbing. You can even wear army shoes that way."

No one commented, and the big man relapsed into silence. Certainly, not one of us prisoners owned a full pair of stockings; we were lucky to have fairly good moccasins.

After midnight, I slept uneasily. The rocking of the boat would wake me, and then I'd dream I was sliding off into the water. When I finally did come wide awake, I could smell the shore odors and hear the sound of small waves on some sort of beach. Evidently, Tyce had given orders earlier, for Hoadley and Allen were at the oars. The sail was down; Tyce stood beside the tiller.

When we had finally lost steerageway and the boat was not moving forward, we sat for a long time listening.

"Scout around a little," Tyce directed Mcfail, who stepped into the shallow water and waded toward the shore. Half an hour later, he reappeared.

"Seems clear, Jim. Help the boys ashore."

Tyce kindled a lanthorn and gave us dried meat, parched corn, a small bag of raisins, and a bottle of whisky. After that, he unwrapped a parcel that contained three fairly good knives and a short musket together with its powder horn and shot bag.

"Cady left them things for you, all but the victuals," Tyce explained.

When we had all gone ashore, he told Mcfail and me to come back on the boat again. Now he showed that, when he wished, he could whisper softly.

"Boys, mebbe God or the Continental Congress knows what you're up to with that man you've got with you. But what I want to know is if he's coming back. Me, I'd drop him in a deep crick with a mud bottom. Do you know that's Doc Hartlin?"

Mcfail only grinned, and the boatman shook his shaggy head.

"Well, if you boys think getting away with Doctor Hartlin is a light thing, like kidnaping a British general would be, you're welcome to your thinking. Now, listen, is he coming back?"

For myself, I had acted on impulse. Hartlin must serve as a guide to the treasure, and I had thought that far but no further. This Tory was a tool, an unpleasant one, but a means to an end. Mcfail answered for me: "No, Jim, he ain't coming back."

Reaching into his pocket, the sergeant gave Tyce three of the four golden coins the man we discussed had given him in Detroit, and our boatman pocketed them before he commented on what Mcfail had said.

"That's good. If Hartlin was to get back, I'd be likely to get my neck stretched, and business is too good on these lakes for that just yet."

The callousness of these frontiersmen was a result of the way they lived. Probably the thing to do with Hartlin was to use him, then turn him over to the Continental authorities. They would probably hang him after due process of law, but neither Tyce nor Mcfail had any idea of that. The man would be dead—one of us would have to shoot him, that was all.

CHAPTER FIFTEEN

TYCE HAD set us ashore west of the British post of Presque Isle on Lake Erie, but he had probably presumed that men like Mcfail knew the country better than we actually did. Our course had to be south and east to strike the Allegheny, but after our first day's tramp, we found ourselves in rather difficult going, and it became worse by the mile. Here were laurel-covered ridges and sharp ravines that took us up- and downhill with every mile.

"Like walking a washboard the wrong way," Allen commented as he puffed up a hill beside me.

The weather had turned raw, for this was still the tag-end of winter in these parts. Along the lakes it had been milder, but here, occasionally, we found snow in sheltered hollows. The only really dry ground we could find was at the base of some big tree that looked toward the sun.

There is a sort of lethargy about men who have been confined for a long time. Our walking had been limited by our prison, and the poor food had left us weaker than we really thought we were. Even I, who had been in much less time than the others, found it sheer labor to walk, at times just setting one foot before the other, knowing that was the only way to reach the Allegheny and later the Mahoning.

We hesitated to shoot what little game we saw, in the vague notion that the sound of the gun's report might bring enemies down upon us. Yet, with glaring inconsistency, each evening we built a huge bonfire that could have served as a beacon to any pursuers within a score of miles. This fire was our only luxury, and we reveled in the heat until our warm bodies were drunken with it. Our clothing would steam, and we turned over slowly to let the warmth search every part of our bodies.

Hartlin had little if anything to say and for the most part walked with young Hoadley, watching his own steps carefully. He did not seem to mind the hard travel, would eat his small portion of food and then sit before the fire, his lean body huddled a little. While he was no longer young, he had started this journey full-fed, for which reason he had so little trouble keeping up with us.

Not even the careful Sergeant Mcfail seemed to think it necessary to post a guard at night, yet had we been normally alert, we would have done so and we could have noted signs that danger followed us long before it struck. For instance, there was the night when we heard a single whippoorwill call and discussed the fact that the bird was early. Again, on another night, after the fire had burned down, there was a soft twittering of birds in the bushes, and so far, we had seen no small birds.

The morning of the fourth day was overcast, as usual, and Frye was huddled on his knees before the fire, trying to get it to burn well, while the rest of us sat up stiffly and tried to wipe the sleep out of our eyes.

"You know," Frye said quizzically, "you could take some of this damned water and boil it down for real good soup, that is, if we had a kettle and mebbe a little piece of meat."

"Dry up," Mcfail growled, but Frye only grinned.

"That's what I tried to do last night, and an important part of these buckskin pants is still wet."

He scarcely finished his pleasantry when he, like the rest of us, heard the snick of gunlocks and the shuffling of moccasined feet in the brush. We were surrounded!

A white man came into our little clearing, and another stepped up back of Mcfail and pressed a cocked pistol between the sergeant's shoulder blades. There were these two white men and ten painted Indians, each with a cocked musket leveled at us. The first white man was standing with his feet set apart, head thrown back, and his pointed beard seemingly aimed at us. It was Girty!

Nothing of the man who had talked so movingly of his old home on the Susquehanna showed this morning. There was ruthless satisfaction on his wide, flat-planed face as he laid his rifle barrel across one arm, but his thumb still rested on the hammer of the piece. From where I crouched, I could see the bright beads of powder with which he had recently primed his gunlock.

"It was nice that you kept the fires going," he said mockingly. "It saved tracking." Then his eyes seemed to narrow.

"I don't want any of you but Hartlin—Doctor Hartlin."

Our captive was sitting up, his hat beside him on the ground, and I could not help but see that his face was grayer than it usually was in the morning. With a slow gesture, he pushed his thinning hair back from his face. My muscles stiffened, for I had brought this man, against his will, into this wilderness, to fall prey to the beast who stood gloating before us.

My right hand edged back slowly. I could not know if an Indian stood directly back of me, but I did get the knife clear of its sheath. It was not as good for throwing as the one with which I had killed the bear, but it was a fair weapon, and I would not miss this leering target before me. What did it matter if they did kill us so long as Girty was gone? My hand snapped back for the throw.

A blow on my elbow sent the knife spinning, and before I could move again, a second one struck the back of my head and I fell forward.

Battle is terrible where men, with their sense of humanity deadened, strive with all their might to kill each other. Then mercy is silent. I had been in the rout of Wayne's regiments above the string of lakes and had lived through the struggle on Long Island and in other places. A bullet had cut into me in one engagement, and I had been on the Paoli hills that night when "No Flint" Gray struck. But when I was conscious again that morning, I was to see a worse sight than all of these, one that made me strain at my rawhide bonds until they cut into my wrists.

Hartlin and I were in another camp with Girty and his Indians. A low fire burned in the center of a small natural clearing, and the packs of the party lay about in the disorder common to ambush. Girty was talking to one of the Indians who wore a white man's long coat and a cap with a bedraggled feather stuck into it. When he had finished whatever he had said to the Indian, he came over and looked down at us. It seemed to me the color of the man's eyes had changed, and the corners of his mouth kept twitching, showing his teeth.

Abruptly, he caught Hartlin by the sleeve and jerked him to his feet, then pulled his stumbling captive a short distance from me and closer to the fire.

"Hartlin, you've been in my hair a long time. This is the end of the road. Do you understand?"

The older man looked into the renegade's eyes steadily, and when he spoke, his voice was even.

"Simon, better let a doctor minister to you. A seizure is coming on; then you'll be crazy for a time. That is what has made you a fiend on this frontier."

"Doctor!" Girty yelled. "Crazy! It's men like you and Crawford that made me what you folks say I am. Crawford is dead, and more will die. Your money won't help you now. You cheated and deceived. I've hob-nobbed with these Indians and helped them take the scalps your money bought."

With his open palm, he struck the doctor so hard he dropped to the ground, blood oozing from the side of his mouth while Girty stood over him.

"Your last trick was this French gold. I helped you get it; you got me tangled up with army orders while you hid those kegs then showed up with a cock-and-bull story about rebels taking them. You've got it hid halfway down one of these rivers, and this morning the doctor is going to tell Simon all about it."

They had topped and trimmed a white oak sapling that stood ten feet or so from the fire. I noticed there was a long blaze in its bark and there was a small cap of mud on the top. At Girty's nod, two Indians lifted Hartlin and tied him to this sapling, his arms being jerked back sharply. They did something else that made the trussed man wince, but I could not see what it was. It must have hurt badly, for there was sweat on the victim's forehead.

The Indian with the coat came forward. First, he took the cap of mud from the torture post and flung it into the bushes, then he seated himself about halfway between the fire and the post. He was now smoking a long-stemmed pipe, which was an odd thing this far in the wilderness, and he looked the trussed captive over carefully while Girty talked.

"Now, Doctor, you know where things hurt, and you'll see what these Indians have learned. Of course, their womenfolk could teach them tricks, but these boys are pretty good."

The blaze in his eyes was more pronounced. He turned sharply on the Natives who were standing, looking on.

"Dance!" he yelled.

One by one, they began, about the post, that awkward shuffling march that Indians call a dance. But one Indian besides the one in the coat had not joined the others; he was simply looking on. Girty turned on him, snarling like a dog, saliva drooling at his mouth corners. With a full swing of his leg, he kicked the warrior sprawling.

"Dance!" he yelled again.

The Indian came to his feet, trying to draw his tomahawk, but Girty snatched the weapon from him and beat him until he joined the shuffling.

Round and round they went until my head was whirling from their monotonous movement and the blow I had taken earlier. They had my arms fastened back of me, my legs drawn straight out in front and tied to a sapling, and I was seated in such a manner that I could not turn my back or shoulders against the spectacle I had to watch—the gray-faced man hanging there in his bonds, dried blood on his face.

The master of ceremonies, the fellow in the coat, gave the signal to stop, and the dancers stood, faces wet with sweat. The look in their eyes was like that of caged animals when they see meat. One of the younger warriors darted behind Hartlin. There was no knowing what he did, but the tortured man's body writhed, and the Indian was making a growling sound like a dog with a bone.

Hartlin sagged loosely in the bonds, and the warrior came in front of him again, spitting something on the ground, either a fingernail or the tip joint of a finger.

It must have been about noon when they finished with his nails, his hands, and whatever they did to his eyebrows. They left him hanging there while they sat about the fire, eating with gobbling noises and laughing among themselves. My whole mind was on Hartlin. Regardless of what the man had done, no human deserved the cruelty that he was subjected to, and I retched as I looked at the blood on his hands and face. It did not occur to me that I might be the second performer in this infernal drama; my feeling of responsibility was too great for that. The meal finished, Girty again faced his victim.

"Now, Doctor, tell me where you hid the gold, and I'll have them end this with a hatchet."

Hartlin made no reply; it was as though he had retreated somewhere inside the aura of his suffering.

The awful work went on through the afternoon. Nausea gripped me until I could scarcely see and my head swam. I must have strained on my bonds, for I felt warm blood on my arms. All I craved was a moment's freedom to choke the life out of one of these torturers before a hatchet ended my account.

No sane man would ever tell others all that went on during those hours. If the victim at that stake had done evil, he paid for it all and to spare. Hartlin broke about midafternoon when he could no longer see. Then he would cry out at each new piece of deviltry. Blood and tears washed over his sightless face, and I remembered his expressed fear of blindness. He had long since gone beyond any power to tell his torturers what Girty wished to know and beyond all consciousness save only the instinct to scream.

There were shadows under the trees when Girty strode forward and spoke to the seated Indian, who shook his head. Probably he had exhausted his repertoire of evil suggestions. Girty faced the victim he had known so well, and as he did so, he breathed like a man who has run a long way. With one smooth gesture, he cut Hartlin's body free and watched it sink to the ground like an old and almost empty sack. Then he approached me and severed enough of my bonds so he could drag me to my feet and slap my face. I realized that my time had come.

Abruptly, the second white man jumped up and strode forward to us. His eyes were cold, pistols were thrust through his belt, and his musket had a bore large enough for a small swivel gun. In addition, he carried a knife and an ax, but his eyes were what looked dangerous.

"There's been enough deviltry here today, Simon. Hartlin bought scalps, as you say. Maybe he did and I said naught, but if I see you or these Indians break another white man's body, I'll split some skulls—yours first, you crazy fool."

Girty stared back at the man for a long moment until his face seemed to change. He walked over to a tree, looked at the ground for a while, then his body retched and a spasm shook him until I thought it would tear him apart. Quietly, the Indians picked up their things and filed away into the darkness. Girty, with bowed shoulders, followed when he could walk again, looking neither at Hartlin's body nor at me. The second white man had gone with the Indians. It seemed as though the coming darkness had swallowed up some evil crew from another world.

I called to Hartlin, but there was no answer. The fire had burned down to coals, and I could see the hurt man lay inert, like a heap of clothing. My conscience hurt me for having kidnapped him; I did not know until long after that his agents had set Colbert's crew at us on the river, nor of his dealings with the Natives in the interest of his fur trading.

Girty had partially freed me, and by rubbing my bonds back and forth on the tree bark, I finally released my hands. Both wrists were bloody; it was a long time before I could free my legs of thongs. When I tried to walk, both ankles were so numb that I fell, and I had to chafe them until I could stand. After that, I built up the fire so that there would be light to do what must be done.

Hartlin had been breathing when he was cut loose, though it was hard to believe life could linger in a body so abused. As I sought to straighten him, one of his hands brushed my face and I started, shocked at the cold touch. There was a fluttering pulse indicating a spark of life still left. Lifting his head, I spoke to him.

"It's Richtier, Doctor. They've gone."

Twice I repeated my words, bending over so my lips were close to his ear, and then I heard him mumbling words so low I had to place my own ear almost on the battered and torn lips.

"Lost," I thought he said, and then something about "paid."

I had no sense of what he was thinking from the disconnected words; indeed, I was not sure that those were heard correctly. The man should not be struggling to speak; he should be released from his misery. His hands moved about feebly; there was one more word, but I did not catch it.

Involuntarily I glanced around; somehow I had the feeling that this dying man was trying to warn me. But we were alone, and when I looked more closely, I saw that Thomas Hartlin was dead. His body and face were broken, but there was about him that awful dignity that follows the passing of life.

I managed to dig a grave in the loose ground under the big trees, for I knew the doctor would want his body out of sight as soon as possible. Then I tried to put his clothing in order and I took the things from his pockets. There was a small clasp-knife used to sharpen quills, four gold coins, and a snuffbox in the coat. In the waistcoat was the heavy gold watch he had taken from his desk in Detroit when we took him away. I put the timepiece in my pocket, intending to give it to Hester when I gave her the power of attorney paper. The other things went into the dead man's grave, together with the fourth gold coin Hartlin had given Mcfail and which the sergeant had handed to me. I wanted nothing that had belonged to this man.

The forest was now a wall of blackness about the small firelit space, but I could not stay here in sight of that charred and blazed post. Walking unsteadily, feeling a desperate weakness, I plunged into the woods, wondering now what had been done to the others and where they might be.

After I had traveled a hundred yards or so, my fingers fumbled in my pocket and I found I had not placed Hartlin's clasp-knife in the grave but in my pocket. I took it out and threw it as far as I could into the dark woods, then hurried on.

With a woodsman's habit, when I found a small stream, I followed it, sitting down often with my back to a tree for the rest I needed. But after a little of this, I would rise and go on, for pictures of what I had seen during the day would come into my mind.

Gray morning light was filtering through the woodland when I found my friends in the camp where I had been captured. All of them were tied and I hurried to loose them, thinking of the knife I had thrown away, which would have served so well now to cut the stubborn knots.

None were hurt, but their muscles were cramped from their bonds and all looked pretty solemn, sitting there rubbing arms and legs to win back circulation. Occasionally they looked at me. After I had looked

about a bit, I found our captors had left us the poorest of our knives, one
tomahawk, and a pistol with its horn and shot bag. All of these had been
left on a stone a rod or so from where our fire had been. Mcfail looked at
me curiously, and after he could walk, helped me get a small blaze going,
about which we all sat; then the sergeant asked his question:

"Is Hartlin dead?"

I nodded. We sat around for another hour until two things happened
to change everything. The sun came out, warm and bright, and later,
Simeon Cady, who had helped us in Detroit, stepped out of the brush
and stood looking at us.

The small, brown-faced man was most understanding. Almost before
he had greeted us, he had his small kettle filled and over the fire. When
he had dusted some powdered tea leaves into this, he took venison from
his pack and set it to roasting, after which he anointed our chafed wrists
and ankles with some kind of salve.

We all felt better after we had eaten and had our portion of tea from
the kettle. Then I leaned back against a tree and told what had happened
to Hartlin, while their eyes stared at me incredulously, although I could
not tell them everything. Mcfail's big hands twisted the stick he had been
holding while I talked until it broke. Cady spoke: "Girty is crazed at such
times. A fit like you see in dogs comes over him. The man is sick."

I remembered the Indian who did not wish to dance and the lights in
Girty's eyes. Mcfail twisted his stick and broke it a second time.

"Me," he said with emphasis, "I'd like to give the man his last sickness
and that of lead or steel poison."

"No," I answered. "The man belongs to me; also the Indian with the
overcoat and the skin cap."

None of us seemed to have the energy to wonder at the appearance
of Cady. We just accepted it, and he finally told us that Brodhead had
sent him to Detroit, which we knew. After that, he had come overland,
learning from Tyce where he would find us. Then he had followed but
had been too late to save us from Girty.

CHAPTER SIXTEEN

IN OUR strained mental and physical condition, we accepted this little man as one of us, and he did wonders to relieve our situation. There seemed to be no bottom to the buckskin haversack he had carried; from it, he would take a mixture of pounded beans and corn from which he made a thick, savory soup. This, with venison, was fed to us twice each day until we were all much stronger physically. His little kettle was always bubbling over the fire.

While we did improve physically, depression rode us, for we had not recovered from the shock of being captured by Girty and the awful death of Hartlin. The responsibility for the man's being in the wilderness rested on us, no matter what we told ourselves of the justice of taking him. Even the man's theft of the gold was not enough to justify the way he died. The woods about us seemed filled with terror, for we did not know when Girty might strike again nor what plan might be maturing in the renegade's twisted mind.

We might have trusted a bit more to Cady, who had already done so much for us. He was the most alert person I had ever seen, and no matter what work he might be doing, his heavy rifle was never far from his hands. He always slept some little distance from the fire, and several times when I woke at night, I would see him sit up and listen, the rifle in his hands.

Selin Frye, ordinarily taciturn but a cheerful person, shared our depression. One afternoon, as we sat about the fire, he began to talk.

"My mom used to keep chickens, but the hawks was plenty. I recollect one time the red hen had six peeps, and when they was about half growed, a chicken hawk moved in on them and took one a day, no matter what Mom did to try to scare him off."

Mcfail scowled, knowing as well as I that such gloomy talk did not help our morale a bit.

"Your old man should have shot the flying varmint," he said sarcastically.

Frye straightened his shoulders and dramatically held up the wooden spoon he had been fashioning,

"But—"

At that moment, Cady spilled some water on the fire and the resulting steam made such a commotion that the thread of Frye's story was broken. I noticed that when the little man turned away, he was grinning. Also, I am sure the sergeant winked at him. That afternoon, I loaded our pistol carefully and went hunting.

For close to an hour I moved in ever-widening circles about our camp, searching for game, but more than that, trying to find if I could learn something of Girty and his crew. There were some squirrels and a few grouse, but I did not want to shoot until my scouting was finished. Finally, I stopped circling and followed a small stream, my moccasins making little noise, for here the snow was but lately melted and the ground was springy.

Presently, the hollow through which the stream ran divided into a north and south branch, and at the "V" made by the two ravines there was a low rocky point. There, with his back turned to me, sat a man!

Minutes later, when I had worked within fifty yards of the still figure, I recognized the long coat and the skin cap worn by the master of Girty's devilish ceremonies. Over the Indian's shoulder, a rifle barrel showed.

Here was game that needed killing, game that took delight in torture. It did not matter that my pistol was not too accurate; I felt sure I should kill this man, and there was a dryness in my mouth as I edged a little closer.

The brush thinned until the space between me and my quarry was open. The man must have been asleep or very tired to have remained so still. Now, eagerness was making my hand tremble a bit; this business had to be finished quickly. I uttered the hiss of a barnyard goose.

The Indian whirled and faced me, the single feather in the skin cap standing straight up like the hair on a scared dog's neck. The flat face was unpainted; the man's mouth was open in surprise. There was no doubt this was the fiend who had squatted on the ground, giving directions for Hartlin's torture. Likely the man had been at many burnings and had become an authority on causing pain. His fingers snatched first for either a knife or an ax, then for his gun.

The weapon had not come halfway to his shoulder when I shot him, and this time the pistol carried true. The bullet struck fairly in the evil face, and the man's body slumped slowly forward on the rocks.

When I turned him over, there was the sharp odor of whisky, and there was an empty flask in his coat pocket from which I also took a little corn. On the ground, at the foot of the rock on which he had been sitting, was a quarter of a deer wrapped in the green hide. When I left, my burden was the meat, the man's musket, together with its furnishings, and the skin cap with the feather.

My friends crowded round me when I came into camp and threw down what I carried. They had heard my shot, but when I pointed to the cap, their eyes widened.

"God," Mcfail muttered, "that's number one."

Even a little success has a tonic effect. These men had become so dispirited that they were content to sit and listen to stories like that of Frye's about the hawk and the chickens. Now they talked and laughed as they roasted and ate the game the Indian had killed. We had scored against Girty; we had another gun and felt stronger. The cause of our fears seemed farther removed.

So, when Cady proposed in the morning that we start for the Allegheny, there was no dissent. Before we started, he drew a map on the ground to show us the course of the river and its main tributaries.

"First, there's the Toby, a good-sized river; then Red Bank Creek, which is smaller."

He tapped the map with the stick; he was showing us the streams coming in from the east. Then he indicated the third of these.

"That's your Mahoning, crooked, long, with a big Indian village two days up from the mouth. The Shamokin Path follows the creek."

"Mahoning," I said with satisfaction. "We'll go that way."

I studied Cady's information as we walked along. The gold could have been taken as far north as the Toby, but if Hartlin, as Girty and others suspected, wanted to take the gold down east, it seemed he might have followed one of the great paths because he must cross the line of ridges to come out on the Susquehanna or the Juanita. This same Shamokin Path would be the shortest way to the big rivers. Excitement rose in me, and I had to repress it and pay attention to traveling.

We crossed the Allegheny at a deep and poor ford and slept that night without fires, for Cady, like all good woodsmen, distrusted the vicinity of a ford. Just about noon of the day following, we sighted the wide flatland, which Cady said marked the mouth of the Mahoning Creek. Beyond the stream itself and across the open space of natural meadows stood several buildings, and I wondered how we had missed seeing them when coming north on the military mission for Brodhead.

Our sorry-looking crew broke its single-line formation when we came to the opening, and all started running toward what we felt was our goal. At least one of our number, Allen, had been a prisoner for more than a year, and the rest of us for months. We were bearded, ragged, dirty, and most eager to meet any of our people from the outside. Cady, with his trim woodsman's dress, was the only presentable member of our group.

We had not gone fifty yards in the open when a file of soldiers rose up from where they had hidden in the brush and tall meadow grass, and we were stopped by the sight of their muskets, but only for a moment; then their sergeant, a big, neat-looking man, bellowed, "All right, men! I see John Mcfail, beard and all!"

The sergeant proved to be Ed Murthree, once with the Lambs, now regularly enlisted. He had a dozen soldiers with him, and more stood back at the building.

"The word is that Girty's about here somewhere, which accounts for our stopping you," Murthree explained. "Come on to the house; we've been waiting for you."

The house was a long log building with windows set just below the eaves, and under them were gunports. The doors were massive pieces of split oak, and one of them swung open as we came up. Out of it came

Hester Jordan, running to meet us. Her hair was loose about her face, her eyes shining. Both of her hands closed round mine while I stood, ashamed of the dirt and tatters in which I appeared.

"I'm so glad, Martin, so glad."

She went from man to man of us, shaking our hands, and she patted Cady on his narrow shoulders.

"We have everything for you," she said. "Food, clothes, weapons."

A few of the soldiers remained out in the meadows to do guard duty while the others helped us, heating water for baths, getting out clean clothing, and producing shaving tackle. In an hour after our arrival, we were a vastly different-looking group. Mcfail, of course, did not shave, but Sergeant Murthree trimmed his hair and beard with some scissors.

"She's waiting," Murthree said when I had finished, so I hurried on into the building and found her seated at one of the windows. She rose and took my hand again, which pleased me.

"We've been prisoners so long it took time to clean up," I told her, and she gestured to a seat close beside her.

First, I gave her the power of attorney paper, which I did not understand too well but which pleased her immensely; then I handed her Hartlin's big watch, and she listened gravely while I outlined what had happened since I had left Fort Pitt months ago. As I talked, she curled up in her chair until she no longer looked like a great lady but like a child listening to a fairy tale. Of course, I did not tell her the details of Hartlin's torture, but I did tell her that I had buried him. When I finished, she wanted me to take the watch, but I refused it, trying hard to keep her from sensing the horror anything belonging to the dead Hartlin roused in me. Presently, though, I felt she understood the whole experience, for she placed her hand on my sleeve.

"Martin, whatever the man went through, he brought it upon himself because of what he had done out here and elsewhere. That, you and I must believe. And you have your farm again; that surely should help you."

I thought of it, the level fields with the line of hills beyond, the small stone house with a figure in the doorway, but I shook my head. This girl to whom I talked and to whom I now owed so much could negotiate with great people for French gold and entertain in city houses. There was no place for such as her in a small stone farmhouse. She began to speak again, and I was glad to stop such thoughts and listen.

"Doctor Hartlin robbed me of more than half my father's property. My uncle, Oliver Pollock, has checked and found that to be true. He also was hand in glove with Indians to destroy frontier homes so the fur trade would be better. He robbed me and our cause and died because of his theft. But—you and I will find the gold."

After a little, she asked a question.

"Is it true about Mcfail and Colonel Gibson?"

There was no use covering the matter. I nodded, and she looked grave.

"Colonel Brodhead will have to arrest our friend on sight. The town is wrought up about the death of its hero, and I am wondering what orders Murthree has in the matter, if he has any. Why did John do it, Martin? He and the colonel had fought together."

"Because of his sister," I explained. "Eben Drough was his nephew."

She listened gravely to the sordid story, my prejudices against Gibson and my liking for Mcfail making me a little less than fair.

"The way Drough died hurt Mcfail terribly, and he probably blamed himself for not being with us. Most of all, he had the notion that Gibson had tricked us all as he certainly had me."

Hester nodded as I finished, and I did not know exactly what she thought, but the men were coming into the room, and our chance for talking passed.

There seemed to be ample stores at this outpost, and soon we were all seated about a table, eating beef, potatoes, and a huge mess of greens gathered along the stream. There was good black tea, and when we had finished, Murthree brought in a small keg of wine made from wild grapes. It was a real occasion to those of us who had had no contact with the outside world for so long. But the main attraction was Hester, gracing the head of the table, smiling, and talking to us all in turn.

"Sergeant Murthree, give us the war news; we've had none for months."

The big man drained his cup.

"It has not been too good but is more promising now. Washington lost a great battle at Germantown through a blunder that made our men fire into each other; then the winter has been bad at Valley Forge. There, men died from hunger and the bitter cold. The enemy lived well but it is said the poor in Philadelphia suffered even worse than Washington's men. The good thing is that our men were drilled all through the winter by Baron Steuben, who comes from Prussia. The farmers would sell the army nothing except for gold, then Wayne took a hand. Farmers who hoarded grain were made to have it threshed and milled or to sell it in the sheaf for the price of straw. With Wayne in action and given authority, the army is better fed and clothed."

He stopped, glanced at his own well-dressed men, then scowled. "The great need is for gold and silver money. You see, when we began to issue paper money, the British printed a great deal of it so the country was flooded. It was a clever trick, one that hurt our credit sorely. If the French gold stolen from Pitt could be found—that would be a victory."

Here it was from a non-commissioned officer, the information I had heard from General Wayne and others high in authority. Gold would buy the strength that comes from victory in heightened morale and support of the people.

After the dinner, we gathered about the wide fireplace and each of us, with the exception of Cady, who sat aloof in a corner, was plied with questions. Allen told of the prison house and the way the men organized. Hester spoke when he had finished.

"It's good to know those men will likely be exchanged soon. Colonel Brodhead has captured two British captains and has something to offer now to impress Colonel Hamilton."

The talk went on until Hester rose and excused herself. After she had gone, Murthree explained.

"Twenty of us were sent up here under Lieutenant Brown. We waited two weeks, then the lieutenant had to leave with part of the men. Will you be ready to go to Fort Pitt in the morning?"

I saw his quick, uneasy glance at Mcfail, but he looked at me directly.

"No, Sergeant. We'll go over our plans in the morning. It may be that some of us will want to go, which is all right, but I have another mission."

When everyone but the sentries seemed to be sleeping, the men in an old barn on piles of sweet-scented swamp grass, I walked down along the stream to the point where it empties into the river. Hester was there as I had hoped she might be, and we sat on a rock for a long time, watching the reflection of the moon on the water.

"Martin, Colonel Brodhead has been wonderful. He sent east for Cady. You do not know him, but he has some wonderful way of getting through Indian country. So he was sent to Detroit and will, I believe, help you search for the gold. The colonel thinks the gold is not far from here, somewhere near the great north bend of the Susquehanna."

I bent forward eagerly.

"How does he know, why does he—"

"Don't be so eager and excited, Martin. All the colonel has is a story that an Indian, grateful to some backwoods farmer for food, told that he and some others had taken three canoe-loads of small kegs from a pack train close to a spot called Hart's Sleeping Place. Does that mean anything?"

"Yes; that is the head of canoe navigation on the West Branch of the Susquehanna. An old trader by the name of Hart used to camp there."

She continued: "They took the loads and traveled for long, weary days on the river until a canoe was nearly wrecked. Then the white man gave them a small keg of brandy and told them to go back the way they had come, which they did."

"Yes," I said with some bitterness. "The Indians drank the brandy and do not remember just where they left their canoes."

She chuckled, a soft pleasant sound in her throat.

"That's the story exactly. The farmer has not seen the Indian since, does not know his name or tribe, but thinks he was a Seneca."

I almost forgot my companion in the silence that followed, for my mind was reaching out over the vast wilderness to the east. This tale was fanciful, but it fit and could well be true. The white man would have been Hartlin, taking his gold bullion in the direction of the coast. There were thousands of good hiding places open to a man who had the help and sympathy of the Indians, as he probably had. The route named was right. Suddenly, I was on fire to go, to travel up this crooked creek and over the mountains to the Susquehanna, then push my search down its entire length, if necessary. I must not fail His Excellency.

"What are you thinking about, Martin?"

Her quiet voice actually startled me so much that I jumped; she laughed and tossed a pebble out into the water.

"Our ensign is getting nervous," she gibed gently.

"This is what I am thinking," I said earnestly. "That I must get to that river and follow it, wherever it flows. I lost my key to the search when Girty killed Hartlin, but I must find the gold."

"You will not fail me," she quoted the words of His Excellency.

"No," I said. "I'll find it; a man hid it and men can locate it. It's the time it takes and the time already lost that bothers me."

We talked with Cady in the morning, Hester, Mcfail, and I, Hester telling the story of the Indian, and I offering my plan. The woodsman heard us through, then he sketched on the sand a rough map of the rivers.

"The Susquehanna goes north, then east, then south. There are many mountains through which it breaks, there are swamps and other rivers entering it," he said, then his eyes narrowed. He tossed away the stick he had used to make the map. "My friends," he said deliberately, "I believe the story of the Indian, and somewhere on that river there will be a sign where the gold is hidden."

Mcfail spoke doubtfully. "How can we see a sign when we do not know where it is?"

Cady grinned at him and showed excellent white teeth.

"It is like hunting, my friend. A man does not look for a deer but for something different from the woods; a touch of brown or white or a movement in the brush. Any of those may mean the game he seeks. So with us; we will search the river and its banks for something different."

Mcfail nodded in agreement, and Hester smiled, though I wondered if she really did understand. When our conference broke up, I went to Murthree. It seemed that our party that had come from Detroit would do the hunting for the gold, but I did not know about Allen. When I spoke to him, he smiled.

"Me," he said, "I want to see what a keg of gold looks like." Hoadley, Frye, and Mcfail were Lambs; they had been trained to see jobs through so I had not doubted but that I would have their help. To us was added this man Allen, whom we all liked, and Cady seemed about to go with us, judging by his interest in finding the treasure.

Brodhead had been thoughtful in sending my personal things up here, and there was a quantity of provisions such as dried meat, flour, beans, pemmican, and, of course, parched corn. There was no reason to go to Pitt to be outfitted. There was enough here, including weapons, for all of us.

Murthree was polite about leaving, but his lieutenant would be expecting him. The gold was our business; he probably had his orders. I saw him talking to Mcfail; since they were close to me, I heard part of their conversation when they shook hands.

Murthree muttered, "He had it coming to him, John. There were other girls, too."

The soldiers had packed the stores we would not need into their four canoes, and they had placed Hester's small leather trunk in one of them. Finally, she came out of the house wearing the costume in which I had first seen her and which she had worn when she warned us of Lafayette's dilemma. It was a boy's suit of soft buckskin with a small round cap, and a red scarf was at her throat. Her small-sized but high moccasins were ornamented with quills, and in her wide belt were a pistol and knife. In one hand she carried a light rifle.

"You are ready, Mistress Jordan?" Murthree questioned. "Thank you, Sergeant. I am going with the other party."

We all stared at her; all, I believe, with some dismay. The way we would take was rough and dangerous; no venture for a girl.

"But," Murthree stammered, "you can't go gallivanting off with them. Colonel Brodhead will—"

"See the wisdom of my act," she finished for him. "I know what I am doing, Sergeant Murthree. The lost gold is partly my responsibility. Goodbye, Sergeant; you have been most helpful."

I, for one, knew there was no arguing with this girl. Most anything might lie ahead, but she had traveled everywhere and had been in much danger. Besides, my heart beat faster when I saw her swing away up the trail back of John Mcfail, carrying her own pack and rifle, matching her steps to those of the sergeant.

CHAPTER SEVENTEEN

COLONEL BRODHEAD understood men and situations, so he had anticipated what I would attempt on release from the British prison. It was for this reason that he had sent us all we needed in the way of supplies, thus saving the time required to return to Fort Pitt to secure such necessities. Nominally, because I had been an officer and because I was committed to finding the gold, I was in charge of the little expedition. But, there was little formality; we just picked up our gear and started. Cady would be the guide, and he seemed very sure of himself and cheerful about what lay ahead. John Mcfail would take over any fighting that would be pushed our way. Cady advised me about the route.

"We'll follow along the Shamokin Path. It is a Seneca road, and those people have not used it since the war started. The Delawares and others always use the Kittanning Path farther to the south."

He glanced sharply at Mcfail and me.

"Punxsutawney village is two days' marching up this creek. They do not like Girty, those people, nor will they like us, so we'll bypass their town, going over the ridges and down to Hart's Sleeping Place."

"How far?" Hoadley had just come up and asked his question. Our guide wrinkled his forehead, made some marks with a stick on the ground, then delivered his opinion.

"Two days to the village, one more to the river."

"With luck," Mcfail said dryly, and Cady grinned.

Our sergeant was eager for action and, his feud with Gibson ended, was as light-hearted as he had been before. But he permitted no carelessness from himself or us. Each night he inspected all firearms, seeing to such matters as bad flints and unpicked touchholes in rifle and pistol locks. Hatchets and knives had to be kept sharp to please him; when they were not, he used a whetstone.

"A man can even get along without a razor if he keeps his knife sharp," he insisted; sound advice from a man who wore a beard.

Hester Jordan knew men well. On the march, she would walk a while with Allen, talking, gesturing with her hands, asking the questions that would permit him to show off his small store of wisdom. When she walked with Mcfail, neither of them would say a word for as much as an hour. With Hoadley and Frye she usually bantered, and she was aloof from Cady. Frequently, she helped in the preparation of meals, though this was usually Allen's job.

One day I walked with Cady for a long time. That morning he had been so cold to Hester that it came close to rudeness. Half serious, I rallied him about it and he stopped abruptly.

"Martin, it is a woman's place to keep silence as men plan. When the red squirrel chatters, the business of the woods stops; so it is with women."

He had started and taken two steps before he added, "Now when I marry or have business with women, I always choose an Indian. They know their place and do not tag along on war trails. Women are a convenience and easily forgotten."

He angered me, but as I watched the swing of his narrow shoulders, I knew he lived in a narrow world of efficiency. Forest trails were places for business, not for social amenities. Not long after his outburst, he found a beautiful piece of moss, which he patted with his fingers as he showed it to me. His eyes shone. This man of the woods, Simeon Cady, had odd traits.

Without his seeing it, I left the moss by the side of the trail where Hester would see it when she passed.

The trail we followed showed little signs of use, for grass grew in the actual path and there were many trees blown down across it. Blazes on fresh bark had become brown, and there were no traces of the hoofs of pack animals that would be found here in normal times, for traders always used these great paths.

We lived well for woods travelers. Cady supplemented our provisions with venison. One day I watched him; he loaded his big-bored gun with an extremely light charge of powder; that, I knew, was so the report would be light. Following him cautiously, I saw the deer browsing. It would reach out, select a leaf with its tongue, then chew for a moment. Cady moved when it did, was still when it looked about, and he had come within a score of yards from his quarry before he fired, striking the deer in the neck with his bullet so that the animal was down in two of its long bounds. Cady was hunting meat, not sport, and to him this was business.

Hester kept up with us very well but we traveled at a sensible pace, without driving ourselves as I had done on the Natchez Trace. We were almost certain that Girty would follow us and we did not wish to exhaust ourselves; rather, we conserved our strength, knowing we would need it when all the cards were down.

Hart's Sleeping Place was a bit of natural meadowland between the narrow river and a hill. From a distance, the yellow wild grass looked like a grain field. Hills and mountains tumbled away to the east, but the river broke through a defile to the north.

Mcfail explained to the others that Hart was an old trader, beloved by the Indians, and this was the end of his usual route collecting furs.

On grim days, with the wind blowing, it seemed more natural to be watchful, but ours were those of a kindly, if early, spring and there was much of interest as we tramped along. We saw arbutus, and Hester usually carried a sprig of it thrust into her belt. I showed her wild anemones and explained that we called it "windflower" because its stem was so delicate the bloom moved each time even a light breeze touched it. I kept thinking how she would love the profusion of wild honeysuckle along the stone fences of my farm. They are a common thing in my country and fragrant beyond belief.

Hester had the gift of interest, which the men soon learned. During the day they would pick up and carry with them little things they found. In the evening, these things would be shown her gravely. There might be bits of twisted wood, fresh wintergreen leaves, or pieces of stone. Hoadley, in crossing a brook one day, found a nearly perfect bit of quartz that we call a "glass stone." It had facets like a diamond and was almost as clear.

"Wood diamond," she called it and tucked it away in her things, while Hoadley beamed at having given her pleasure. Perhaps because of her we were dawdling, but she certainly did wonders in keeping our small company in good spirits. Wayne would have driven us to make ten miles a day more had he been in charge.

The river was growing larger with each mile and each feeding brook or creek. In the morning, we saw a cut far ahead in the hills through which our river and our way would go. We marched toward it all day, and by midafternoon, the ground was growing much rougher. We could see that our stream went round the point of the ridge and swung away left toward a far blue mountain. We walked on the right of the river, and our path followed a low bluff with benches above it on the ridge that formed this small valley's one wall. Our side was covered with trees and brush, but on the other, the steep-pointed hill was rocky, with large boulders scattered about in profusion.

Our company was well stretched out, with Hester and me to the front. Cady had slipped out of line, probably bent on doing some hunting. Mcfail was next to us; Frye was the last man, the other two walking together between him and the sergeant. Then, with no warning, the first shot fell.

None of us doubted from whom the shot came or what sort of attack we had to face. Simon Girty was a competent partisan leader, able to manage Indians, and we had realized that he would follow. Now he may have grown weary of doing so, or perhaps the Indians simply wanted to break the monotony.

"Down!" Mcfail yelled, and I pushed Hester behind a rock just as another bullet struck a boulder near Hoadley and whined away hungrily in this echoing defile. There was more firing on the part of our attackers, but we had not, as yet, loosed a shot because we saw no targets. Then, after about ten minutes, there was some sort of movement high up the hill and both the sergeant and Hoadley fired, almost together. Hester caught my arm and shook it.

"Look back; they've hit Frye."

She had half risen from her shelter, and I pushed her down again. Frye was lying out in the open and he did not seem to move. There was brush close to him, and I knew that in the next moment a warrior would come out for the scalp. Thrusting my rifle into Hester's hands, I jumped up and started running, weaving back and forth to make shooting at me difficult. They tried hard enough, but I reached the prostrate man unscathed.

Selin Frye was not a big fellow like Allen, for which I was thankful as I flung him over my shoulder and started back, the burden making it impossible to do any more dodging. Once I felt Frye's body twitch under the continuous fire they kept up from the ridge, and there was warm blood on my hands where I clutched his legs. It seemed to take me hours, but I made it back to the small circle of rocks into which Mcfail must have brought Hester. Hoadley crouched there, his rifle pushed forward and his eyes searching the hillside for a target under the puffs of smoke.

Selin Frye was not dead, but his breath came in fighting gasps and his fingers loosened from the rifle he had held clutched in his hands as I carried him. Hester leaned over him and wiped his lips with her handkerchief. Mcfail glanced at Frye just once, and his lips formed into a straight line.

"Folks, we'll have to make a break for the bench above us. They can shoot down on us here. Break and run when I call your names."

"Hoadley." The young Lamb was on his feet and running. There was movement on the hill and Mcfail fired. While he reloaded, he called the second name.

"Allen." The big man was some little distance from us and showed now that he was not a good runner. They were pitching a slow, methodical fire at us, and halfway up Allen stumbled, rolling back a full rod. We thought him hit, but he was up again and made the shelter of the rocky bench at his second try.

"Hester."

Mcfail's voice faltered a bit as he spoke her name, then he and I faced the hillside where our enemies were. I fired at a movement; Mcfail finished his reloading and fired another shot before we saw that Hester was safe. Then we both dropped to our knees beside Frye.

"I'll take him, John. You cover me."

He snatched the rifle from my fingers and faced round, while I took a long breath, then shouldered the wounded man. A rifle cracked, seeming nearer to us, and I thought I was hit, but what had nicked my neck was just a tiny spawl of stone kicked off by a bullet.

The slope was a hard one for a man unencumbered, and my heart pounded under the exertion of climbing with my burden. Vaguely I realized rifles were firing from above and Mcfail was shooting to cover me from below. Fighting up the slope, breath almost gone, I had nearly reached my goal when I saw Hester's face through the fringe of brush, her hair falling forward and almost hiding her features. Her lips were open as though she were panting. When I had struggled until I was within one yard of my destination, with the weight dragging at my shoulders, the blackness of complete exhaustion came down upon me. As I was about to fall, hands reached out and grasped me.

I did not lose complete consciousness, but my head rested on Hester's lap while I fought for breath. After a minute or so, I could see the men at their stations. Somehow, Cady had managed to rejoin us, and Mcfail had scrambled safely to our cover.

"You're lucky, Martin," Mcfail grunted. "They pitched bullets all around you."

I sat up, still a bit dizzy.

"Frye?" I questioned anxiously.

"Going fast," the sergeant answered, and we crawled over the few yards to where they had placed the dying man on a bed of green leaves. His eyes were open, his chest heaved rapidly, but he smiled.

"Good try, Martin. I'll tell—Eben."

Hester's eyes were wide and dry as she watched me bend lower so that I could hear anything our passing comrade might have to say.

"Mom's chickens," he whispered. "The hawk got every one of 'em. Just like—"

We thought he was gone, but his lips still shaped the ghost of a smile as he added one more word, which finished what he wanted to say:

"Me."

We left the dead man and went back to the edge of the bench where we began shooting grimly at every puff of smoke that appeared.

Hester had moved over beside Mcfail, and I heard her speaking. "Had Selin no people, John?"

"Only his brother, Benjamin. They came from over the mountains near where Colonel Cresap had his post. Both were raised on a mountain farm then drifted over the hills and joined the Lambs— for excitement, I guess."

She crouched for a while, with her small chin cupped in her hand, then she spoke pensively.

"It's hard—dying on a lonely mountainside with a battle going and only a bed of leaves to ease one. What did he mean about the hawk that was so important—the last thing in his life?"

Mcfail glanced round. Most of us were listening and remembered the story Frye had begun back there in that sodden wilderness camp. The sergeant scowled.

"Oh," he answered callously, "likely it meant nothing; he was sort of out of his head."

"But," she insisted, "it was hard."

When the big sergeant spoke this time, he summed up the matter in a few words: "He was a Lamb."

Breon had spoken of these men, enlisted to fight and die with never a thought of odds, and I had come to know them. Now the organization was broken, with Gibson dead on a nameless creek, shot for his sins, his followers scattered. Often the friendliest face these men of the frontier would see when horror had overtaken them, was that of death.

Sergeant John Mcfail knew how to fight Indians. After darkness came, he had us kindle fires down the slope so our attackers could not creep upon us in the shadows. We watched in pairs through the long night to a bright morning. He and I talked together when it was our turn on guard.

"There's a good many of them," he said. "I figure there's three white men because most Indians can't shoot as well as that gang's been doing. In addition, there's a good score of warriors over there." I did not comment, for his tone made me feel uneasy, as though he was touched with desperation. Much of my own thinking had centered about Selin Frye, whose grave we had dug with knives and then covered carefully so he would not be dug up for his scalp. The story of the hen and her chickens bothered me, and I was particularly concerned for Hester. If the attackers, with three white renegades, captured us, it would be hell for her. At the last moment, it would be someone's duty to give her the mercy of a bullet.

They rushed us about midmorning, a long line of them crossing the stream below. Now they were creeping up the hill, sheltered by the bushes. The sergeant had been right; more than a score of attackers moved upward toward us. We held steady. Mcfail would count to twenty, which was time enough to load a rifle, then name the man who should shoot. I can hear him yet, his tongue a bit thick because of the pipe in his teeth:

"One, two, three . . . twenty—Allen—"

We used a bullet and two buckshot and kept up a steady searching fire, with pistols held as a reserve in case they got too close. The cover was too dense for us to see how much execution we accomplished, but we had fired at each good mark and from this distance would not miss.

For ourselves, Allen had taken a nick in the shoulder and was proud to have Hester dress it for him. Another bullet had ripped through a haversack, spilling parched corn about.

The day was warm with a high sun, and by noon we were very thirsty since we had eaten dried meat and the remnants of cornbread. By the afternoon we were parched, more so because the river, with its murmuring of cold water, was so near to us, yet so far!

Simon Girty was a good officer and thoroughly understood our predicament, for on three different occasions, when one of us tried to move down through the brush, we attracted a withering fire from among the boulders. At dusk, Mcfail drew Cady and me close to him and pointed to the hill over the stream.

"Look."

Years before, a heavy storm had cut a swath through the small timber, and now there was a big pile of dead and dry brush angling up the hillside on which the enemy lay.

"Girty's going to try fire tonight. Let's beat him to it. We'll light that brush and have a man slip down the gap and start a blaze there. Fire will burn hard—uphill. Then, if we can make them pull foot, we'll break for the valley above, where we'll have more room."

We had two small kettles, one of them belonging to Cady and which had done such yeoman service after our escape. After nightfall, we filled these with live coals and prepared two bundles of resinous dry wood. Cady and I expected to make the try at firing the brush and the woods. We tossed a coin; Cady got the job with the brush row and I the one around the point of the mountain. His was the riskier task, but I knew he was a far better woodsman than I.

Each carrying a kettle covered with green brush, we slipped out quietly, bearing only our sidearms so as not to be encumbered. Nothing happened to me until I reached the river, which I crossed under the heavy shadow of a big tree. There I wanted to stop and drink, for my lips felt dry and cracked, but I thought of my companions who were just as thirsty. Hester had moistened her lips often, and I once had seen her put a small pebble in her mouth. Foolishly, I hurried on without touching the water.

The rattle of the stream covered any small noises I probably made as I went through the gap. Then, by the glow of their fire, I saw that Girty's camp was just beyond the crest of the ridge. From this protected place, he could send his men over to fire at us. The camp was in a grove of small pines that I could see against the light. If I could set fire to that clump of trees, I'd burn out the hornets' nest.

Two things helped me, one being a drift of dry leaves by a rock, the other a dead pine from which I stripped the branches. Huddled there beside my mass of kindling, I blew on the coals in my kettle until I was able to fire the leaves from them. The flames leaped up like live things, running through the tinder in a long line and then advancing up the hillside, driven by the breeze that one always finds in a mountain gap. From Girty's camp I heard a yell, then muskets crashed and spurted their stabs of fire toward my position. Beyond the mountain, rifles pounded twice.

Running now, and flinging what was left of my coals where I felt they would do the most good, I came around the mountain point and to the place where I must cross the stream.

The Indian must have been assigned to keep watch over our camp and, blinded as I was from the fire's light, I plunged right into him. His arms clutched me, and neither of us could draw a weapon since I was pinioned fast and he was using both of his arms to hold me. Twisting about, I tried to force his sweaty, greasy body back, but he writhed clear, letting go his own hold for a moment; in that flash of time, I swung the iron kettle, which I had not dropped. It was solid and heavy for its size; when it struck the shaven head of my antagonist, he yelled in pain, stumbled, and fell into the water.

He would be up and at me in another moment, so I splashed across the stream and was halfway up the slope before I remembered about the water. Indian or no Indian, my people were thirsty. This time, I filled the useful kettle and had a drink myself, then I climbed up the bench and placed my treasure in Hester's hands. I had seen nothing of the Indian I had struck and fervently hoped he had drowned.

It did not seem possible that we had managed to start such a holocaust in so short a time; Cady had kindled his fire in the windfall, and the whole side of the ridge seemed ablaze, leaves and brush burning like tinder. Through the gap, we could see that that side of Girty's vantage place was aflame.

When we felt sure the fire would keep our enemies busy, we filed diagonally down the mountain bench, with Cady moving first and Mcfail bringing up the rear. About us clung the acrid smell of wood smoke. When we reached the water we halted while we all drank deeply, then bathed our hands and faces in the cooling flow.

"Noble stuff," Allen commented with water dripping from his chin. "Better'n any whisky I ever drank."

Dawn found us entering parklike country through which our river meandered, to disappear in a range of blue hills to the north. Here we stopped and set about making a better camp than usual.

It would be hard for Girty and his henchmen to attack us over the more or less open terrain, and we meant to rest after the strain of our recent experience. We were fairly confident; this was our second encounter with Girty, and we felt we had come out of it in good shape, even though we had left Selin Frye back there on that lonely and unnamed ridge.

CHAPTER EIGHTEEN

DESPITE A HINT of rain, the morning was fair, with bright sun, so that we ate our breakfast comfortably in the deep grass beside the river, taking our time and feeling secure against attack because of the open country about us. But we had scarcely finished when the sky clouded over. Reluctant to leave our comfort, we remained so long, listening to the onward march of the rain, that we finally had to run for a mixed stand of oaks and chestnuts.

Hoadley and I rigged our one small oilskin as a shelter for Hester and put our food and ammunition under it with her. Putting the deerskin lock covers on our rifles, we settled down to take the discomfort of a wetting.

A light shower was followed, after an hour or two, by a terrific thunderstorm, which brought down rain in such torrents that we had to huddle close to tree trunks until the force of the downpour was spent. With everything soaked, we had a hard time getting a fire to burn, and when night came, we had to use sodden blankets.

It was some satisfaction to know this rain would have quenched the forest fire we had set, also that it would hold our pursuers in their camp, wherever it was. But the weather did not clear for two more long days, during which time we had to rig bough shelters and to pad the wet ground with leaves and grass. One of us stayed by the fire at all times to keep it going. That blaze was our only comfort.

Cady and Hester were the only ones who kept up their spirits, for the reaction of battle held the rest of us. Allen was grumpy, Hoadley irritated by small things; Mcfail fell into silent moods that lasted for hours, and my own mind was on the passing of Selin Frye. The responsibility for all of us was mine, and I had to weigh that against the business that had brought me here: the recovery of the precious gold. Somewhere back of us was a force able to pick us off one by one or overwhelm us in a single rush if the opportunity presented itself. I was sure Girty would wish to capture me in order to wring from me whatever information he thought I might have obtained from Hartlin. My major worry, however, was Hester; the men knew the forest and its risks. With her, it was different. Even her staunch courage would avail little in the final struggle when it came.

Cady turned entertainer. He could do odd tricks with his hands, making grains of corn disappear and then reappear in unlikely places. He fashioned a set of whistles made of chestnut bark, on which he played what he claimed to be a tune. His last stunt was to capture four black crickets and he got thoroughly wet in the grass doing so. Before he caught them, he had fashioned a small yard of woven grass and smoothed the ground inside. Hester had watched him closely, and he explained to her what he planned.

"This is the dance of the crickets."

He lay down close to his enclosure and breathed softly into his whistles. Whether the air coming through these forest pipes stirred the insects or something else disturbed them was hard to tell, but all four of the little creatures began to hop about.

Allen was so delighted that he slapped his heavy thighs and laughed until there were tears on his face. Hoadley tried to maintain his dignity but gave it up, and even Mcfail brightened. Cady watched us all, pleased with his act.

"The Shawnees called me the Cricket," he said, and I remembered that was what he had called himself back there in the cemetery at Detroit.

In the evenings about the fire, we debated our problem. Cady confirmed what some of us had heard, that the Shamokin Path left the river somewhere up ahead and cut across country, coming out on the main stream below the great north bend of this Susquehanna. We did not know which was the wiser—to follow the path or the river. Our stream was already bearing toward the north.

We had not settled the question when the rain stopped and we took the trail again. Our damp clothing was uncomfortable, and every tree and bush against which we brushed drenched us all over again. But it was more pleasant for me to move than to sit in camp brooding.

Our big valley narrowed, and here Girty gave us a reminder of his presence. Again it was rifle fire from the hillside, but this time one of the Indians made the mistake of showing himself; instantly, Hoadley and Mcfail dropped to their knees, the long barrels of their rifles swinging with the running man. When the reports sounded, the Indian dropped and rolled down the slope. A concealed marksman howled, then I saw what looked like a feathered headdress show itself, and my bullet kicked bits of stone from the rock where my target had appeared. As I reloaded, the Indian leaped out, and Allen missed him as he ran for shelter.

We did not say much about the attack, but we all realized we were in for a long-running fight, and for a pitched battle if we located the gold. Our only safety lay in lessening the odds against us by the most sustained vigilance.

We finished the day's travel a little low in spirits, but as we sat around the campfire, there came the accident that gave direction to our journey.

Hoadley owned a small boxed compass and took it out to show it to Hester. He demonstrated how the needle would follow the point of his knife about the dial when he held the steel close.

"Then," she commented, "a man with a rifle could not trust the instrument."

"No," he said. "He'd have to lay the rifle down a little distance from the compass."

She struck her hands together.

"I know a better thing. You take a watch and point the hour hand at the sun. Halfway between the minute hand and the twelve o'clock mark, going the longest way round, is the north and south line."

She had caught our attention completely, but we did not fully understand. Hoadley scratched an ear and even Cady looked doubtful.

Allen shook his heavy head. "Never had a watch so I wouldn't know if she's right or not."

Hester came to her feet in that smooth movement characteristic of her and glanced over toward me.

"I have the watch that Martin brought to me from Doctor Hartlin. It's running, for I have kept it wound."

She brought the timepiece from her things and held it in the firelight while we all crowded close to see.

The watch was a heavy one of gold with three fobs dangling from the ring on the stem. One of these carried the winding key, one held an ornament, and the third was a tiny chisel-shaped piece of steel to open the closed case. She held it out to me.

"Open it, Martin; the lid sticks."

I took the big timepiece from her slender fingers and used my knife instead of the metal pick. The case was double, and I had opened the back instead of the front, so here was a second smooth lid with an opening in it for the key. But I had pried rather hard and the second lid was ajar. Abruptly, Hester cried out, "Look, Martin, inside the second cover!"

I stared down stupidly at the instrument I held cupped in my hand until she took it from me and opened both lids as wide as they would go. There, pasted inside the second cover, was a small piece of paper with markings on it.

"It's a map!" she cried. "It shows the river. We've found it, we've found it!"

Balanced on the tips of her moccasins, she spun round and round, brandishing the watch and its seals above her head. Her hair was flying, her eyes sparkled in the firelight. We gathered closer, and when she had stopped, she gave us a better look at the paper.

The tiny chart showed a river running north to a great bend, then southward, a tiny arrow indicating the direction of the flow. High up on the bend, a second river entered from the northwest and an arrow pointed up its flow. Some little way up this stream two letters that looked like 'RI' showed, and directly across the stream from them was a cross that had a wide bar, as though the pen making it had slipped.

"The gold's on that north river," I muttered and was surprised to find my voice shook. Hester placed the timepiece on my hand, and as I heard it ticking away, I thought of that awful spot in the forest where I had seen a man die so terribly.

No doubt about it, Hartlin had valued this watch. He had chosen to take it with him above anything else in his officelike room back in Detroit. Whether he wished to or not, Hartlin was now about to guide us.

The fire died low as we stood there, passing from hand to hand the timepiece that had marked the march of hours for Doctor Hartlin.

Perhaps some among us wondered about this man who had worshiped property and wealth and who, in the end, had received such a diabolical return from all his ill-gotten gains.

We set no watch duty that night; our minds were too full of the import of our discovery. I lay on my back for a long time, looking up into the dark sky. Somewhere on one of these wild forest rivers rested the price of victory for His Excellency and our forces. We few were approaching this triumph, not with cannon and uniformed troops, but at the risk of our own lives.

No one lingered in the blankets next morning, and I even had to insist that a breakfast be prepared and eaten. Our treasure hunters were eager to take the field at once, and delay was painful, even if it was for eating. When we finished, Cady, at my nod, set the pace. Once, Hoadley passed the woodsman, but the little man kept up his steady, unhurried stride.

The twisting river took us through a long, deep, turning gorge where it was hard to keep one's balance on the narrow stony beach. Above us, rock walls lifted almost as sheer as though they had been carved by some great cutting tool. Here would be a place for Girty to attack, so we walked with rifles ready, as men will when hunting deer. As we stepped along smartly, Hester seemed oblivious to her surroundings, carrying the watch in the pocket of her hunting shirt, the fobs dangling just below the ends of her red neckerchief.

It was a relief to be out of that gorge by evening, and that night we camped in a small cove. We had sense enough to set a guard. After one hour of brisk travel in the morning, we rounded a rocky point and came to a dead stop, all of us crowding together. Directly ahead, a high, bold mountain turned our river toward the right, and to the left was a broad, blue stream coming down a long, straight reach and emptying into our Susquehanna.

"The Sinnemahoning," Cady muttered, and I turned on him quickly.

"Do you know this country?"

He shook his head and answered, "Only from hearsay. It is here the Indian paths fork, one going north to real Iroquois country; the other is the one we have followed. Neither would be in use now while the Senecas serve the English."

Without hesitation, we started up this new river, finding on its sides flatland covered with brush. I walked with Hester, and occasionally she took out the watch or tapped the pocket where she carried it. Once, she had me open the case with the little pick so she could glance at the map itself.

"We'll make it by night, won't we, Martin?"

I grinned at her, for she was like a small child, too eager for her own good. She had taken the toil and danger of this march as bravely as any of the men and much more cheerfully. Without reason, I thought of my small stone house with its divided door and how her face would look as she stood framed there against the interior. After that, I thought of Wayne's house with its high ceilings, the beautiful walls, and the elaborate furnishings. This girl belonged in such a dwelling with the silver and mahogany, not in a Dutch farmhouse.

She had put back the watch, and I plodded along with my head down, trying to close my mind to these thoughts. Suddenly, she clutched my arm, her fingers digging into the buckskin of my sleeve.

"Look, Martin, look!"

My eyes followed the direction of her pointed finger to the very tip of the great mountain overlooking the rivers. High up, almost at the crest, was an Indian. He stood there quite calmly, secure in the fact that he was out of rifle range, and it was certain that he could and did see us. We all looked at him for a while, then he picked up a blanket from a rock, flung it over his shoulder, and disappeared.

"Well, I'll be—" Mcfail checked his oath after a glance at Hester.

"So Girty knows," I said, and Cady nodded before he spoke.

"They've cut across country and saved miles. Now they watch to see on which river we go."

Hester broke the spell of our disillusionment. "Let the man wear his filthy blanket. We'll find the gold and fight for it."

We moved fast, the flatland narrowing until we had to climb over the end of a ridge to follow the river. Before us, from this slight elevation, was a panorama. The rise where we stood was on the left bank. Across the stream and farther up was another bold headland almost as high as the mountain on which we had seen the Indian. It was covered with forest and broken by great gray rocks. At the base of both our ridge and the one across from us, streams emptied into our river, which was very wide here. In its center was a small, wooded island, perfectly round in shape.

Again it was Hester who was faster than the rest of us. She pointed to the little island.

"Look, men; it is round."

We stared at her a moment, then I understood, and at my word, she took out the watch, opened it, and showed the two letters, RI.

"That's Round Island," she declared emphatically.

"Let's go," said Hoadley impulsively. "I want to handle one of them gold bars."

I held up my hand.

"Listen, everybody. We'd better scout this place carefully. It isn't likely Hartlin would leave his gold without guards, and we've our hands full with Girty. The sergeant and I will go down there first!"

We found the stream down below us wider and deeper than expected, and it was overhung with a growth of black alder, so the water moved through a tunnel of greenery. We scouted a mile up the main stream, flushing grouse and sending at least one deer bounding away into a thicket. But we saw no person nor sign that people had ever been here. We crossed the main Sinnemahoning some little distance above the island. Here, on the bluff, was an old trail running north and south. Like the one on which we had traveled, this showed no signs of recent use, but directly across from the island on the bank of the tributary stream was an old camping place with a litter of charred wood ashes and stones cracked by heat.

"Nothing here for a long time," Mcfail commented, and I had to agree with him.

"But, John, it has to be about here somewhere."

He stared at the ground and shuffled the point of his worn moccasins.

"Martin, I keep thinking about this man Cady. Do you figure he knows something?"

"Well, he puzzles me, but we owe him a lot. His advice has always been good, and he's been sure all along that we'd find the treasure. I think I'll ask him right out."

Mcfail shook his head emphatically.

"No, the man's too Indian in his ways. Try to pump a Red Stick and he dries up on you. Just wait."

We made a careful and, for us, elaborate camp, with good lean-tos for everyone. Hester's was set back a bit from the others to give her some privacy. It would be necessary to cover every square foot of this region in our search, and a good base was essential, so we took time to make one. Hester liked her place with its bough bed over which she spread a blanket, and the small oilskin served as a good door. Allen fashioned her a bark bucket, and she was surprised that the clumsy-looking object actually held water.

In the evening about the campfire, the talk was of the treasure. Each of us had another good look at the map, and I told them for at least the twentieth time of the kegs with a brass tack set in each of them as I had seen them on the flatboat.

"What would it weigh?" Allen asked, and I laughed.

"More than we could carry. Twenty kegs at fifty pounds each would weigh close to half a ton."

He whistled.

"No wonder Girty's got half a tribe with him. It would take his whole crowd to heft it and pack it out."

Hester had left us some little time before, and we had heard her moving about at her lean-to. More or less absently, I noticed that she had walked toward the creek, and I had heard her steps until they were lost in the sound of the water. Likely she was trying her new bucket. Hoadley was asking some question of Mcfail when Cady touched my arm.

"She did not come back."

I looked at him, puzzled for a moment; then I was on my feet when I realized what he meant. Fright laid its cold hand along my spine. We should have planned to set our sentries earlier and not at bedtime as we usually did. With no explanation to the others, I plunged into the darkness, but Cady was beside me before I had gone ten feet, and someone else, likely Mcfail, was coming from the camp.

The lean-to was empty, and we saw that the oilcloth flap was flung up over the edge of the roof, and at the stream, where we had obtained our water, Cady fumbled about and found the bark bucket. Not more than ten minutes could have elapsed since the girl was here, and it did not seem possible that she had been spirited away with no sound.

Crossing the stream, we searched the bank in the darkness, dreading what we might find. Cady seemed to have eyes like a cat, and the longer I was away from the fire, the better I could see.

"Listen," he hissed, holding me by the sleeve.

Diagonally up the ridge was a light sound of breaking sticks, and I flung off his hand to start running up the slope. Both of us knew the danger; if Indians had captured Hester and thought we would overtake them, it meant a hatchet in her head. Cady caught my arm again.

"Wait!" he said imperiously. "Don't rush up like a damned fool. Let me get round in front of them. And don't make so much noise."

His fingers closed on my arm painfully.

"Then we'll strike."

He was gone from me like a flitting shadow. Ahead, the light noises continued like the brushing of clothing against leaves. Above me, the bushes and timber were thinning against the sky. In another five minutes, I saw a dark moving mass.

I had a choking sensation, and my fingers searched my belt, finding the big knife Eben Drough had used. Ahead of the moving shadow, a branch cracked sharply and whatever was before me stopped. Trying desperately to make no noise, I came closer. Hester was there with her captors; my least mistake would mean that she would die.

A second stick broke and the shadow divided so that I saw a feathered head against the skyline.

Closer and closer I came, even holding my breath lest I make a sound. There were two warriors standing some little distance apart, with something dark on the ground between them. Their attention was centered on whatever was stirring up there ahead. Then I was upon them, plunging with outspread arms so that I might knock them off balance.

One warrior did go down to flounder in the brush, but the other slid from my arms like a trained wrestler and I saw his ax flash as he yanked it from his belt. Crouching, I went under his arm, trying to trip him, but we both fell with a force that nearly knocked the wind out of me. His body was under me, but he was twisting clear. Down on the ground it was darker, and I felt his fingers clawing for my eyes. I slashed at him with the knife and heard him groan, but he twisted again. He had cleared his ax but missed his stroke, the flat of his weapon striking the side of my head. In spite of my giddiness, I held fast with my free hand and was clear in a moment. Then I used the big blade, not driving the point into him, but slashing from side to side with that razor-sharp weapon. He gave one awful yell of agony and surprise and jerked spasmodically from my grasp. But I was after him. Now I drove the knife home again and again until he was still.

"Martin?" It was Cady whispering.

"Yes," I panted. "Is she all right?"

"Stunned," he answered. "The other got away, but I cut him with my ax."

Wiping my bloody hands on the leaves, I gathered up the unconscious girl. She seemed very slight in my arms to have come so far and endured so much. I was enraged that one of that filthy crew had dared to touch her. So we tramped down the hillside with Cady leading the way. As we crossed the stream, Hester stirred in my arms.

"Martin," she whispered, "I knew you'd come. They—struck me."

The others met us, and we went on into our camp where Cady examined her head by the firelight and found she had a bad bump but no serious injury. The blanket had saved her.

"We'll brew her a cup of yarrow tea," the little man said. "It will be good for the headache she will have."

Hester shuddered when she drank the bitter brew he prepared in his small kettle. She told us they had flung a blanket over her head and twisted it so she could not cry out. She had been struck when her captors heard the first sound of our pursuit. When she became drowsy, we escorted her to the lean-to and promised to stand guard. Before very long, her regular breathing told us that she slept.

Cady had something to say, and his dark face was grim as he stood facing us.

"Men, there's only one reason they did not kill the girl; Girty wanted her as a hostage. He planned to trade her for whatever we know of the gold."

I stared at the man's brown face without seeing it. There was a sick feeling at the pit of my stomach as I wondered what I would do if really faced with such a decision.

None of us slept that night, for we lay listening to every sound and starting at each slight stir or whisper. But no danger came out of the shadows. Perhaps Girty and his men were concerned about two warriors, one with a tomahawk gash in his shoulder, the other slashed with a razor-edged knife until the life ran out of him on the dead leaves that covered the mountainside.

CHAPTER NINETEEN

THROUGH THE night we talked things out and came to a desperate resolve. All of us were tired of this situation in which Girty's crew could attack at will and pick us off one by one. Before anything else happened, we would carry the war to the enemy. We remembered Hartlin, taken from us and tortured, and fresh in our memories was Selin Frye, dead down there on that mountain bench. The seizure of Hester was our greatest worry, and our only remaining decision, when morning came, was which one of us must remain behind to be a guard for her. That was settled as such questions were in the prison at Detroit, by casting lots. Cady lost.

"We can hit them hard enough to send them off balance," Sergeant Mcfail assured us. The details of our action were up to him, for he knew best this business of frontier war. A man did not come to be a sergeant in Gibson's Lambs without both fighting experience and judgment.

"This will be a deer drive, boys, no more," he explained, grinning. "One man tops the ridge, the others flank him; one on the riverside, the other two back in the woods. We'll move quiet as a thin wind getting through the trees. Load with buckshot, and when I yell, pour it at 'em."

The ridge on our side yielded nothing to our grim hunting, not even a flushed deer; then we crossed the Sinnemahoning above the island and moved northwestward on the old trail until we came to the creek, which entered the river from that side. It was larger than the one on which we were camped and more heavily screened with alders. As we moved up this, preparatory to mounting the ridge, we made our find. About a quarter of a mile from the creek's mouth, under heavy overhanging trees, was moored a flatboat such as we had taken to New Orleans, though this one was much smaller. It was made of whip-sawn pine lumber and looked new.

One man covered us with his rifle while the rest went on board, moving cautiously, but there was no one there. The craft was well equipped with oars, sweeps, and cordage, but there was nothing else on board, not even a water-beaker.

The hair on my neck prickled as I looked about. Outside of the map, here was the first definite discovery we had made so far in our search. This boat was here for a purpose. It was a cargo carrier, and there could be nothing around here to take down the river except those kegs of gold. Hartlin was a careful man; this boat could well have fitted into his plans. Hoadley volunteered an opinion.

"She was built somewhere on the river, Martin, and poled or dragged up here with a rope."

He had noticed that there was no sign of building about here, and, of course, if the flatboat was to be hidden, it would have been built where no signs of its construction would reveal its hiding place.

"Them little kegs is close," Allen declared jubilantly. "I heard tell gold is soft like lead. I wonder, could I hack off a piece with a hatchet and carry it in my war bag? Then I'd never feel poor again."

Mcfail broke in on our conjectures.

"Boys, Girty's seen this, too. Them Indians wouldn't miss it. Let's try for his watchers."

The second ridge was different. Back of its bold front on the river, the ground dropped only a little to a broad, lightly timbered tableland. We had not gone far before I smelled smoke. Holding up my hand, I signaled the others to stop. They sniffed like hunting dogs.

"Fan out, men," Mcfail directed, "all on this side of the ridge." A man was busy cooking a strip of meat over a tiny fire little bigger than the broad black hat he wore. A big fellow, he was dressed in a cloth hunting shirt, leather breeches, and moccasins. Hoadley's sharp eyes had seen him first; we moved in slowly and surrounded the simple camp.

Here, as sometimes happens in these hills, a spring broke from the rocks and a tiny brooklet wound away, nearly hidden in the ferns. The man we watched poked into the ground the end of the long stick that held his meat so the cooking would continue, leaving his hands free. He partly filled a tin cup with water, took a bottle from his pocket, and held it up to the light to note its contents, after which he decanted some of the liquor into the cup and drank with relish. We had a good look at his smoothly shaven face, scarred across the forehead. His eyes were light in color, too light; it was an evil face.

"My God, Martin, that's Joe Trigg!"

It was Mcfail, whispering softly close to my ear. I had heard this name in Pitt; that of a known renegade who was drummed out of the place for stealing powder and attempted rape. Again the sergeant's whisper:

"My meat, Martin; you've had your fun."

Our quarry's rifle and tomahawk lay to one side, but his knife was in its sheath. Trigg was not drunk, but his palate had been pleased with the first drink. He examined his meat, then prepared a second draught. Mcfail had laid down his rifle and crawled in an arc that took him back of the unsuspecting man. When Trigg raised the cup, the sergeant leaped.

Probably few men ever had much of a chance with John Mcfail in a rough-and-tumble encounter, for the man was large and had tremendous strength coupled with a will to win. But Trigg, knocked off his feet, eluded the clutching arms thrust out to grab him. Rolling, then leaping to his feet, he seized his hatchet and threw it, but Mcfail twisted his own body sideways so the thrown weapon missed him by a very little. Before Trigg could snatch up his rifle, Mcfail plunged forward again. The two men clinched and staggered back and forth, tearing at each other whenever their hands were free. Hoadley raised his rifle and sighted carefully.

"No," I remonstrated, "John would never forgive you."

Next instant I was sorry I had prevented the shot, for the sergeant slipped so that Trigg threw him heavily, then was on top of him, knife out and high. Mcfail rolled, and when Trigg lunged, the sergeant's feet lashed out. It was all over; the renegade was knocked prone, and Mcfail leaped on him, choking the man until he begged for mercy.

Our captive would not talk at first, and Mcfail, his face grim, signaled for Allen to draw Trigg's arms back of him and to hold them tightly. Then the sergeant drew his own knife, tested it on his thumb, and moved toward the trapped prisoner. Trigg's eyes followed the blade and he gulped.

"You're John Mcfail; I'll talk. I know—"

The sergeant's cold eyes stripped him.

"Yes, you know too much about a morning near Pitt when the Radel family was butchered. Trigg, you were there with the Indians."

The prisoner's eyes widened in greater fright.

"I—" he gasped.

"Where's Girty?" the cold questioning voice continued.

Allen jerked the man to a more erect position, using his long hair for a better grip.

"At the point, below here."

The answer was given eagerly, and at the sergeant's nod, I took over.

"How many with him?"

"One other white man and fifteen Indians."

"Loosen up," I told him roughly. "Why are you up here?" Trigg cleared his throat, and words tumbled out of him, while Mcfail, who had seated himself, was touching up his big knife with a tiny sharpening stone. Trigg's story held together; they were after powder, twenty kegs of it. The Indians were to get the kegs not marked with brass tacks; there were to be four of them. The other kegs were to be loaded on the flatboat for transportation down the river with the three white men. He said he did not know who had built the flatboat, claiming that they had just found it. Likely it belonged to the man who hid the powder. I drew closer to him; the prisoner took another look at Mcfail and the knife.

"What does Girty want with all that powder?"

"It ain't powder!" Trigg cried. "Them little kegs is filled with Spanish pieces of eight that you fellers brought upriver. Girty and us would slip them downriver to where we could get a pack train at 'em."

I stood up, recalling my interview with Girty at the smithy. The man was clinging to his original idea, and if he did reach the lower river with such a treasure at his command, there was no telling what he might accomplish among those where the need for hard money was so vital. Two hundred thousand dollars could purchase a pardon and the chance for the renegade to live in the place he loved. Also, the man was known to have betrayed his closest henchmen. If the three went downriver, certainly only one would arrive at the post Girty had selected. His two white companions were as good as dead when, and if, they started on the trip.

Allen had released Trigg's hands, and he and Hoadley were calmly eating the strip of meat the captive had been cooking. I remembered that Mcfail had left his rifle back in the brush and went to get it.

Afterward, I suspected that the sergeant had planned things to happen as they did. Trigg was now seated on his heels. Suddenly, he was up, running like a frightened deer. The renegade must have realized what was going to happen to him, so he took the slim, desperate chance that seemed open.

"Hoadley," Mcfail snapped, "you saw the Radel family—take him!"

The young Lamb flung down his piece of meat, grabbed his rifle, and then dropped on one knee for a steady shot. I waited, holding my breath; the running man had already covered a good deal of ground. An instant more and the big rifle crashed, echoing in the hills. Trigg dropped, his big body rolling inertly into the brush.

"Back of the neck at the shoulder," the young rifleman called his shot. "Just about where they clipped Radel with a hatchet."

He was right; Hoadley had aimed accurately; it was an ugly and decisive wound.

We searched our victim and found one carefully wrapped scalp, which would have meant eight dollars delivered at Niagara or Detroit. He carried nothing else of value, excepting a silk scarf and a good clasp-knife, which Hoadley claimed. We buried the scalp under a big rock but left Trigg for the buzzards; all of us but Allen had seen the dead Radel family in that cabin at Fort Pitt.

Surprise would have been our only weapon against Girty's number, so we gave over an attack and went back down to the hidden flatboat. After we looked the craft over, admiring the craftsmanship of its building, we recrossed the Sinnemahoning and reached our camp.

Hester was relieved to see us. She was cooking over an excellent fire that looked as though an Indian had built it. She said her head did not bother her anymore and glanced toward Cady, who was sitting on a rock. Having fashioned another chestnut whistle, he was trying to coax a tune from it. Both, however, forgot what they were doing and listened while we told of our encounter on the hill, and of the flatboat.

"We're right then," Hester declared. "The gold has to be here."

While we ate hungrily, she sat on a stone, took out the watch, and studied the map, bending close so she could follow the faint tracing. Finally, she looked up at us.

"Nothing to guide us but that RI and the cross mark."

I went over to her and looked at the tiny crude map.

"It's a regular cross," I said half-aloud. "It's not an x. Only the crossbar is wider than the upright. Maybe his pen slipped when he made the map."

Cady had finished eating and had carefully cleansed his fingers on a bit of moss. When he beckoned to me, almost slyly, I rose and followed him down to the shore of the river and into the fringing brush. There, dramatically, he raised his arm and pointed with the chestnut whistle, which he still held.

I glanced at him; he stood erect. There was something military about the man.

"I said there would be a sign," he said quietly. "Look."

Well up toward the point of the ridge was a bar of grayish rock, which I remembered seeing when we climbed up that way, searching for Girty's men. Now, following this man's pointing, I saw something else. Directly in front of the rock stood a tall pine clear of branches almost to the top, which is so common to old trees. I saw it; the tree trunk against the background of the gray rock made a cross, one with a wide crossbar, as the map showed.

Excitement was so strong in me that I gasped.

"The gold," I muttered. "It's there. Your Excellency—"

Cady was looking at me so sharply and sternly that I stopped and stared at him. Suddenly, my suspicions rose; I remembered Mcfail's question about the man who had served us so well but about whom we really knew so little.

"Who are you?" I demanded. "Did you know the gold was there?"

He shook his head. He was smiling a bit as if my heat amused him.

"No, I looked for signs and saw them today."

His fingers disappeared into the breast of his hunting shirt and came out holding something that he thrust into my hands. Stupidly, I took it and stared at him. Looking more closely, I saw that what I held was not just a paper but a parchment; it was a captain's commission given for meritorious services to one Simeon Cady.

"You should know now, Martin. When Brodhead asked His Excellency to send a man to get you out of Detroit, he wanted me because, since I am blood brother in some of the tribes, I can come and go pretty well. The man we serve has used me on other missions, therefore, because the gold is so important, he sent me. Between us, he said—"

"We would not fail him," I finished.

He nodded, then our hands clasped. But before we turned to go back to the others, he cautioned me.

"No word of this to the others. There will be other missions. To them, let me continue to be Simeon Cady, woods runner and sometimes one good with herbs and other remedies."

When we came back to the camp, I called out, "Cady has something to show you."

They gathered about us, Hester close to me, and the small brown-faced man pointed again to the cross on the hillside. Hester picked it out first.

"Martin, Martin, the cross!"

All of us were woodsmen, but we had not seen what lay before our eyes and we stood silent, staring across the river at the landmark set down on the dead Hartlin's map. I saw Mcfail's broad palm drop on Cady's narrow shoulders in a gesture that meant a great deal.

In spite of our excitement, I would not permit the men and Hester to go over at once to investigate our find, and Cady seconded me.

"We'll have to be careful. If Girty knows we've located the kegs, he'll attack at once. He's watching all the time."

With the others finally agreeing, we did not cross until the following morning, and then we did it cautiously at the ford above the island. We loosed the flatboat and allowed it to drift down to the mouth of the creek, as though that was our purpose in coming over. We moored the craft out in plain sight and tied it fast to the bank of the main Sinnemahoning, after which, keeping a sharp lookout, we climbed the ridge.

The tree we sought stood on a narrow bench on the mountain's slope where the ground was so heavily covered with pine needles that it was spongy under our moccasins. Close by were other big rocks, but there was no sign of any digging nor of a hiding place big enough for twenty kegs, each holding half a hundredweight.

Allen had climbed a little above the bench in his search and now let his big body slide down the bank, using his heels for brakes. We paid little attention to his clumsiness until he cried out, "Look!"

His big feet had made two deep furrows in the thick mat of pine needles, and there we saw what had made him cry out: the brown of sailcloth! In a moment we had seized this and flung it aside. In a wide fissure of the rocks on this stony ledge lay the kegs, twenty of them. First they had been covered with the sailcloth and then pine needles had been thrown over that to hide the treasure.

Cady grinned.

"We might have known there were too many needles to be under one tree."

Hester counted carefully as we turned over our find. There were twenty kegs and all but four were marked with brass tacks. These four, according to Trigg's story, were to contain powder.

The whole group was looking at me, Hester with her lips parted a little like those of an eager child. Hoadley just stared; Allen was licking his lips and brushing pine needles from a keg; Mcfail's eyes were bright with excitement, but Cady's face wore a look of profound amusement.

At my nod, Allen lifted a keg and went to work on one of the tough oaken staves with his tomahawk until he had chopped a fair-sized hole; then Hester pushed her hand into the opening, pulled out some straw, then a curved yellow slab a few inches wide, not an inch in thickness and about as long as my knife blade, which I knew to be seven inches.

Gold has a subtle power over men; the look of it, the weight, its vast potentiality stirs men, and this power showed on the faces of my friends as the small ingot went from hand to hand. They had come so far through so many dangers that they appreciated the precious metal the more, considering what it had cost us in endurance. I wanted to do something for them as I looked at them. A glance at Hester and Cady brought no help, so I decided.

"We'll each take a chip. That much won't hurt. Allen, do the cutting."

The big fellow's wish to have a bit of gold in his war bag so he would never feel poor again had lingered in my mind.

It was amusing to see this hulk of a man sitting on the ground like an Indian girl sewing moccasins while he drove the edge of his knife with a stone into the soft metal. He took off the four corners, then a thin shaving, possibly two inches in length and the width of the ingot. This last, he divided lengthwise. Gravely, he pocketed one of the corners, then gave the three others to Hoadley, Mcfail, and Cady. The two flat pieces went one each to Hester and me.

While they admired their bits of gold, I shaped mine into a ring and smoothed it with my knife.

"Here, Hester," I said. "Wear this for good fortune."

She looked at me oddly; her eyes were wide and I thought they had a hint of tears in them. I was about to drop the crude ring into her palm, but she shook her head.

"No, Martin; you put it on so the luck won't be spoiled."

The narrow band slipped onto her finger, and I was so tremendously stirred that I was afraid the others had noticed, but they were too busy with their own small shares of the treasure.

Cady and Mcfail took charge of reconcealing our find, for we had no plan as yet for its disposal. We all helped, but it was Cady's fingers that spread the final layer of needles, obliterating all traces of our having been there.

When we finally got back to the others, I knew it would be an hour or so before food was prepared and ready, so Cady and I went down to the creek.

"You cover me," I told him. "Somebody will have to look that island over."

The water of the creek was not too deep, though I did step into a hole that dropped me in up to my chest. I found the island bank lined with thick bushes through which I pushed, coming out into a comparatively open space where there had been many campfires, judging from the ashes and blackened stones. The whole island did not contain a full acre, and the trees were water birches and elms. But on the side opposite our camp, I made another find. In a narrow, brush-fringed channel lay a bateau made of new lumber. This was also like the craft we used on the Mississippi, but much smaller, with the midship cabin really tiny. All the proper fittings of oars and poles were there, each in its proper place.

Looking at this second boat, I saw clearly that Hartlin had meant to get this golden fortune through to the coast with no regard for his British friends. Somehow, he had probably brought the ingots this far and had hidden them. Perhaps he first planned to use the flatboat; later, he may have felt he needed speed and had the bateau built. There was no use speculating on how he had obtained the craftsmen—here were the boats with no signs of building about.

Time passed as I looked at the bateau; then I had an uncomfortable feeling as though someone were watching me. Turning swiftly, my hand reaching for my hatchet, I saw an Indian a scant ten feet from me. He made no signs of hostility; merely stood there, his face grave.

Over one shoulder was an unstrung bow. A quiver, showing arrow feathers hung over the other. There was a knife at his belt, but he wore no paint and his hair hung loose over his ears and neck.

I shoved my tomahawk back into its place a bit shamefacedly, for the Indian had spread his palms in a gesture of peace. It was plain, too, that he was an old man. Seemingly, he did not understand English, but he did follow me to the bank from where I signaled Cady to come over. After the captain had talked to the old man for a little, he translated.

"He watched and kept the boats hidden for Hartlin. Now that they are discovered, he says it is his duty to take that word back. He is not to fight, merely to report what has happened."

"Where was he to go?" I asked, and Cady translated, only to have our acquaintance shrug his shoulders. Clearly, he had finished talking. Turning abruptly from us, he entered a small bough house from which he emerged in a moment, all his meager belongings in his hands: a blanket and a small sack that might have contained food. He touched his chest.

"Go," he grunted.

Cady nodded and I made no objection as the Indian went to the side of the island and stepped into the water. He walked diagonally over this arm of the creek, evidently following a rock ledge, and he did not look back from the far side but walked north on the old trail.

I saw that Hartlin's watcher had been careful to keep the brush fresh about the hidden boats, and there must have been some appointed rendezvous where this Indian was to report to the doctor that the treasure and the boats had been discovered.

There would be no one waiting now for the old Indian. Hartlin had made his gamble and lost. He had played each side against the other in this war, worshiping property more than people or country, and his last scheme had killed him as surely as though an arrow had been driven through his spare frame.

We shared with our companions the excitement of our new discovery and talked about the possibility of loading it with the kegs and making a quick dash downriver, defying Girty and his riflemen. For a reason we could not quite express, neither Cady nor I mentioned the old Indian and this new connection with Hartlin.

CHAPTER TWENTY

THAT EVENING, tension made us nervous, for beyond the creek on the mountainside was the treasure that meant so much to us for the cause we served. His Excellency had explained to me how much gold would bolster the morale of the army, providing payment for the men and improving the confidence of the people in their new government. And there on the hillside it rested.

Girty and his crew might locate the kegs; perhaps his watchers had seen us upturn the pine needles. We were outnumbered three to one in fighting men, yet gold breeds confidence, and I believe it was that which made our campfire talk optimistic. No word was said about failure; the talk was all about plans for moving the precious store.

Half a ton of precious metal was a pack-horse job if it went overland. Hartlin had provided a way to use the flowing road since horses were out of the question. But the Tory doctor had been in no hurry; probably he was willing to wait out the war, then move his stolen treasure. With us, time meant everything. The armies would be moving; now, after a winter like that at Valley Forge, gold would pour life into the Patriot cause.

John Mcfail was emphatic in answering Allen's question.

"No, we couldn't run the river in the bateau with riflemen on that point. The flatboat would be worse because it is slower. Remember, they could fire down at us. Our job's to even the odds and fight through."

"Well," I broke into their conversation, "our first job's to get the stuff down and across the island. We could hold that place a month if we must, and we've plenty of powder. They couldn't rush us across the water. And we'll keep the bateau hidden."

In the morning we had something more than conjecture to concern us, for Girty attacked just a little after daybreak. Hoadley's vigilance saved us from being overrun. I had been waking and dozing while I wondered what time it might be. Then the spiteful crack of a rifle brought me and the others to our feet. Hoadley told us afterward that he had walked over to where they had kidnaped Hester and had seen the movement of figures he was sure were not deer. He had fired immediately.

They were around us on three sides, clear to the edge of the water, and were making a deal of racket with gunfire and gobbling noises. However, they kept well out of sight, having had hard experience with our sort of shooting. They did keep us pinned down in the shelter of the rocks and the timber, and we held our fire, excepting when one of us saw a movement.

"Keep loaded," was Mcfail's word passed along the line, and we watched so that no two fired at the same time. If they rushed us, we would need every firearm. Our pistols, as in our other fights, were held as a reserve.

Hester was not far back of the big rock that was my shelter, and she crept up to me.

"Martin," she whispered anxiously, "do you think he's located the gold and this attack is to cover his getting it off the hill?"

That was a real possibility, but I was not going to admit it, even to her.

"No, Hester. Likely the only way he can keep these Indians interested is to have some action now and then. Besides, Girty himself can't stand pressure; he wants to get things over."

She seemed satisfied and turned her attention toward watching the woods. She looked so small and slight, lying there with her rifle ready. It startled me to think I had answered the girl as casually as I might have one of the men who had made the same query. And her question had nothing to do with either her own safety or comfort; she had been concerned for the mission that had brought us here. Thinking about her, I knew that we might have faltered in our quest had it not been for her high courage, this slim girl in her boyish buckskins, watching through the trees to find a target for her rifle.

The chaotic din rose and fell. Our first concern had been defense, to keep ourselves from being overrun by numbers, but after hours of strain, our tempers were getting short. Mcfail and Hoadley were edging deeper into the brushland about us as they found trees to cover them, and I moved forward to keep the line straight. Just as I leaped behind a large pine, the sergeant's big-bored rifle roared, to be answered by a yell of either fright or pain.

"Nicked one!" Mcfail yelled, then, "Watch, Hoadley!"

The second rifle cracked; men were running in the woods and I got one snap shot at an indistinct target. There were one or two derisive yells, then the forest about us was empty once more. The widening circle of our scouting found nothing, and we all returned to the camp area.

We wasted no time in argument but gathered up our scanty equipment and waded across to the island where a watch would not be so difficult to keep. I carried Hester with her arm about my neck. When I stumbled, she tightened her grip and I almost lost my balance completely. As I set her down on the bank, she patted my shoulder.

"Next time, Martin, you better carry powder or blankets."

"I'd much rather carry you," I blurted.

"Dear, dear," she commented mockingly, "these strong men do so love to labor."

For a moment, she was again the exasperating young woman she had been back there on the flatboat in the scene that had ended with me in the river. Abruptly, she placed her hand on my shoulder and, when she spoke, I knew the same incident was in her mind, only this time her voice was kind.

"Now our Martin's all wet again, but in a better cause."

It was thinking about her and how soft her hands had felt that kept me from planning or doing anything until John Mcfail approached with a question.

"Martin, can we ford to the other side from here?"

"Yes," I answered. "There's a sort of ledge all the way over." When I pointed to where it lay, he looked at me curiously as if he were about to ask me how I had learned this fact, but he seemed to think better of it and gave his reason for asking about a ford.

"We'll have to get that gold to this island and do it after dark. If they see us carrying one keg, they'll make an all-out attack, not the kind of thing they staged this morning."

The idea seemed to be a good one since we would be more comfortable with the treasure under cover of our rifles. We could, of course, load the flatboat with the kegs and so transport it, but that also meant precipitating a major battle.

We crossed the ford that afternoon, going again to the flatboat, but this time Hoadley slipped downstream to watch, and Cady went to the north of us. The rest of us climbed up the hillside and tackled the job of getting the kegs down. It was hard labor on the steep slope, especially since we had to screen our movements behind trees and bushes. Allen, with his great strength, did more than either Mcfail or I.

Dusk was showing when we had the last keg down on the flatboat; then our watchers along the river came in, reporting that they had seen nothing of either Girty or the Indians. Cady had killed a small deer, and because we were hungry from our labors, we built a good fire and cooked some of the tender meat, after which we feasted to repletion, regardless of the danger of watchers in the crowding forest about us. Mcfail talked to us when we had all finished.

"I've a plan. Girty's crew may still be on the other side of the river where they attacked this morning. But by some time tomorrow they'll figure we've made a find, no matter what we do. Those Indians will be quick to read signs. Maybe they'll figure the kegs are right here on this flatboat, which is exactly what I'd like them to think. But, we'll take the gold kegs over to the bateau when it's good and dark. The powder will stay right here."

To me, there did not seem too much sense in the plan, and I interrupted impatiently.

"John, we couldn't run the river after night. They'd make it hot for us, and we can't run the risk of losing the kegs if we crack up the bateau on the rocks."

"Exactly," he agreed, examining the piece of meat he had broiled but had not eaten as yet. Then he gestured toward the kegs.

"There's close to two hundred pounds of powder in them four kegs, and we'll leave it until the gold is over. We'll make some dummies so it will look as if all the stuff is still right here. Then, when they jump on this flatboat to finish us in the dark, we'll touch off that powder." He chuckled softly before he finished. "That'd blow Girty closer to heaven than he's ever likely to come again."

The sergeant was a good man, and this was no time to count risks or weigh chances. His plan might work. The only objection I saw was that we would have to wait another full day and so chance an attack in force, pushed home with real determination, and we would be only a few rifles against many.

Once more we carried kegs, this time over the ford, feeling for our footing with our feet, floundering at times under the awkward loads. But this time we had Hoadley and Cady helping us, and we managed the job in four treacherous trips. Hester, checking with the big watch, said it had taken us just an hour and a half. In order to make our hoax look better, we broke open some of the gold kegs on the island and placed the bars in the lockers of the bateau. The empty containers went back to the flatboat. Hoadley took over the last load and remained to guard the treasure while the rest of us stayed on the flatboat, with Hester sleeping inside the cabin, according to my strict orders. The night was quiet, and as I lay there, watching the stars and the dark stream, I almost convinced myself that we could run Girty's gauntlet. But there were only six of us, one a girl. Ahead lay long miles of river travel, when every man would be needed to handle the boat. Also, we had seen Frye die; I would not risk another precious life if I could possibly avoid it.

Night and the river; far down, there would be pleasant fields, quiet towns. There would be pack trains to hurry the gold to His Excellency, to Wayne, or to the Congress. I had spent months on the task and was already too long delayed, when one remembered the need of our fighting armies. I fell asleep finally, lulled by the soft lapping of the water against the planks of the boat.

Morning presented nothing new, but I grumbled because they had not roused me to stand my watch. Allen grinned.

"Figured you needed sleep, what with doing the worrying and lugging kegs, you must have been tired. Now, work don't hurt a man but bothering about things just plays him out."

The hours of the day dragged out since most of the time we had to remain on the flatboat where we lashed some of the kegs in plain view at the ends of the deckhouse. We puttered at chores such as mounting the big sweeps in their pole-crotches at prow and stern, driving wooden pins here and there as though strengthening the planking, generally creating the appearance of getting the craft ready for the river.

Hester, at Mcfail's direction, was busy with the needle and thread she carried, making long cloth tubes which, filled with powder, would form the fuse we needed. This would be led out through a hole in the boat's planking and along the ground to a clump of bushes where a watcher could fire it. We laid other trains of powder about the flatboat until the whole craft was a potential bomb.

"She's set and set well," Mcfail said with satisfaction. "Now let's hope Girty brings down his lousy pack tonight."

"If he doesn't," I announced with sudden decision, "we'll run the river tomorrow. That gold must get out where it will be doing some good."

Our tasks were allotted. Hoadley would remain on the island and have the bateau ready. One of us would fire the powder fuse, all the rest having crossed to the island after dark. We even made three dummies, one to sit on each end of the boat, and one on the cabin to look like watchers. For my part, I scarcely thought we would fool Girty much, but I was willing to back Mcfail's judgment.

Dusk came and with it the familiar tension that comes after too much waiting and watching, knowing that any moment danger would raise its head. We had made the final preparations, which included filling a small kettle with punky wood and setting a live coal in it so there would be fire to ignite the fuse. This was placed in the thicket. We were now all standing together in the first darkness of the evening.

"All right," I said in a low voice. "Now get over to the island. I'll take care of the fuse."

Mcfail stepped closer to me.

"That's my job, Martin. I planned this thing!"

The others sensed the tenseness of Mcfail's statement and moved uneasily. Then, Hester spoke.

"I was thinking about that earlier. We'll draw lots; I have five sticks here. Short stick fires the fuse."

"Not five," Mcfail said roughly. "You're out, Hester."

He took one of the sticks from her hand and tossed it into the water. A mumbling assent came from us all.

"Go ahead; cast the lots."

"All right," Hester said, her voice a little strained. "There are four sticks; draw."

Fumbling in the poor light, we drew. Allen poked his head forward.

"Mcfail it is," he announced. "That's good; Martin's most as clumsy as I am. Cady brought us all that meat, and we couldn't risk him. Hell, John, you're elected and you can turn the trick if anybody can."

It was a long speech, and the big sergeant chuckled and poked me in the ribs, but I was in no mood for pleasantry. The others had moved away a little.

"Martin," he said, "swap knives. If there's a mix-up, I'd like to have Eben's blade. I know the blacksmith that made it."

We exchanged before he spoke again to give us curt directions.

"Just after the boat blows up, I figure to cross to the island fast. From where I am in the brush, the underwater ledge reaches right over to you. But—if that way's blocked, keep your boat well in toward the bank all the way down to the point. I'll see it. Listen for a whip-poor-will that doesn't finish his cry."

One by one, we reluctantly stepped into the water, which felt cold to us now. Mcfail's arrangement for his escape seemed pretty sketchy to me, but then I knew the man's resources in a tight corner, and he would have those minutes of confusion on the part of our enemies to slip away.

Allen led, and we waded carefully to avoid splashing, bent over so our silhouettes might not show above the dark water. Hoadley was waiting at the edge of the island when we arrived.

"Ready to shove off, Martin, and all's quiet here."

I was afraid in this night dash the bateau might strike a rock and sink with its valuable cargo. This stream was not too wide and certainly not very deep. Yet this seemed the best way. The explosion might deplete Girty's force and demoralize his riflemen left in position at the point so that we could slip safely through. However, I planned that we would tie up until morning as soon as we gained the wide reaches of the main river.

Shivering a little in our wet clothing, we lay in the brush where we could look across to the dark mainland. The night was not especially dark, and there were faint reflections of starshine on the water. Mcfail was over there alone, and it would be eerie, nerve-wracking business, even for a man of his iron resolve. I felt a deep guilt at not being the one to fire the fuse, yet I knew the sergeant had made up his mind about the plan and would have quarreled to get his way. Chance had put its finger on him, and danger was like wine to him.

Presently, Hester drew close to me. We were a little distance from the others, and as I turned, she sat down beside me.

"Martin," she whispered, "you are thinking that you should be over there?"

"Yes," I answered shortly. "It's my place."

She touched my arm, then her fingers tightened.

"No, John is cool and will not take the reckless chances you will. Remember, you carried Frye back. John is the man for the job, and it's his plan."

When I made no reply, she was silent for a little. Her voice was thoughtful when she did speak again.

"Yours is the responsibility for this gold, a charge from His Excellency. John couldn't go down the river with it. George Gibson stands in his way."

In the press of things, I had almost forgotten about George Gibson, dead on that nameless creek. At times I had wondered what could be done about Mcfail but could see no solution. I dismissed the matter, planning to take it up at some later time, after we had saved the treasure. Hester was going on.

"John talked to me earlier this evening. He thought you would object to his firing the charge, so I fixed the lot, Martin, as he asked me to do."

What she told me startled me so much that I leaped to my feet. Then I sat down when I realized that it was too late to cross over the water again.

It was too late for anything, as Hester probably realized when she told me the fact. I was bitterly angry. Girty would be moving in any moment now, and I was impotent to stop him. Hester touched my arm lightly.

This girl had seen much of men and events. She had known that commanders often send men to certain death. She, perhaps, better than I, understood the size of the stakes for which we were playing here this night on a lonely river. The safety of the treasure we had to bear back to those who faced the might of England rested in the hands of that bearded sergeant, crouching alone over his little firepot in the darkness. Hester had heard him and agreed that he should take the risk. I forgot my anger in wondering if she might have any other reason for keeping me safe and was ashamed of the thought at a time like this. Suddenly, she gripped my arm.

"Something's moving over there," she whispered.

I saw nothing until Hoadley came close.

"There's a canoe over there, moving downstream. It's close inshore."

I could see it as we all crowded together, watching. The canoe meant Mcfail would find it hard to get to the island. In minutes, what we expected would happen. Over there, flitting shadows would be coming through the timber, bearing bright axes and sharpened knives. Hester was tugging at my arm, almost shaking with excitement.

"Sure of the boat?" I asked Hoadley.

"All set," he answered.

The shadowy canoe vanished in the deeper darkness at the creek mouth. Girty would strike two ways, from the land and from the water. Then the stillness was abruptly broken by the vacant laughter of the cry of a loon.

"That's Girty's signal," Cady muttered. "Now—"

It came as he finished the word; first, a flash of fire that lit up the flatboat, showing figures upon it, so many of them that they crowded it. Then there was another flash and a heavy dull boom that shook the ground under us here on the island.

A great sheet of flame leaped up against the dark background of mountain and forest. In the fire we saw, tossed high, bulks of lumber, bodies, and other things we did not wish to identify.

"My God," I cried, "he was too close!'

I knew that awful burst of fire had reached the clump of bushes where the sergeant lurked.

Minutes passed. We heard one long shriek like a man tortured with awful pain and, afterward, silence. None of us had anything to say, standing there close together, hoping and listening for the sound of someone in the water. Our minutes stretched to an hour until all of us were sure Mcfail was not coming over. We boarded the bateau, according to our plan, and were about to push out into the stream when I stopped the movement of the boat by thrusting my set pole into the mud at the bottom of the cove.

"No, we'll wait for morning. I can't leave him like this. He may be hurt."

No one objected. Perhaps some of them may have slept, but I sat thinking. By waiting, I might be throwing away all that Sergeant John Mcfail had gained for us over there. It could well be that the success of the expedition was slipping away in the shadows. In my heart, I was sure our sergeant of the Lambs had died over there in that great flash of light. But I could no more leave him until I was sure than he would have left me had he been in my place.

Keeping a safe distance from the small creek's mouth and the scene of the explosion, we crossed over in the bateau in the gray of the dawn. A little distance below, Cady and I landed and walked back, rifles ready.

There was nothing at the creek mouth we could identify, though some timbers smoldered and a heavy smell of burning hung in the air. The thicket where Mcfail had planned to hide was now a collection of charred sticks, and I stared at the place until Cady plucked my sleeve.

"Martin, I must tell you what I could not before the others. John Mcfail talked to me."

I stared at the captain impatiently and was about to ask a question when he continued.

"It was days ago, after he learned just who I am. He had his suspicions all along. We spoke of Gibson, and John knew he could never go home. Gibson was supposed to be a hero, you know, and John had killed him."

I looked again at the charred thicket, a bit impatient with Cady. Then he finished.

"We talked again this afternoon. John wanted to be certain. He never intended to hide in that thicket but was going to stay on the boat and take them with him. I had to be sure first, but now I know he carried out that plan."

Aghast, I stared at the little man in his brown buckskins. That filled out the story. No wonder Mcfail had been so confident the plan would work; no wonder he would not yield to another man. This would be his moment, here on the lonely Sinnemahoning. We turned slowly. Then, facing the charred scene, Cady stood straight and raised his hand in a salute. After a moment, I joined him.

In this early dawn, there was still one pale star shining high above the mountain, but it was fading in the gathering light. Somewhere up there, John Mcfail and Eben Drough were foregathering and chuckling at what had happened to Girty and his crew.

Back on the bateau, we dropped slowly down the river, watching the shore as if we expected to see Mcfail. Yet all of us knew, from the utter violence of the explosion, that he could not be alive. In three hours, with no sign of our friend or of the Indians, we came to the river.

We traveled all the remainder of the day, anxious to be out of this wild, dangerous country where so much had happened to us. None of us talked much, I least of all as I thought of John Mcfail's sacrifice, which he had so carefully hidden. Cady was cheerful. He knew that danger was as familiar to John Mcfail as the sights on his rifle. He knew, too, that the sergeant would be pleased with the success of the plan. So the whole matter had ended well, and after all, it was not every man who could choose how he would die.

Our spirits lifted with each day's travel. The river was a blue pathway down which we glided, winding about the bases of wooded mountains, and occasionally refreshed and increased by the entering of another creek.

After we had passed the old Indian camping ground on the Great Island, we began to see an occasional house with its clearing. In our hurry, we did not tie up at Fort Augusta, but we did pull into shore, for Cady was leaving us there to take the lower part of the Shamokin Path on his way back to the army. I stepped out on the bank with him and we clasped hands. There did not seem to be any adequate way to thank this man.

"I'll go straight to His Excellency," he assured me. "I'll tell him you did not fail him, that you bring victory in many little kegs. He will be grateful to you and your fellows. Belike the general will have a better appetite for the cold mutton he loves so much."

Grinning, and with a wave for all of us, he walked up the bank toward the fort, a spare, small figure who would never be out of our minds.

Our river broke through the hills in an arrogant fashion, from Augusta to Harris Ferry. We noticed the place where Girty wanted to spend his old age. It was only a short distance above the ferry.

At the next great river crossing south, we would leave the bateau near the town of York. Pack horses would carry the gold from there; the gold for food and for munitions; gold to raise the hopes of those who had fought so hard and were so weary.

On what was to be our last evening aboard the bateau, the men had all gone to their bunks. We were tied up where we could see the light from a farmhouse that stood in a clearing. Hester and I stood in the prow of the boat as the moon rose.

"Hester," I tried to say casually, "tomorrow you will be a great lady again and wear silks and satins instead of a boy's buckskins. You will have your hair piled high on your head—"

She laughed, a low chuckling sound deep in her throat, and her fingers tightened on my sleeve. She pointed to the farmhouse light.

"No," she answered, "silks and laces would be in the way of a woman who lived in a house like that. She could not wear them while she cooked dinner for a hungry man who had toiled all day in the fields."

My breath caught for a moment. While I did not fully understand her, my longing got the better of me and I caught her close until she was breathless and begged to be released. Then she rumpled my hair with her fingers.

"Martin, Martin, so Dutch and so slow to see! I thought I would have to drop you into the river again."

"Hester," I whispered, filled with awe and wonder, "did you care then?"

Her small hands were firm on my shoulders as she answered, "Almost from the first, Martin Jon Richtier, though why, I cannot tell."

Nor could I, yet I was satisfied.